Also by Will Aebi

The Wedding Day

Jonathan's Journey

A Pius Wake

The Curse Of Mullagh Na Sidhe

An IBEA Book

Library of Congress Cataloging-in-publication Data

ISBN-10 0-9719641-3-0
ISBN-13 978-0-9719641-3-6

IBEA Publishing
www.ibeapublishing.com

Printing Company:
Adibooks
181 Industrial Ave. East
Lowell, Mass

Manufactured in the United States of America

The Curse of Mullagh Na Sidhe

A Mystery

Will Aebi

The UnGnome Author

This book is dedicated to my mother, Adele Gertrude Aebi, a true spirit of love during a time of strife. For always loving me even though I was a spoiled brat. For calling me Butchie-pie when I was good and Cow-pie when I was bad. For all those sons who might have treated their mum better; I wish I had. Peace and love to you now, if you can hear me,

Your son, the Ungnome Author, Will (Butch) Aebi

ACKNOWLEDGMENTS

Jan Aebi, a tender soul, in a time of turmoil.

Karen Chaplin, the supreme editor.

The owners of Caroline's Café in Bundoran, Ireland; Breege & Tommy MaGuire, for their hospitality & good food.

Patricia McGuinness, an international ambassador of good will & delightful waitress.

Holly Crissinger, photographer of the Ungnome Author, for her skill with the camera and capturing the author in his natural habitat.

Wim Schimmer, for creating the cover, an artist of exceptional talent.

Prologue

Mysteries abound in this thriller about people living on a fairy hill in Ballyshannon, Ireland. It's 1999 and superstitions are as persistent as the fresh Atlantic breezes off Donegal Bay. Evil comes in many forms, as the good folks find out when they decide to live, uninvited, on a fairy hill. An American man visits his friend in hopes of renewing their friendship, and in the process discovers a sinister mystery. Folklore rears its ugly head, forcing Will Bonner and his friend, Eamonn Gallagher, to solve the mystery . . . or die. A simple search for rational answers rapidly becomes the need to solve a deadly puzzle.

One—Alone on the hill

In the small village of Ballyshannon, Ireland the rain beat down, the wind blowing in off the Atlantic to the west. Seeping in through the cracks and crevices, an old woman gave a shiver. A widow in her sixties, Margaret O'Neil was tired. Tired of the pain in her head and feeling so depressed it made her heart ache. *Not one person in Beal Atha Seanaidh (Ballyshannon) cares a hoot,* she thought. *If I go to me mortal resting-place, there'll be no tears lost. Me husband, bless his eternal soul, will be waitin',* she mused bitterly.

Seated in the worn chair her husband had used for some ten years past, she wondered if her leaving would appease the evil floating around her head. Would her offspring live a better life for it? *God knows,* she thought. *Me kids won't give a fiddler's damn, long as they gets the house.*

Outside, the wind blew cold rain against the small window in her living room. A chill ran through her bones as she looked at the gray sheet draped across the crude beam overhead. She had tied one end to the large knob on the door.

Slowly she got up, her arthritic hands quivering as she carefully climbed up on the chair propped against the wall. *Maybe now I'll find some peace,* she thought tiredly. Lightning struck some unknown spot as the rain beat down. Joining her, the elements seemed to scream in pain as she placed the rolled sheet around her wrinkled neck. Fearfully she looked at the floor, searching the room one last time to see if anyone was there. Her legs began to tremble and shake as she tried to steady herself. Not quite ready to end it, she prayed the pain would soon be gone. Her right knee gave way and for a moment she wished it was over. Her will to live strong, she reached vainly with both hands. With agonizing slowness the chair slid out from under her. The noose around her neck tightened, then squeezed tighter as she gasped for breath. Her legs flailing she knocked over the rickety chair, eyes bulging with fear as she tried to loosen the knot. Gasping, blood spilled from her lips as her eyes glazed over. A figure appeared ever so slowly in her peripheral vision. Hopelessly she tried to catch her breath. Her heart beating slower, she saw her tormentor for a moment then gave up the ghost.

Blood running down her chin, she hung quite still. Urine escaped her bladder in slow dribbles as muscles went limp. The rain poured down while cold eyes stared at her for a moment, then were gone.

Two—Long lost friend

Will Bonner sat at his computer terminal trying to figure out how to translate a few phrases into the Irish language, Gaelic. Frustrated with his lack of knowledge, he stared out across the field at the river rushing past his home in an eternal push of white water. Since retiring to southern Maine, his life had never been so busy. Annie, his beautiful wife, loved it too. The quiet, good neighbors, the serenity of nature, had a calming effect on both of them. Money wasn't as plentiful, and his hopes of getting published as a mystery writer seemed more a dream than reality.

Pondering this problem reminded him of a friend from his former company; someone who had certainly left an impression. For years he had talked to his wife about the Irishman, using colloquialisms of almost-Irish phrases; faith and begory, kiss the blarney stone and arrg me matey, *which is probably more English than Irish,* he thought.

Over the last seven years he and the Irishman had written back and forth, each trying to outdo the other. *Torture*, Will mused. Shy in many ways, he was not inclined to visit uninvited. *It seems wrong to impose, I can't take advantage,* he thought. However now he'd brave it, risk rejection if need be, as it seemed right to reach out and call. He'd take the bull by the horns and contact his friend. A visit to Ireland would certainly be nice, fun actually. It had been awhile since he had seen Eamonn, but a friend made is a friend worth keeping. At least that's what he'd heard somewhere. *Besides,* he thought, *who knows more about the language and history of Ireland than Eamonn Gallagher.*

Eamonn had married since leaving the states. Los Angeles had taken down more than one good soul in its existence, so his leaving was in a very real way an escape back to life. He certainly was mellower in his letters than he used to be. That's not to say he was ever wild, maybe a little off sometimes. *At thirty-five he's still a kid, a young whippersnapper; well a kid to me,* Will thought dryly. William Bonner had just turned sixty and was feeling his age. It was more difficult now to work a full day, and with age he had to watch his fat, and cholesterol intake so his blood-pressure wouldn't rise. *No matter, tomorrow I'll call. Early though, Ireland's five hours ahead,* he thought.

Morning came quickly as he had taken an herbal sleeping aid to knock himself out. Always thinking, he had to have a little help. The wind rattling the shutters woke him early. "Time to eat and read," as he always referred to breakfast and the daily newspaper.

At precisely nine a.m. he called the number on Eamonn's letter of eight months earlier. Long distance static seemed strangely missing as a voice answered "Eamonn Gallagher here".

"Yes, this is Sir William of Orange, then Anaheim Hills, Pomona and all its lands, now of Steep Falls, Maine. I've called to torture you."

"And torture it is, Sir William," the voice on the other end replied with a merry twinkle.

"Well, perhaps a torture of time," Will responded. "I was thinking I'd . . . me and the wif' would like to come and visit the self and his family." With much emphasis he used his best Irish accent, which sounded more like a cross between a Piccadilly Square guttersnipe and the deceased Irish actor, Barry Fitzgerald.

"Ah, now that's a grand idea. You can stay in me summer cottage by the sea. It has a good view of the bay."

"That sounds great. I'm thinking of changing my name to Finnegan Bonner, go back to me roots," Will said solemnly.

"I'll be givin' you roots," the Irishman said with a smile, then continued in a more serious vein. "Plan on staying as long as you like."

"I don't want to be a bother now. I was thinking Annie and I could come in May."

"That's a ways away, Sir William."

"I know it's four months, but I need to plan ahead; get me house in order."

"Ah, yes, the house," he laughed, then went on, "good stuff, that'd be great. I'm thinking the only time we will be using the cottage is in July, so anytime 'til then."

"Thanks, Eamonn," Will said earnestly. "It's good to hear your voice after all these years."

"Yes and yours too, Sir William. We'll be lookin' forward to your presence. Send me the details of your trip and I'll do the same with a map to me house." Quiet for a moment, Eamonn continued, "Yes, well then, we'd better ring off, this is expensive."

"Good point, I'll send you a letter in two or three weeks."

"Aye, that'll be grand," Eamonn said.

"Take care, my friend," Will replied as he hung up the phone. *Well, we've got our experiment now,* he thought. A little apprehensive, he hurried in to tell Annie, who was busy cross-stitching her eighth Victorian angel. She enjoyed her hobby. Except for framing it was inexpensive and kept her creative juices flowing. *Now writing, that's another story,* he thought, smiling to himself. Annie watched the daydreaming man, waiting expectantly for him to speak.

"Well, I finally did it, I called my friend in Ireland."

"And?"

"He's receptive to the idea, so I thought we'd go if it's okay with you."

"Yes, of course!" Annie said, "Who's been pushing you to call?"

"Our neighbor?"

I'll give you neighbor, it was me!" she replied.

A conservative when it came to travel or finances, it was disconcerting to figure out all the finer details of taking a month away from his busy schedule of writing and remodeling their Victorian house. *How would the bills get paid, who would watch our house? Where should we put important papers?* His mind went from item to item. *Then there are airline reservations, car rental in Ireland,* he stopped for a moment and laughed. *Gads, I need a glass of wine.*

The next four months passed quickly as plans were made for every contingency. A very thorough man, William Bonner put his affairs in order.

Three—No rest for the weary

The incessant banging of a shutter irritated Michael McGinty more than the overriding feelings of fear that filled his soul. Living in Ballyshannon had taken its toll. He had heard about Margaret O'Neil's untimely death and felt sad. *God in heaven,* he thought, *I hope she's found peace.* He felt trapped in the small bedroom he shared with his younger brother, Malachi. Wind whistling through the cracks of his window to the outside world only added to his depression. His last job at the grocers had been over nine months ago. They said his attitude needed improving. *Fecking dick, he wouldn't know the truth if it hit him in the arse,* Michael mused tiredly. *Feck it, I won't take me medicine today. If me mind wants to sit in the shite, so be it.*

Staring out the window he watched the rain come down. Never ending, it seemed to press in. *Damn the rain, and the feckin' dampness, and feckin' clouds. I'll not need a bath, if this keeps up.*

Tired of sitting he decided to go down to the pub. *Maybe I'll be meetin' some sweet young lass wantin' company.*

Putting on his worn, long coat he headed down the narrow street towards the only escape he knew. Having a pint or two always made him feel better before his mind started churning. Same old feelings of guilt and remorse. *If I could right the wrong, I would. Nobody's consultin' me when they desecrate places two hundred years ago; now*

I gets to pay. Looking around the busy bar he wondered who would mess with him tonight. *Who'll go down for the count?* He wondered. *Maybe if I bloody enough noses, this damned fog will let up. Just for a day,* he thought. *Oh, that'd be grand, it would.*

A voice from behind made him stiffen, "Michael McGinty, out spongin' off your friends again?"

The whirling dervish slammed into the face connected to the voice, interrupting the barroom laughter. Screams and yells filled the air as the angry young man flailed wildly at his tormenter. Exhausted, he stared down at the terrified bloody face. Predictably, angry men threw him to the floor, holding him until the Garda arrived.

No one knew his pain, nor cared really if he suffered. *If only this cursed feeling would leave me brain, I could be off the pills.* Rough hands dragged him away as he muttered to himself, wishing he was dead.

Four—The best laid plans

Will had arranged for them to be picked up at four p.m. in Steep Falls. He decided to call the shuttle service again to verify its arrival.

It was ten to four when he heard the service pick up the phone on the other end, "Hello?"

"Yes, this is Will Bonner, I'm checking to confirm that someone will be here at four to take my wife and me to the airport."

"No, Sir, we have you down for a six-thirty pick-up."

Silent for a moment, Will felt his pulse quicken.

"There must be some mistake. I specifically told the lady to schedule us for four p.m. It takes at least two and a half hours to reach Boston."

"We're sorry about that, we'll send a driver right away."

"And how long will it take him to get here?" Will asked impatiently.

"Forty minutes, tops. He should be there by four-thirty."

"Our flight is at eight-fifteen and the airline wants us there two hours ahead of time."

"We'll get you there, Sir."

The minutes ticked away as Will nervously walked from room to room in the old house, while Annie checked the roadway from time to time hoping to see their ride arrive.

All that planning, then the shuttle screws up, he thought tiredly.

It was now four forty-five, five minutes past the new expected time of arrival. His patience ebbing, he called the shuttle service again.

"Yes, Sir, the driver has run into heavy traffic. He's in Gorham on Route 25."

"So realistically he'll be here at five-thirty. How will we make it to Logan Airport, check our luggage, and get boarded on time? We'll only have fifteen minutes leeway. I may have to cancel the flight," Will said with a finality even he didn't like.

"No, Sir, don't worry about a thing. The driver says he'll get you there."

"Okay, please hurry. We could lose our airfare. You understand we're retired, we're not made of money."

"I'm very sorry, Sir. Someone screwed up, but we'll get you there on time if it's humanly possible."

The scrunching sound of gravel alerted Annie that the shuttle had arrived at last. It was five-twenty-five.

Gads, what a relief, Will thought, *let the trip begin.*

It seemed almost festive racing down the back roads of Maine towards the interstate. The driver kept up a running patter in a futile attempt to pacify his passengers. Explaining how he normally didn't work days at all, but they needed a fast driver for this run. To make matters worse, it had started to rain. The weather looked very depressing.

"I hope the airport isn't fogged in," Annie worried.

"I checked on the net, just clouds in Boston, no fog," Will replied.

"That's good," the demure woman said with relief.

It seemed they were finally on their way. The miles ticked away as the old cab raced towards Boston at seventy-five miles per hour.

Luck of the Irish, Will thought grimly.

They arrived without mishap at ten minutes to eight. Will hurriedly paid the driver, reluctantly giving him a tip. *The screw-up wasn't his fault, and we will need him to pick us up on the return trip,* he reasoned.

The trip to Logan Airport had been Mr. Toad's Wild Ride, but thankfully the check-in went smoothly and they were waved directly onto the plane.

Talk about close, Annie thought.

Seated in two seats by the window, they breathed a collective sigh of relief. They were finally off to Ireland.

The L10-11 took off with much jingling and clanking, racing down the runway. Reminiscent of a giant albatross flapping its wings wildly, then smooth as silk once in the air. With the exception of two chunky young women behind them constantly bumping the back of their seats, asking that the seats not be put back too far so they could repeatedly go to the head, the flight seemed pleasant. *The occasional grabbing of Will's head notwithstanding, the flight is wonderful,* Annie thought philosophically. At long last they had found an airline that had its act together. The excellent food and free drinks made Will smile, Aer Lingus was a great airline.

"Gads, it's been years since I've had service like this." he marveled. Flying in the U.S. had become a real drudge. At best squeezing normal size people into miniature seats. The pretense that everything was wonderful when it wasn't seemed deceitful. *No matter, that was then, he* thought watching the movie, Patch Adams. *Gads I'm tired, of being bumped, if only those creatures behind us would settle down.*

Mercifully time passed quickly. "Ladies and gentlemen, we'll be landing briefly in Shannon. All passengers going on, please stay on board," the stewardess announced over the intercom.

It felt good to sit quietly for a few moments while passengers left the plane in Shannon. The fates being kind, the chunkies behind them, doing their best Irish accents, left the two weary travelers to their own devices, as they had reached their destination.

Twenty minutes later they landed in Dublin. Going through Customs went smoothly enough. Thankfully the airport luggage carriers made retrieving their suitcases easier. Arriving at the car rental desk, Will gave the man his paid receipt.

"Sir, would ya be needin' theft insurance?"

"Theft insurance?"

"Yes, if the car is stolen you'll be owing a thousand punts."

Will looked at Annie standing behind him. "It's up to you my love, I'm not sure there's much theft where we're going."

The agent looked intently at Will. "Sir, some thugs might just run off with the car. It's for your own protection."

"We're going to Ballyshannon, County Donegal. I was under the impression it's quiet there."

"Ah, true, but theft can occur anywhere on the isle," the overstuffed man said with finality.

Sighing, Will paid the extra ninety-three punts. *If I ignore him, it would be just my luck,* he thought ruefully.

As prepared as he thought he was for operating the small Fiat with the steering wheel on the right, stick shift on the left, driving on the wrong side of the road was terrifying to both of them. "My God!" he said under his breath, almost hitting the oncoming barrage of miniature trucks and cars before swinging quickly into the left lane.

"The map sucks," he said, panicking as he swerved towards the curb.

"These roads must have been designed by the little people," Annie groaned as she watched oncoming traffic come perilously close to Will's side of the car. *We'll never make it,* she thought, *I've come to Ireland with this man to die on the wrong side of the road.*

"Oh, God," Will cried out, flinching as a large truck crossed the centerline and aimed straight at them. With no thought of crashing, it needed more room and took it. Pulling dangerously close to the ditch, he all but stopped. After several minutes of driving aimlessly about, trying to get onto the M50, he was finally successful. That was short-lived, as he realized they were headed north instead of south. More time slipped by as he searched for an exit similar to the ones in America, finding only roundabouts instead. After several attempts, they finally headed south towards a toll booth. Eighty pence was asked and gladly given. Unfortunately, he didn't realize the very next exit 'roundabout' was their turnoff to N4, going toward Galway, the west, and the way they wanted to go. So another thirty minutes was spent taking two more roundabouts to return to the M50 and then to Lucan Road, hence the N4 towards Ballyshannon. To say that leaving the M50 and Dublin Airport behind was a relief, understated things considerably.

Unable to stop her hands from shaking; Annie clenched them tightly on her lap. While the N4 was marked clearly enough, in size it could definitely be considered the narrowest of highways. *Allowing only a small margin of error, only a wee person could drive it,* Will thought.

"Phew, that was close," he said, driving helter skelter down the roadway.

"You're getting too close to the ditch on my side," Annie said nervously.

"Just tell me how much room I've got. The trolls keep crossing into our lane when there's no room in theirs."

"Well, stop then," Annie said in frustration.

The sky was overcast with clouds and rain. To the Irish drivers it seemed perfectly natural to pass a slow moving tractor or car on a collision course with the two bedraggled Americans. Time passed as the countryside became more what they had in mind, dotted with an occasional thatched roof cottage or European styled gray brick house with many chimneys. Rusted tractors from the early 1900s were a common sight as traffic all but stopped several times on their road to adventure.

"Arrgh, me mateys and matettes, the wee folk are here for sure," Will said.

"Don't look for wee folk while you're driving," Annie replied firmly.

Feeling like salmon swimming upstream against opposing traffic, sure they would crash and burn at any moment, took its toll on the couple. Not having slept in twenty-four hours Will found himself nodding in spite of his fears. Opening the window, the cool air was refreshing. Never having driven in a foreign country he wondered if they would survive. Each crisis of the road seemed a little more extreme as they finally reached the narrow streets of Sligo, then Bundoran and Ballyshannon. It was a relief to stop the car. Even though it was raining, they were here. Near a telephone, in a public parking lot and safe. *I'll just call Eamonn,* Will thought tiredly.

Five—The ledger

Quietly the small hand wrote the list again, adjusting the names according to family; name, age, address, state of health, living/deceased. Seated at a large wooden desk, the diminutive figure read the list aloud to the group assembled in the great hall. A candle flickered as he spoke almost inaudibly.

"Margaret O'Neil, age sixty-three, Market Street, deceased."

Carefully the name was checked off the list.

"Maggie Gibbons, age 35, Back Street, deceased."

As with the last, the name was marked off.

"James McGurran, age 51, Castle Street, deceased."

Meticulously each name was verified as the seemingly endless series of names was read. More often than not there was a murmur of approval. Stern black eyes silenced any sounds as he continued. "More than enough remain livin', when they should be dyin'."

Calmly now, the reading began again,

"Horace McBride, age 33, College Street, in fair health; Frances Murray, age 47, Mall Street, in fair health."

A wrinkled hand marked off the names.

"Patrick McDermott, age 51, Market Street, in good health; Peter Culmore, age 56, Erne Street, in good health; Michael McGinty, age 20, Castle Street, a troublemaker in good health."

The reading went on for a long time as street after street was checked off. Beginning with Back, then Castle, Chapel, College, Erne, Maine, and Mall, Market, Bishop and Martin's Row. With a sense of finality the voice stopped. It was finished. Staring at the faces, the man smiled cruelly then bid them go.

Six—The meeting

The phone rang its static ring.

"Hello?"

"Eamonn, it's me, the William from Steep Falls. I'm in the Mall."

"You're here! Good stuff, stay where you are and I'll be by directly."

The phone went dead as Will hung up. *It seems strange Eamonn doesn't have a street address. He lives in a house and no one knows where. Oh well, different country,* he thought. *Maybe it's like our unlisted phone numbers, here it's unlisted houses,* he mused. *No matter, he's coming to get us.*

Across the narrow street a large clock was being repaired in an old bell tower. The hustle bustle of Main Street was added to by happy children excited about being out of class for the day. *It's refreshing to see smiling faces. Ballyshannon seems truly blessed with good will,* the twenty-year-old stuck in the sixty-year-old body thought.

It was two p.m. and bells from somewhere up the hill were ringing. Standing by the telephone booth Will thought how odd it was to see his friend of seven years ago, hardly changed at all. Time had been kind to him. At thirty-five, Eamonn Gallagher looked young and healthy. Near six-feet tall, he strolled up and gave Will a hearty hug.

"You look younger since you cut your beard off," Eamonn said with some enthusiasm.

"I had to, it was aging too fast." Will responded.

"You look younger anyway." Eamonn replied.

"You're no old man of the sea either," Will said, looking at his friend. "With the store you must be quite busy."

"Aye, there's no time with work and supporting a family," Eamonn said tiredly. Studying Will for a moment he lit up, remembering, "Your wife, I've not met the little woman."

"Oh, I'm sorry, we're parked around the corner." Motioning Eamonn to follow, Will hurried to the rental car where Annie was waiting patiently.

Will opened the car door so she could get out to meet his friend. "Eamonn, this is Annie."

"Ah, it's grand thing, your coming," Eamonn replied with a smile.

"Yes, I've heard so much about you," Annie said brightly, "it's a pleasure to meet you too."

"The pleasure's all mine."   Distracted for a moment, Eamonn continued, "Did your flight go all right?"

"Yes, it was wonderful," Annie replied, "except for the trip out of Dublin on the M50 with a man who doesn't know how to drive on the wrong side of the road." Out of breath, she rolled her eyes at her husband.

"I'm surprised you found Ballyshannon from there."

"I just followed your instructions," Will said.

"Yes, he did that," Annie said tiredly, "dodging cars all the way."

"Well, you're safe now," Eamonn replied, "so let's be getting you both back to the house to meet the wife. I'm thinkin' she's more excited than I am."

The drive up Main Street went slowly as Will followed the Irishman dodging around this or that vehicle blocking the lane. Eamonn's Jeep Cherokee squeezed through the smallest of openings, while the Fiat Will was driving seemed much wider than his mini-truck in America. Bright green foliage crowded the narrow roadway as they followed the elusive black and white SUV. Unsure of where they were, it didn't seem to matter as they finally stopped in front of a Chateau-styled house. Brick with two chimneys attached to the outside and two protruding from the center of the roof, it was a wonderful old edifice of times gone by.

Leaving their bags in the car, Annie and Will followed the jubilant young man to the front door, then down a narrow hallway, the high ceiling belying the length as they walked to a closed door at the end. Entering, Will saw a beautiful Irish woman sitting with a baby on her lap. Slender, with short brown hair in a ponytail, she wore soft beige slacks, a light colored blouse, with a bright silk scarf around her neck. She looked over with a smile as Eamonn introduced his wife and daughter.

"This is me wife, Katie," he said with a slight wave of his hand, "and me darlin' daughter, Mollie."

Will walked over and shook hands with the lovely person smiling at him and Annie.

"It's so nice to meet you after all these years of Eamonn carryin' on," Kate said in the melodious voice of the Irish.

A little shy Will looked out the window towards the Mall Quay and muddy shore of Ballyshannon Harbor.

"Yes, well, the pleasure is all mine. Actually Annie and I have looked forward to coming here for quite some time. Somehow I just never got up the nerve to do it."

Annie patted him on the shoulder. "He's always been kind of a homebody, traveling about Maine's alright, just doesn't like to fly."

Kate nodded as she offered to take their coats.

"Looks like you just got off the boat with your tam and overcoat," Eamonn said smiling, "could be you're immigrating to the Emerald Isle?"

"Yes, me and ten thousand fairies from America."

"We'll not be needin' that kind of immigration here," Eamonn responded.

The dazed couple sat at the antique kitchen table gazing out at the beautiful scene below. The tide was going out and Ballyshannon Harbor had the look of ancient times with small boats rolled over on their sides. While Kate busied herself preparing food, Eamonn held their eleven month-old daughter on his lap. Mollie wiggled in her father's arms as she surveyed the strangers.

Quiet for a moment, Will sat admiring the wonderful kitchen. Pots and pans, hanging from a rack directly above a wooden cutting table, had the well worn look of constant use. Cutting loaves of French bread, Kate filled a basket to the brim.

"You must be thirsty after such a long trip," she said softly. "I'll put the kettle on."

"Oh, that would be wonderful," Annie said exhaustedly.

"Tea, Sir W?" Eamonn asked, already taking out four cups.

"Sounds great, thanks."

Seeing that Kate was busy, Eamonn offered to put the water on while she prepared a salad of Romaine lettuce, sliced carrots, tomatoes, small green onions and other secrets native to her recipe.

"Is there anything I can do?" Annie asked the young woman working at the kitchen counter.

"Oh, no, I'm just finishing up. Thanks anyway."

Perhaps it was the hot tea Eamonn had prepared or just the historic setting, but Will felt very small looking out the window at Inis Saimer, an island in Ballyshannon Harbor. Eamonn explained how ancient Donegal chieftains had once occupied it.

In a flurry of activity the table was set and food arranged. A lunch of crab salad, strawberries and pineapple mixed, cold vegetables with oil and vinaigrette, bottled fruit juice, French and stone-ground bread, rhubarb pie and hot tea was greatly appreciated by the weary travelers. Fresh lettuce leaves with a sweet sauce tasted wonderful.

Will had been worried about what to expect after not seeing Eamonn for so many years, relieved that it was so easy talking to him. He enjoyed hashing over all the good stuff that had happened.

Taking a bit more salad, Will turned to their hostess, "This is good."

"Yes, it's all wonderful," Annie added.

"Would you like some juice or water?" Kate asked.

"Water would be fine," Will replied.

"Just tea for me," Annie said quietly.

"Milk in your tea?"

"Oh yes, I'll try that," Annie answered.

"I wasn't sure what Americans drink," Kate said, "Preconceived notions, you know. I thought they all drank beer," she added laughing.

Smiling Will looked across the table. "You know, until you said that I'd never thought of myself as anything, let alone an American."

"Well you are," Eamonn said with a grin, "and don't forget it."

"No, seriously. In America we have all these people with roots from other countries, but there's a large group of us who are just Heinz 57 variety, no rich Spanish tradition."

"I give you rich Spanish tradition," Eamonn replied dryly.

"No, it's true. You guys go back thousands of years. You've got history, a heritage and culture you can be proud of."

"So it's pride you want," Eamonn said with a fiendish glare. "We've been conquered or enslaved ever since there was an Ireland. Least ways, our time here. It's always the same, someone wanting control and power. In Ballyshannon it was the Ui Neill clan in the fifth century; kings that owned the land. Then the O'Donnell clan sprung up in 1215, and in 1423 built the castle of Ballyshannon. Then it was kings killing kings. The O'Donnell clan was divided and weak and in 1605 King James of England conquered them. So it went, back and forth, Ballyshannon was controlled by someone different. Then to really screw things up there was the battle of Erne Fords that took place near Belleek in 1593. Irish and English forces defeated Hugh Maguire. That was one of the early fights in the Nine Years War. It ended with the overthrow of the Gaelic Kingdoms of north-west Ireland."

"Maybe that's what started the British wanting this place," Will said.

"I don't know what got the feather up the British arses, but they just never let go after that."

"Maybe they got the hots for Irish stew."

"I'll give you the hots," Eamonn said dryly.

"I read in the Portland newspaper that one in every thousand Irish commit suicide. Maybe unemployment is too high."

"I don't know the answer to that," Eamonn replied. "I reckon at least one out of every family here abouts died or is on medication for depression."

"That's frightening," Will said, "it seems folks would want to live."

Seven—Always watchin'

Peering through a closed blind in her kitchen, Elizabeth Gillespie was fixated on a house further up the curved hill facing the harbor. *That Eamonn Gallagher's having company and I'm not knowin' from where,* she puzzled. *Could be one of herself's sisters and husband.* Clouds covered the sun as she tried to see. *Could be they're in there plottin', keepin' to themselves like they do, there's no way of knowin'. They're blow-ins for sure.* The pain running through her head seemed to increase as she struggled to think. *Them and their private ways, could be the curse on me head. Everyone knows they avoid the church and God's cursed us all because of it.*

Her mind buzzed like a thousand bees flying endlessly in the small space reserved for her brain. The constant noise was driving her insane. For twenty years she had lived with her sister Mary in this house. As siblings go, she had always been a good woman, then ever so slowly started changing. *Visitin' friends to all hours of the night, going to the pubs.* Elizabeth felt the despair as she tried to reason, *her taken to the Guinness after all these years, then disappearin' like that without a clue, it had to be that Eamonn Gallagher and his secrets.*

The wind had started to blow, sifting through invisible cracks. Rubbing her arms together she felt clammy. *Someone's been watchin',* she thought with a worried frown. *I'm sure that Eamonn's got spies all over.* Visions of staring faces ran through her head as she tried vainly to block them out. Her hands moved unconsciously to open the bottle standing on the kitchen counter. Putting it to her mouth, she tipped it up. Chewing and swallowing, the bottle was almost empty before she realized what she had done. Her face pale, the forty-seven year old woman fell to the floor. The fast-acting drug worked quickly, slowing her vital organs. Each beat of her heart felt like a drumbeat as she lay staring up at the cold face above her. Like an over wound clock her heart stopped abruptly. Her brain registered fear as she noted her tormentor and was gone.

Eight—Visits

Eamonn sat sipping his tea while Will, Annie and Kate enjoyed the last of their meal. Almost in concert, rain drops pelted the kitchen window. *I'll not be needin' to clean that,* he thought.

Interrupting the quiet, Will asked, "Where are all the grownups? On our way here from Dublin we went through deserted towns. Except for the children, everyone seemed gone."

"Oh now, don't be worrying about that. All the folks are working or staying inside. There's not enough to be running around all times of the day like in L.A."

"I know you're right, but it seems strange when you're used to people on the streets," Will said philosophically.

"Different world," Annie said affectionately.

"Well, that could be why fairies have survived so long. No humans," Will said flatly.

Eamonn took a deep breath. "The fairies don't need humans. They'd exist if every man, woman and child disappeared."

"Why here?" Will asked. "I mean, why not in west Texas or Oklahoma?"

"Now that's something I'll not be able to answer, maybe they like it here because it's green and cold.

Legend has it they were here before the Gaelic kingdoms."

Eamonn rubbed his brow, then continued, "It's too difficult a question you're asking. I don't know when they started."

"I don't think they're friendlies," Will said, rolling his eyes. "We've got a book on fairies and it seems they would rather not have intercourse with humans."

"Aw now, that's obscene," Eamonn replied, "no sense testing the fates."

"Maybe fairies secretly love us," Will said stoically.

"Oh God, I wouldn't want to get one excited now."

"Okay, they're not attracted to humans, but maybe it's the other way around. Why else are there so many books and stories?"

"It's just pagan beliefs from the past," Eamonn replied.

"Yeah, but you believe in them, don't you?" Will asked.

"Sure and you believe in little angels on your shoulders and all that other new age stuff," Eamonn replied seriously.

"New age subscribes to a universal God without the dogma or catma of organized religion." His little attempt at humor ignored, Will continued, "No controls, complete freedom, Gandhi, Buddha, Jesus, Mohammed; all teachers. Allah or God, Protestant or Catholic, all the same. It's just that in this case the Protestants are British, or blow-ins, and that sucks. Anyway, that's what I read back home."

"You're right about that," Eamonn said smiling. "Whether or not you believe, this hill is Mullagh Na Sidhe and some say that when the Episcopal Church was built here that's when all the trouble started."

Eamonn looked tenderly at his daughter with her cherubic face. "The wee folk don't like intruders and there's no getting around that."

With some confidence he smiled at his guests, then bent to help Mollie with her toys.

"Eamonn mentioned you're a writer," Kate said, "that must be interesting."

"A writer of unpublished stories."

"Well, I wish you luck," she said softly.

"Thank you, I need it." Will said reluctantly, "If the current story I'm working on flies . . . I was hoping to do some research here on Irish attitudes towards the English."

"Might be better to ask their attitude towards us," Eamonn volunteered.

"I guess they're kind of stuffy," Will replied, thinking out loud. "Besides, they never know when to give up. That must be why England was never occupied during the Second World War."

"The reason they were never occupied is because the yanks were here," Eamonn said with some conviction.

"Well, they must think highly of themselves," Annie interjected.

"Yes, they do that, they love themselves." Will added, giving himself a hug.

"Snobs, is more the true of it," Eamonn said.

"Could be," Will agreed. "I met a large Englishman in Martinique and he treated me like a specimen. When he called the waiter over to order coffee he kept saying 'selene', I imagine it's Greek; a lunar deity or something used for belittlement."

"There you go again, generalizing. They can't all be snobs," Annie said patiently.

"I know, but look at the British newspapers."

"It's a national attitude, national snobbery," Kate added dryly.

"Maybe it's national paranoia."

"The self and all the Irish are a threat?" Eamonn asked, unconvinced.

"Hmm, that sounds like another story," Will said with a smile.

"Yes, it does, so don't be pulling the strings," Eamonn retorted, the fencing with words begun.

Will looked at his watch surprised at the time, seven p.m. and the sun was still shining brightly. He and Annie hadn't slept in over twenty-four hours. Feeling a chill of fatigue he looked at his friend with a tired smile.

Eamonn, Kate and Mollie led the way to the cottage in Kate's Citron. The going was slow through the resort town of Bundoran. Will stared at the jumble of cars parked in the southbound lane while the drivers talked to some friend, causing all to wait until the oncoming traffic cleared so he could go around them.

My kingdom for a bed, he thought tiredly. His eyes burning from lack of sleep would soon get some rest. As he followed onto the turn-off to Eamonn's cottage a sign appeared, Mullaghmore, four kilometers.

The wonder of hidden dreams lay open, as they saw how green everything was. Passing beneath a canopy of nature's beauty, scenes quickly changed. Pressing towards the sky, shrubs and small trees reached vainly, grasping for the light. Two white swans glided along the reed-filled surface of a murky pond. Oblivious to the hurriedly passing strangers, each was more intent on eating some rare treat found on the marshy bottom. On the horizon a castle appeared. Built high on a hill, it looked magical in its lonely setting three kilometers away. Eamonn had said it's privately owned. *It won't be closer for our eyes,* Will thought with a twinge of regret.

Soon they turned left up a steep hill overlooking Donegal Bay. Near the top they pulled off to the side. The green of many rains covered a block wall partially enclosing a garden of grass. Standing alone in its very center was a rustic cottage, the thatch on its roof newly replaced. Eamonn led his guests into the cheery entryway. Cozy and well kept, it looked wonderfully romantic to Annie.

Having been closed up for the winter, Eamonn opened the curtains in the living room. The view of Donegal Bay with the mountains in the background was stunning.

I like the fireplace, Will thought.

It was much more than they had expected. Everything was provided, from shampoo to linen. Peat logs for the fire were neatly stacked on the hearth. Kate had provided groceries to hold them over until they could go shopping. It was greatly appreciated not having to rush out for breakfast in the morning.

Will felt a sense of relief seated in the living room while Annie took a quick bath. It seemed quite a feat to have traveled three thousand miles and still be in one piece. The impressionable writer was thinking about all the things Eamonn had told him. The talk of fairies seemed far fetched at best, but then if the whole country believed . . . *no matter, I'm not here to change my beliefs, just enjoy my friend.*

Snuggled next to his wife, they whispered their love for each other as they drifted off to sleep. The sound of the wind buffeting the windows was comforting. Suddenly a loud crash shook Will's senses as his body froze wide-awake.

"What was that?" Annie asked, her voice shaking.

Listening to the silence that followed, Will whispered, "I'll go check."

Except for the wind whistling through the cracks, there was nothing. He carefully checked the doors and windows while Annie turned on the lights.

"It would seem that we have a sound without visible cause," he said, obviously troubled.

"Well, it had to come from somewhere," Annie replied.

Giving her husband a hug, she tugged on his sweatshirt. Unable to explain the sound, he followed his wife back to bed.

Immersed in a sleep of the dead, as Annie always called it when one was zonked out, Will awoke early, still trying to figure out where the loud noise had come from. Going into the bathroom he noticed the toilet-seat cover was closed. Neither he nor Annie ever put the cover down at home, and he hadn't last night. *Strange,* he thought, *when it's upright it can't possible fall forward by itself. It even leans back a little.* Testing his theory a few times it was obvious it had to be pushed. *How, when it stands securely in the upright position?* For now he'd wait for Annie to wake. He'd check with her later, maybe she had put it down for some reason.

More bothered than he wanted to admit over something so silly, he sat alone in the living room with the sun shining brightly in, finding it all the harder to imagine anything other than some very logical answer. Suddenly, a squawking moan emanated from the fireplace. As he happened to be reading a book on Irish folk tales, he wasn't really sure if his mind and ears had taken a holiday. The hair on the back of his neck prickling, he listened in spite of himself. As though to verify its existence, it happened again. Holding his breath he nervously approached the brick fireplace. Seeing nothing only added to the tension spreading through his chest. *What in God's name is that,* he wondered? Waking Annie, she grumbled something about being on vacation.

"Listen, it's important," he said seriously to the face still filled with sleep.

"That noise last night was the toilet seat cover. I'm positive."

"I never touched the seat-back dear, you know I always leave the cover up," Annie said, coming fully awake.

"Could be the fairies did it because you were inquiring about them," she added with a smile.

"Not funny, Magee," he said sourly. "That's not the half of it."

"What do you mean that's not the half of it?" Annie said, keenly aware that her husband was in no mood for playful banter.

"While I was waiting for you to get up I heard a grunting noise like a duck or a goose; or a troll."

"Troll?"

"Yeah, a troll. And it wasn't in its best voice either," he replied sarcastically.

Sitting in the living room with their tea, both tried to ignore a sound emanating from the chimney, looking at each other as it repeated itself.

"That's a bird," Annie said, with a sigh of relief. "You silly, you had me going there for a minute. There's a bird nest in the chimney."

"Well that doesn't explain the loud bang and the toilet seat falling with no one there."

"I agree, sweet one, but at least it doesn't have a voice yet," Annie answered softly.

Nine—A traveler's way

Flynn sat at the small table in his trailer, staring out the window, yellowed with age. *It's time,* he thought. *She's old enough. I've supported her, fed her well.* Snapping his fingers at an old woman, he whispered something to her as she scurried out.

His mind drifted to another time when he was somewhere else. *Seeing a young man running on the beach, chasing a young woman, then sudden fear as men rode up with pistols drawn. Shocking thunder and painful darkness. Then him waking in an unfamiliar place, a captive now learning a new way, one filled with pain and physical satisfaction. Eat, drink and be merry, for tomorrow never comes and yesterday's gone.* A traveler now, he smiled grimly.

The banging of the screen door brought his mind back to the present. Standing in front of him, a fifteen-year-old girl waited with the innocent look of a child. Eyes as dark as the long black hair hanging down her back looked way, while fully developed breasts pushed out from the loose sweater she wore.

Clearing his throat, Flynn looked out the window. At forty-five, some things were still enjoyable. "Yer well fed?"

"Aye," she whispered.

"Sure and it's time ya went to a job."

Nodding, she looked at the mustached man seated at the window. Waving his hand at the old woman to leave the room, he slowly unzipped his pants.

"I'll be needin' you to work for me to repay the self for all the time I took care of you."

Standing mute, she watched Flynn stand up. Taking her by the hand he led her over to a chair by the table. Her breath came quicker as he lifted her sweater over her head, revealing full breasts. Moving with each inhalation, dark nipples hardened in the chilled air. Her eyes wide as saucers, she watched in fear as he took one of them in his mouth and began to suck. Undoing her belt he pulled her jeans to the floor. Chill-bumps formed on her thighs as he removed her panties. A cluster of pubic hair covered her untried sex. Unsure what to expect, she protested slightly as he bent her over the chair to expose her slightly moist slit. The curve of her bottom extended as she held tightly to the chair seat, trying to stifle her tears.

From behind, Flynn stood briefly eyeing his prize. His pants on the floor, his exposed sex seemed larger than normal. Moving closer to the hapless virgin's rear he rubbed the bulbous head against her crack, then pushed. Her moan increased to a whimper as he went in further, until he was fully embedded in her flesh. Crying with pain she trembled in fear, as he slowly withdrew, then plunged in over and over, deeper with each thrust. Large balls gathered up, tightening against her slit as he went faster and faster, ignoring her cries. The peppery scent of her sex filled his nostrils. Her breasts swayed back and forth as the wide-eyed female cried out in pain. His pace quickened as the virgin lips clung to his engorged unit. In a burst of hot fluid wave after wave of pain exploded inside the young woman, then it was over.

Her training had begun, Flynn had broken her in; the first of many times that he would use her before sending her out to work for him.

Ten—Gypsy law

No one moved as they sat around the giant bonfire waiting for their leader. Each knew the penalty for not following the law. Broken, it was a curse for life, no matter how long ago the offense occurred. Since the time of the Gaelic kingdoms the laws had been passed down, held sacred by all, each and every one.

It was a hard life for those who fought it. Always they traveled, tonight at the ruins of a castle, two days from now they would stay in Mullaghmore, then Rossnowlagh.

Flynn felt a betrayal. A man had ignored his order; the old oracles had been violated.

"Someone has betrayed us," Flynn said, tucking in his shirt. "Someone has revealed our quest."

Heads turned as each looked accusingly at the others.

The wind blew as tall grass danced in willful patterns. His eyes glazed over, Flynn turned within seeing a small man with a beard speaking rapidly to a woman in her late thirties.

Mary McNulty listened to her father's friend, a traveler. Fearfully she glanced around as he spoke in a hushed tone. "You have broken the covenant."

"I didn't think I did," she said.

"Ya must have told someone."

"Only me son in case I die."

"There's no telling. If me leader finds out, I'm cooked."

Thunder slammed the earth as lightning lit up the sky. Seated near the fire Joseph McGowan started to tremble. Drool ran from his lips as he tried to still his body. Fearfully, he stood and ran towards the darkness, the fire followed his flight, glowing bright and alive. A knife glimmering with heat from Flynn's raised hand, aimed at the fleeing man. Obedient to his desire it moved surely towards its target. Joseph staggered as it settled deep within his back, piercing his heart. The earth trembled as thunder shook the ground once more.

Evil thoughts filled Flynn's mind. *The woman must die too.* In the tall grass, the dead man laid quite still, a wisp of hair flitting in the breeze.

Eleven—Dreams & lunch in Sligo

Exhausted from staying up all night Annie agreed they should flop, as Will put it. The case of the chimney noise resolved, the world felt safer today. Near noon they journeyed out to a local grocery store.

"Look at this, Annie," he said, pointing to a loaf of crunchy soda bread.

Nodding her head in agreement, she watched him place it in the basket. Eggs in a six-pack and rashers of bacon delighted the fascinated couple as they browsed through the tiny store. Collecting the few things they needed, the lady at the counter carefully added up everything in their basket. Arms full, they returned to their rental car in the parking lot.

Heading back to the cottage Will watched the road closely. The rain hadn't stopped since they had arrived and learning to accept oncoming cars in his lane took getting used to. *He who out-bluffs the other,* he thought tiredly.

To the east clouds covered the peaks of mountains shrouded in mist. *Looks lonely,* Will thought. *Maybe it's trying to tell me something.* Barney's Hill came into view as he shifted down. Only their second day, it seemed a magical time in their cottage by the sea. The wind blew gusts, buffeting the small house. Like the moan of an old woman it invaded his mind. Looking out at the glimmering silver bay, he tried to shake off the feeling. *Jet lag, that's all,* he reasoned. Convinced, he excused himself to take a nap.

Annie nodded, smiling at her husband of many years. She loved him dearly. *I'll finish this chapter then join him,* she thought as she turned the page in her Dean Koontz novel.

The sands of time fell away as Will slept, troubled dreams filling his mind. *Standing near a clump of trees, he watched the marching soldiers. Helmeted and armed with swords and spears they moved forward with shields extended. High on a hill, an army of villagers stood ready to defend their homes. Great in numbers, they stood fast as the hoards approached, the soldiers marching forward, winds howling through the heavens. Fighting valiantly, the villagers died. Wave after wave, the endless slaughter continued through dismemberment and death. Only moments, it seemed an eternity.*

Urging his soldiers on, a large goblin with wicked teeth and vicious red eyes spoke rapidly, then faster and faster. Too late to stop, the villagers fell, their hearts cut out. Cries of pain filled Will's ears as he felt cold steel enter his chest . . .

Suddenly awake, cold sweat covered his brow. *God,* he thought trembling, *that'll be enough of the folklore. What I really need to do is start my story. Maybe if I just get the outline done, that'll get my mind off the fables.*

After working on his novel and a dinner of hamburger and chips, he felt better. *Fatigue's causing the dreams.* Tired of thinking about it, he decided to go to Sligo the next day and check out the shopping. Kate had said there was a large food store there with a much better selection. *Annie will love that,* he thought.

The next day came early as his internal clock was still five hours off. Lying in the dark, he wondered if he'd ever sleep normally again. Slowly but surely the dawn arrived. In the beautiful sunrise Donegal Bay looked like a brilliant blue jewel stuck in a mound of bright green.

The drive to Sligo was easier as his driving skills improved. Parking on a narrow street across from the Garda, Annie thought it was safe enough from car theft. Looking in antique shops and music stores delighted the treasure hunters.

"Remember, whatever rare precious you find has to fit in our bags. No end tables or lamps," Will said nervously.

"Oh silly, we can always have it shipped," Annie said. "Just kidding," she hastened to add. Seeing the look on his face, she laughed. It was still fun teasing him.

Passing an occasional old man in a suit coat, sweater and vest, hat perched on top of his head, seemed more a remnant of tourist advertisements than reality to Will. School children wearing uniforms of blue with emblems on their jackets and shirts were more prominent now. There seemed to be no shortage of money as they lined up for candy and sweet shops. Will watched the twelve and thirteen-year-olds smoking cigarettes. Nonchalantly trying to appear older and more sophisticated, he supposed. Happy talk laced with *feckin' this* and *feckin' that* was everywhere.

Oh well, he thought, *it was ever thus. It's a shame so many have to grow up suffering lung maladies.* Horns honked as he led Annie across St. John Street to a family eatery.

"The Helm, that sounds like a nice place to eat," she said brightly as they pushed the door open.

Standing in line at the cafeteria-style counter, a sharp-eyed man with disheveled hair looked at the selections with a suspicious eye. Chicken, coleslaw and sliced hard-boiled egg on a sandwich with lettuce and tomato; or ham, coleslaw and sliced hard-boiled egg on a sandwich with lettuce and tomato; or today's special: fried chicken thighs with mashed potatoes, vegetables and bread. Two punts or four, respectively.

"Gimme the ham sandwich with chips on the side; and don't be skimpin' on the ham now."

"Aye, Sir," the spindly red-haired girl behind the counter replied.

Turning, he eyed the two foreigners behind him waiting patiently to be served. The redhead looked to Will and Annie for their order. "What'll you be havin'?" she asked tiredly.

"The chicken sandwich," Annie replied. "May I have that on wheat?"

"Don't have wheat," the girl said impatiently.

"Okay, white but no onions please."

"Yes, I'll have the same," Will said as he watched the girl put their sandwiches together.

Seeing that all the tables were filled with dirty dishes, Will looked at the girl.

"Where do we sit?"

"There," she pointed, "ya clear your own table if ya wanna eat here."

Annie rolled her eyes as she found a table and cleaned it.

The food was surprisingly good, and that was all that seemed to matter to the crowd packed inside. The stained and dirty carpet did little to discourage the hungry shoppers. It was a culinary experience, but Will thought he'd 'give it a miss' the next time. Smiling to himself he remembered Kate saying that about something she'd found less than pleasing.

Twelve—Fear of the Unknown

Only two blocks to go, Mary McNulty thought to herself. She wanted to get home before her husband of seventeen years. Their son Sean had just graduated and she wanted to make him a present.

"Faith in the mother, it's cold," she said under her breath.

More than once lately she had taken to talking to herself. The fear was always there now. "Damn that Joseph McGowan scaring me half to death," she mumbled.

The sound of her shoes clacked on the sidewalk. The harsh cold of the Atlantic blew across her face as she trudged on, crossing the bridge. Below, the Erne flowed slowly over bare rocks, the dam regulating the flow.

The sound of her footsteps was comforting, *almost like a companion* she thought. Not sure why, she stopped suddenly. The sound of footsteps somewhere behind stopped a heartbeat later.

"Sure and it's me imagination," she reasoned.

Quickening her step, she walked on. *Only half a block to go,* she sighed.

Passing a row of brick houses the sound of footsteps increased. Not looking back she hurried towards her house, two doors down. Headlights flashed on as she stepped into the street. Startled, she stared at the rain-filled beams. Before she could think adrenaline pushed her forward as she dashed for the other side, slipping in the wet. The roar of an engine filled her ears just before she fell in the middle of the street. Looking up she cried out in fear. Its wheels spinning, the vehicle raced towards her. The wind gusted, taking her hat. Instinctively she rolled towards the curb, the wind at her back. The deadly machine hurried forward, barely missing the tumbling body in its haste to kill, colliding with a forklift tractor parked at the side of the road. Fearful eyes closed as the lift went through the windshield, decapitating the driver.

Mary cried hysterically as she ran to her house. Dead bolting the door, she breathed a sigh of relief. *Sean must have left the lights on. Oh, me son, I'll not be blamin' you this time. At least I'm safe from whatever fiend has taken a fancy to me. And when will himself be here, I'm wondering?* She sighed, looking at the clock on the wall. *Ten-thirty, he shouldn't be staying out so long. I'll refresh myself,* she thought going to the tub and turning on the hot water. She went into their bedroom to get a gown and clean under-things. A proper woman, Mary McNulty did not parade around the house naked.

The steam felt good in the bathroom as she removed her torn dress. Unsnapping her bra, her beautiful bosom swung free. Hidden in her modest dress she was still a very attractive woman. At age thirty-seven her stomach was flat and her legs shapely. She felt good knowing her husband still loved her.

Saints preserve us, I hope Pauly gets home soon, I could use a hug. Carefully she stepped into the tub, then slowly sank into the steaming water. Sliding back she closed her eyes, relaxing, her fears forgotten in the familiar setting.

Hearing the front door open she called out, "I'm in for a wash luv, be out in a sec." Lying there, she felt a sigh of relief knowing he was finally home. No one dared harm her now.

The footsteps in the hall seemed unfamiliar, "Pauly, is that you?" *Just me silly insecurities,* she thought.

Looking up, she screamed as a small man appeared. Reaching up to the shelf over her head, he turned on the radio. Before she could react he dropped it in the water, smiling grimly. A second later he was gone.

The brief sizzle and smoke from the radio stopped quickly as Mary shook uncontrollably. Her back arched out of the water as she convulsed then went limp, her eyes rolling back in her head. Her legs half out of the tub, blood trickled from her lips as she died.

Thirteen—A special time

Today was going to be special, meeting at the Allingham Hotel in Bundoran; eating out with Eamonn and his family; it all seemed so Irish. Annie walked out to the car as Will locked the cottage door. More from habit than fear of thieves, he turned the key. *Can't have the fairy folk breaking in,* he thought, amusing himself.

Arriving early, he followed Annie as she went on a tour of the lobby. Fascinated with the artwork she studied each piece, giving her approval or disapproval of each drawing or painting. That done in less time than it takes to say "over", she followed Will out to wait in the lounge for their friends' arrival.

Will looked at his watch, one-twenty, then heard Annie, "There's Kate and Mollie." She waved at the young woman.

"Great," Will said, "I'm so glad they could come."

"Hi Kate," Annie called, still waving her hand.

"Hi there," Kate replied.

Mollie clung to her mother's arm, happy and smiling. Dressed in a green and white striped dress trimmed in red, her face fairly beamed out of a floppy little hat.

"Hi, Mollie," Annie said smiling at the small person.

"It's good to see you, Kate," Will said, "I wasn't sure you were coming."

"Oh, sometimes it's a struggle to get out you know, but I wanted to."

Annie pointed to a sports vehicle just pulling into the parking lot. Soon Eamonn hurried into the lobby determined as always, never to be late.

"Oh and it's the workin' man finally gettin' here," Will said in his best Irish accent.

"Don't be funning the host, I'm here aren't I?" Eamonn replied, smiling.

Seated around a wooden table in the pub, the two friends had great fun talking and laughing together. Ordering their food, Kate, Annie and Eamonn had baked chicken with sauce, green beans, mashed potatoes for the ladies and chips for Eamonn. Mollie had fish and chips, while Will ordered trout topped with baby shrimp.

"Good trout, where do they get them?" he asked.

"They find them in streams," Eamonn replied sarcastically.

"Oh, I didn't know there were trout in the streams."

"Well, no, actually they're coming from the fields," Eamonn said with a gleam in his eye.

"Oh," Will said, not really thinking, "brown trout."

Kate looked across at Will then at Eamonn, rolling her eyes.

Eamonn groaned, "Oh, stinky monkey butts."

Kate looked at her husband pointedly.

"I got that from him," he said defensively.

"Oh, it's you I have to thank for that charming expression," she said, smiling at Will.

"I'm sorry," he said, grinning sheepishly.

For all the good-hearted humor, Will couldn't stop thinking about what he and Eamonn had been talking about. Determined not to spoil lunch with talk of bad dreams and such, he thought he'd save it for another time.

After the last bite was savored they walked across Main Street to the seawall. Below, a sandy beach stretched for miles. As far as the eye could see, Donegal Bay covered the horizon. The tide was out and a maze of long flat rocks was visible, smoothed by millions of years of crashing waves. Eamonn explained how surfing was a popular sport in this part of Ireland. The history of the village was quite interesting, situated right up against the cliffs and a fairy bridge. The Bundoran Golf Club was over ninety-nine years old and with the exception of cars crowding the narrow streets, all was the same as it had been for years.

Time seemed to fly by and Eamonn had to get back to work. Will thanked him for the wonderful lunch.

"Listen, on Friday I'll cook for you guys," he said enthusiastically.

"Yes," Annie agreed, "Will's a great cook."

"Oh, you don't have to do that," Eamonn said, trying to give him an out.

"It would be fun, really," he insisted.

"What should I do?" Kate asked.

"You've done so much, just sit back and relax. We'll bring everything," Will replied.

"Are you sure?" Kate asked.

"Will doesn't do well with dessert," Annie said.

"Oh, good, I'll make pudding," Kate offered.

As Eamonn and Kate drove off down the street, the two oldies decided to stay awhile and do some sightseeing. As they walked down the cobblestone sidewalk, Will tried not to notice the diminutive person approaching. Almost a caricature, the small man was dressed in gray bulky clothes; a sweater, green stocking cap, pants with the stains of life shining through and gray bulky boots. As he shuffled by, his hat down to the top of his eyes, he never looked over; his long beard hanging limply on his chest. *He most certainly seems lost,* Will thought.

"Annie, a leprechaun," he whispered.

She looked for a moment, not really going for it, the distraction of the shops too great.

Oh well, Will mused, *probably just my imagination anyhow, Leprechauns don't walk the streets.*

Fourteen—A Mystery

The next morning dawned bright and early. Mullaghmore was laid out in all its glory, sheep and cattle grazing in neatly divided strips of land and fields. Nearby, swans glided across a placid mirror-like pond. Seated in the living room, Will looked down the hill at the splendor of it all. Suddenly his eyes were drawn to huge brown eyes staring at him from a very narrow face. A small rabbit with two very pointed ears was hiding in the tall grass. Staring hard for a moment, it settled back in its haven of safety, at home in the grass.

An Irish rabbit, Will thought whimsically, *seems to be a trusting soul.*

From a field, a herd of cows had wandered down to the shore of Donegal Bay. Wading up to their ankles, some stared out to sea while the rest nosed and sniffed, sand covering their hooves as they walked leisurely up the beach. Relaxed and free, the herd stood on the beach like lost children. Evolution in progress?

Quite strange, he thought. *Oh well, to each his own.*

Smiling, he continued his writing. Excited to be off and running again, the story unfolding, he busily worked his pen taking notes. As he read and wrote about the people of Ireland, a loud rapping sound, then grunting in the chimney caught his attention. Laughing to Annie, he said, "See? That's what I heard."

She nodded skeptically, "That was only a bird."

Unconvinced he turned back to his book, 'The Peoples of Ireland'. Suddenly they heard a clanking, as something fell down the chimney.

"What's that?" he said nervously.

Annie went to the screened-in opening. Eyeing a small narrow object, she reached in and pulled out a bone; dried leathery pieces of meat still clinging to the surface. "A pork chop?" Will asked, smiling. *Now what birds are carnivores? Maybe they like pigs in Ireland. Oh well, I'll not worry about that now.*

Annie smiled at him. "Your over-active imagination should come up with something good for this."

"Well, it does seem odd," he said quietly.

Fifteen—A day trip to Donegal

It was a sunny day, and even though Will had caught cold he decided to take Annie for a ride past Ballyshannon. The N15 wasn't busy through Bundoran and the sky was clear. It was a beautiful day and the narrow streets of Ballyshannon were filled with shoppers off to buy some rare treat. Young people clustered in groups had just gotten out of school.

Past the quaint village the scene opened into fields of bright green divided neatly by yellow gorse, forming hedge-like fences. Decorated by the impenetrable bush, stone walls consisting mostly of flat rocks stacked three feet high, defined clear boundaries.

Hoping to get near the sea, Will turned off at a sign pointing to Rossnowlagh. Driving for awhile it seemed they were going back towards Ballyshannon.

"That's a beautiful house," Annie said wistfully.

"Maybe we'd better stop and ask someone how far it is to the shore."

Will pulled over near a man clearing pieces of building material from a castle-like house. The smell of the sea in the air, he gazed at the open water some miles to the west. While he asked directions, Annie went across the road to photograph the ruin of a small stone church thousands of years old.

"Hello there, nice house you're building."   Will called out as he approached the man. "Would you know if this road goes up the coast to Donegal?"

While he waited for the stranger to get nearer to the edge of the road, a large black dog ran up. Quickly the Irishman issued a sharp command, but not before the animal jumped up on Will's new Levis to greet him. As they talked, the dog brought something in its mouth and dropped it at the writer's feet. While the man gave him directions, Will looked down to see what the dog had brought. At his feet was a rock.

"No, yiz have to go back the way ya came."

The dog stood frozen in front of Will, staring down at the rock between his feet.

"Ya take N15 to Donegal, then yiz can go along the coast," the gray-haired man said.

Will bent down and picked up the stone the dog was staring at and offered it to him. Grabbing it quickly the dog walked around him in a circle then dropped it again at his feet, staring at the rock.

"Oh, thank you," Will said, a bit distracted.

"Ya on holiday here abouts?"

"Yes, yes we are," Will responded as he picked up the stone again and offered it to the black dog who hadn't taken his eyes off it.

"Ya like Ireland?"

"Yes, I do. It's just like in the movies," Will mumbled, not wanting to offend. "It's really beautiful."

Again the dog stood frozen waiting for him to pick up the stone.

Handing it to the expectant animal, Will said his goodbyes as he saw Annie crossing the road to join him. The Irishman issued an order to the dog, then waved at the tourists walking up the road to their small rental car.

The landscape to Donegal was mostly rolling hills of green. In a Norman Rockwell setting, hundreds of sheep and lambs dotted the hillside, their white coats of wool and black faces etched in nature's mural. The town clustered together on a large roundabout, was a tourist haven of Irish knick-knacks. In her glory, Annie roamed the shops filled with talking leprechauns, postcards of Ireland in glorious color for 30 pence, miniature ceramic smoking pipes decorated with clover, fairies and pottery in various shapes and colors.

Will breathed a sigh of relief as they headed back to their car with relatively few purchases.

That evening they relaxed in the cottage, him making copious notes while Annie read one of the several novels she had brought along. More tired than he'd like to admit, it was a relief to go to bed early. *Well, ten-thirty isn't early,* he thought, but at least the sun had gone down. *It'll take some getting used to, reminds me of Alaska. Gads, how do people sleep?* The night went quickly as Will woke at five a.m. Seated in the wooden loveseat he searched the yard for his morning visitor. It had become a ritual watching the brown bunny jumping lightly over the street towards the cottage garden. Today it stopped near the edge of the uncut grass. The wind blew the seedlings as the small rabbit looked towards the street with its ears laid back. Large eyes watched the writer busily recording the strange scene. *Maybe it's a guard for the little people, a sentinel for all the creatures of the yard.* A free spirit, it sat sniffing the air. Quite alone, it explored the tall grass and beyond. Dandelion puffs of white stood like household decorations. A feast for the young rabbit, it tasted a bit of buttercup and clover, then Irish grass. Ears up, then down, its antennas listened for danger.

The wind started to blow hard as waves formed on Donegal Bay. Swells first, whitecaps rushed forward. Will watched with detached interest, trying to think like the Irish character in his novel. It was difficult creating dialog without slipping into English pub slang. *No matter,* he thought, *Mullaghmore is a wonderful place to stay;* the movement of the sea beckoning the adventurer in him.

Waves crashed continually against the cliffs of Bundoran to the north. Far and away the most beautiful sight, the sun broke through the clouds giving color to the now roiling sea. Green near the shore, it crashed in waves of white on the brown sand. Above the dunes, the green of long grass held tightly to the mix of soil and crystalline particles. The shadow of passing clouds belied the changing color of the sea.

Emotions extended in wonder, Will watched the storm play out. A lone white sailboat lay anchored near the ancient rock jetty as white water rode the green in its endless journey to nowhere.

Sixteen—A game of chance

It was a quiet afternoon and Will felt good. "What say we go to Bundoran? We can check out the amusement centers, try our luck."

Annie's face lit up, looking out the large pane of glass towards the glimmering sea. "I'd like that," she said confidently. "Maybe I'll win the big one."

Driving down the narrow highway had gotten much easier for Will. It felt safer.

"I've never seen so many people," he exclaimed.

The town, which had been empty all week, was now filled with families and children running across the street. Sounds of recognition filled the air.

"O'Flarety, ya no good sausage."

"Aye, ya storm in a teacup, when ya comin' over?" A response came flying back.

All the while two little girls dressed in snow-white confirmation dresses danced about on the sidewalk.

Will forged ahead, leading Annie up the sidewalk to the Goldfinger Club. Less crowded than the Olympic, it had an air of elegance. Even though they played two-pence machines, the jackpots paid up to two hundred punts.

"Oh, my," Annie said happily, "this is better than Vegas."

Finding a seat, she sat down to some serious gambling with her sack of two-pence coins.

"Gads, Annie, these machines are not going to kick. They're taking all my coins."

Suddenly her face lit up as two red sevens and a wild card lined up on her screen. The electronic chun chun seemed like music to her ears as the meter went up and up, 467, 540, 799, 1050, 1200, 1400. Her face flushed with joy as the machine reached its limit of fifteen hundred coins.

"How much is that?" Will asked the quiet little man who ran the place.

"Eh, I don't know. Wait a second, I'll be back," he said, muttering something in Gaelic.

Hungry, it was decided to stop the games and find some place to eat. A gloomy day at best, the chill hastened their search. Headed down Main Street, an eatery with a sign on the sidewalk seemed most appealing. Entering Caroline's Café, it felt cozy and warm, the aroma of good food adding to their appetites. In the back was a deli counter for ordering food to go, tables in two rows against each wall. Deciding the later, a waitress came by and gave them menus.

"Oh, traditional Irish beef stew," Will mumbled, his stomach grumbling.

"That sounds wonderful," Annie said to herself, deeply engrossed in the menu.

The Waitress came up to their table with a cheery smile.

"You from America?"

"Yes, how'd you know?" Annie asked.

"You kin' tell easy enough," she replied, laughing.

"I though we'd hidden ourselves with my hat and all."

"I don't think so," she said.

The afternoon crowd was coming in so the noise level had risen.

"What'll ya be havin'," she asked loudly.

"I'll have the traditional Irish beef stew," Will replied, "And a pot of tea."

"That's grand, Mister. And you, Missus?"

"A turkey club on toasted brown bread."

"Would ya like some tae?"

"Yes, yes, with milk please," Annie said.

While the waitress hurried to turn in their order, it occurred to Will he was in a foreign land. The dialog, a mix of Gaelic with a trace of English was hard to understand. Still, with all the laughter and good humor, he felt right at home.

Bringing their tea first, Annie struck up a conversation with the waitress. "My name's Annie Bonner."

Hello, mine's Patricia."

"Patricia, it's great meeting you," Will added.

"This your first time here?"

" That it is," Annie replied, "And there's been more excitement than I'd like to admit."

"Oh, I don't know about that.," Patricia said, turning to leave. "I'll have your order out shortly."

Waiting, Annie started reading the children's menu. "Look here Will, there's a Little Smartie Menu on the back," as she began reading, " Bugs Bunny Burger, Fred's Fish Fingers, Simpson's Sausage & Chips, Casper's Crunchy chips."

Laughing to herself, it seemed lost on her husband, busy people watching.

"You know I'm 14 Euros ahead, Mr. Bonner," she said with a glint in her eye.

"Well, I've lost five," He interjected.

Carrying a large tray, Patricia appeared at their table. The bowl of stew was steaming hot, much to Will's satisfaction. Placing Annie's club sandwich and some bread for Will's stew on the table, she asked if there'd be anything else.

"Nope, that's it."

Left to their own devices, each ate their selection with great pleasure. Finally finished, they sat for a while sipping hot tea.

"That was very good Mrs. Bonner," Will said, eating a last bit of bread.

"Yes it was," Annie said as they got up to leave, thanking Patricia very much.

"Come back," she said.

"We will," Will replied as they left.

Seventeen—Untold secrets

Reilly Currie sat with his back to the brick wall. Except for the flickering of a candle it was dark. It was near the time, five more minutes. The bell would strike midnight and he would pass the note, then they would recite the oath, if only to protect their families. All the illness and death had clung to his heart. *This hill is the curse of us all.*

Thinking of past conversations he ran over it again:

"McCoskey, have you heard anything?"

"No, and I'm sure it's too late," the stocky man had said.

"We're sworn," he had replied, "on me grandfather's grave and his da's as well. There's no telling whether harm's comin' our way."

That was then, and this is now. The tall redheaded man wiped a bit of nervous sweat from his brow as ever so faint footsteps grew louder. Magically it seemed, a small man in a top hat appeared in the light.

"Do you have the list, Reilly?" a voice hard as stone, asked.

"Aye, I do," he said, handing a neatly folded piece of paper to a wrinkled hand.

Others appeared as the frog-like voice spoke, "Now swear again."

Together they formed a circle in the desolate graveyard. The wind murmuring in sympathy, they began, "Spirits of the hill, keepers of the oath, hear us now, this we pledge. On pain of death no word shall pass our lips, no person shall know our deeds."

Gray clouds glided across the moonless sky. "Our oath is set," they whispered. Fearfully each looked at the other and fled.

Eighteen—Another death

Will and Annie hurried from the grocery store in Sligo. Finding the right veggies for the salad, new potatoes and fresh asparagus had been easier than expected. With the French bread and salmon in their bags, it was a relief to have everything bought.

It had started to rain on their way towards Ballyshannon. Passing the burial place of W.B. Yeats, Annie thought of the laureate's Nobel Prize for literature and Irish poetry wishing aloud they could stop sometime to take pictures.

"We will, sweetpea, right now we got to get over to Eamonn's house so I can start cooking."

"Never mind, maybe tomorrow," Annie said wistfully.

Filled with warm feelings, she looked over at the man driving quite well now. The wonderful way he had loved her all these years. Cleaning house when she was tired or unable was a treasure she would never forget.

The gray sky did little to spoil the festive mood as they drove up to the old Parisian house. Annie went ahead of him, knocking on the door. The sound of footsteps followed by Kate's voice interrupted any further thoughts as the door swung open.

"Hi, Kate," Annie said, greeting the happy face.

"Hello, it's good to see you. Eamonn will be here soon." Waving her arm for them to enter, they followed.

"Sit," Kate said as they came into the kitchen. "Did you go see the sights?"

"Actually, we just laid around the last few days. Jet lag and fear of driving has a way of stifling the urge," Will said.

"Ah, but you need to see Ireland. It's beautiful, you know," Kate said dreamily. More to Mollie than her guests, she added, "Aye, it 'tis. The loughs are best in the spring."

"They sound beautiful," Annie said with a smile, "we're looking forward to it."

"When Eamonn gets home he'll be anxious to show you some places to go."

While Annie talked to Kate about memories of childhood and life, Will set up his veggies to cut and cook. As they simmered he continued to chop lettuce for the salad, then taking a large pan from the stack Kate had provided he made the sauces. It was great fun and never ceased to be enjoyable for the aging man. *I should have been a chef,* he thought, *that's it, Chef Finnegan Bonner.*

Time flew by as he talked and chopped. By the time Eamonn got home from the shop, he was working at a fevered pitch.

"Ah, 'tis the great Irish cook, Sir Finnegan," Eamonn whispered.

"Yes, so don't be buggin'," Will shot back. "I've had enough trouble keeping the females out of me kitchen."

"All kidding aside, it's a grand thing you're doing," Eamonn said.

Thirty minutes had passed since Eamonn had come home and the kitchen had started to have the look of unfinished ideas. Even though Will was determined to do it all himself, it became apparent he needed another set of hands to heat bread, peel hard boiled eggs, dice green onions while he made the sauce. Reluctantly he whispered softly, "Annie, I may have to say uncle on this one. I can't do it all like I thought." Looking at her desperately, he smiled as she came into the kitchen.

"Okay, what should I do?"

"If you would stir the Béarnaise sauce and watch the salmon. I can set up the salads and bread."

The wine Kate had opened went well with fish, and her dessert of peaches with a chocolate drop sauce was wonderful.

"This is good," Will said genuinely impressed.

After they had finished eating, Eamonn took Will into the family room overlooking the bay while Annie and Kate cleaned the kitchen.

Over a hot cup of tea, Will looked at his friend. "It's so peaceful here."

"Aye, I'm wishing the same was true for me," Eamonn said sadly. "Me friend's wife died in an accident."

"What happened?"

"The Garda said she electrocuted herself in the tub."

"Carelessness?"

"Oh, I don't think so. Mary was safety conscious. She'd never drop a radio in water she's standing in."

"Maybe she slipped and knocked it. Was the mat in the bottom?"

"That's a good question. Another might be why the radio? Me friend Pauly said it was only there for him, she never used it."

"Did she have any enemies?" Thinking for a moment Will didn't wait for an answer. "Could be someone wanted her out of the way."

"I'm not sure," Eamonn said evenly, "but I'm knowin' one thing, it was no accident."

Will stared out at the muddy bay below. An uneasy feeling was growing in his gut as he tried to rationalize why a radio someone never used had fallen in her bath. Suicides, depression, and what now appeared to be homicide had only increased the puzzling questions.

"If there is anything I can do, I'll gladly help."

"Oh, I'll not be needin' any help going to the funeral," Eamonn replied heavily.

"Would it be all right if I went?"

Eamonn looked at his friend waiting for an answer. "Aye, that would be fine, Sir William," he said with a grim smile.

Nineteen—An investigation starts

The drive from Eamonn's house overlooking Ballyshannon Harbor to Paul McNulty's small flat was slow at best. They didn't say much as they waited behind a double-parked car on Back Street, the narrow cobblestone road affording few spaces to park. A one-way thoroughfare, it seemed to take forever to get by. The oppressive cloud cover only added to the depressing journey. All one-way, they followed Market Street then Castle past the Bank of Ireland and the miniscule Post Office with a bright green postal truck out front. Over what was left of the River Erne, Eamonn took the roundabout keeping a sharp eye out for on coming traffic from the right.

The gray brick duplex seemed deserted except for the lone funeral car parked outside. A block wall surrounded the small yard. Inside the low entryway was a small room with chairs lined up against the walls. In the center on a small kitchen table the diminutive body of a woman was laid out. Candlelight reflected dully off the faded white dress, her slender face pointing towards the cracked, smoke-stained ceiling. From somewhere the haunting melody of Davy Spillane's Sea of Dreams filled the air.

Will strained to see in the darkened space. Cold eyes stared at the two newcomers in the half-light of shadows and candles. Hat in hand Eamonn went over to a man who stood in the corner.

"Dia duit," (God to you), Eamonn said.

The man looked up briefly, then accepted a hug from his friend.

"Dia Muire duit, Eamonn," (God and Mary to you), he replied.

As they spoke in whispers Will wondered if things would ever be the same for his friend. Not wanting to look, he could feel the hostility from around the room. An outsider, he knew he wasn't welcome. It was only natural to resent his coming to the wake of someone he didn't know. His only thought had been to comfort Eamonn. It seemed a good idea at the time, but now he wasn't so sure.

Through talking, Eamonn went to the table lit by candles and gently touched the woman's folded arms. He whispered something in Gaelic that wasn't understandable.

Standing near the door, Will felt awkward and out of place. His head bowed he said the only prayer he could think of at a time like this, the Lord's.

Eamonn backed away from the table then signaled for him to come over.

Paul McNulty looked quizzically at Will. "Cen Tainm ata ort?"

"Your name," Eamonn clarified.

"Will Bonner," he replied.

Reaching out, the stone-faced man shook his hand; the force registering in his white knuckles. Eamonn pointed to a table near the wall and Will followed him to where an old woman dressed in black poured them a drink of dark fluid. Taking the stained water glasses, both men drank the amber whiskey. Not wanting to offend, Will followed Eamonn's lead and drained his glass.

Putting on their hats, they stood near the door. His head spinning slightly, Will watched as each man went over to the table and was poured a drink. Noticeable by his youth, a lanky dark-haired boy followed the last man taking his drink like the rest.

Walking over to the boy, Eamonn spoke softly, "Aye, Sean, I'm truly sorry for the loss of your Mum."

"Thanks, mate."

"You take care," Eamonn added, shaking the sad boy's hand.

The closed-in room was humid and smelled of embalming fluid. Afraid he would gag soon, Will was relived when Eamonn signaled him to go. Near the door, a little man stood to the side. Dressed in a black top hat and coat with tails, he watched them intently.

A cold wind penetrated Will's London Fog as he followed Eamonn to the car. Slowly, other dark forms filed out. A biting rain pelted the lonesome gathering. No one spoke as four men loaded the casket into the hearse. Disappearing around the corner, cars pulled up behind Eamonn's Jeep. Soon the hearse started up, proceeding on West Port to the turn on West Rock to the Roman Catholic cemetery.

Parking next to a crumbling block wall, Will followed Eamonn to the gravesite. Rain dripped off his umbrella as he watched them set the casket on the gurney. Twelve men, women, and close relatives stood around the opening in the earth.

At the head of the casket a parish priest gave a small eulogy, "Mary McNulty was a good mother and wife. It's the Lord's will that she go to her final resting place. May the Holy Father bless her and forgive all her mortal sins. Peace be to her and to all of you. Amen." Making the sign of the cross, he hurried away to his car.

The remaining mourners watched the rain-soaked box being lowered into the ground. Paul McNulty walked over to the edge of the grave and stared down at the coffin. Taking a handful of soil, he reluctantly released it over his love's final resting place.

The wind blew harder as Eamonn approached the edge of Mary's grave. In the background Will looked around the old cemetery with its gothic gravestones. It was darker now as he squinted for a second, trying to see what looked like the shadow of a person some twenty meters away. Lightning flashed across the sky, lighting up the morbid scene. Staring back, eyes the color of granite headstones seemed to pierce his soul. He trembled as he recognized the same small man, top hat and coat with tails, leaning against a large monument to a life long past.

Evilness probed Will's mind as he went over to Eamonn's side. The large man looked at the worried face. "Are you okay?"

"I've been better," he replied nervously.

"I know how different this must all seem, but it's a custom handed down from me father and his father back to the beginning of time."

"It's not that, Eamonn, it's the feeling that we're being watched. That little man who was at the wake, he's watching us now from over there." Will said tiredly.

Turning to where Will had pointed, Eamonn saw nothing but shadows.

"He was there a few seconds ago."

"I'm not sure who was at Pauly's. It might have been someone from Mary's side of the family, maybe an acquaintance."

Seeing the frustrated look on Will's face, Eamonn patted his friend on the shoulder. "I'm thinkin' the self and you had better check it out. We'll talk to Pauly after he's had some time. It's mourning he needs right now." Eamonn looked at Will and smiled, "Okay, mate?"

Will nodded as they left the gloomy place.

If it was truly an accident, why was everyone so suspicious? Even though he was an outsider, he was only paying his respects. Unsure what to think the old man from Maine was glad to be leaving. He'd have time for hashing in the morning, after a good night's sleep. Annie would be missing him by now. She always kept a watchful eye. It used to bother, but now after so many years he knew it was a sign of affection. He knew she loved him.

Twenty—Under the cover of darkness

The sound of waves gently lapping at the shore below was soothing to Flynn. Parked at the side of the road he could see jagged moss covered rocks and broken bits of seaweed brought in by the tide. Others had come for the meet. *Sure and they had better. Fear of pain and humiliation in front of the lads will keep them in line. Damn the man that falters,* he thought. *If it takes me last breath I'll see a secret's kept.*

Carefully, he removed a small blue crystal from a leather pouch and began to rub it with his thumb. Slowly an image grew. The gray sky of evening revealed itself as he saw a broad sandy beach. Soundless, he uttered words in his mind: *"Darkness come, darkness bright, spirits of the night give me yer might, will me yer strength. Stones and heather, pins and needles, let me fly. With wings of prey let me fly through the night."*

Rain fell as the wind blew harder. No one noticed the spirit rise from the entranced man. Rising quickly it surveyed the miniature shapes of the caravans below. Keen eyes looked to the west and Donegal Bay. Flying like the wind he searched the shore. Blown by the winds, past fields of grass and cliffs of stone, he followed the coast. The shapeless wraith passed over Bundoran and the military camp as hundreds of rabbits looked up fearfully.

Traffic on the N15 was light and no one saw. A rush of wind blended with the spirit of darkness nearing the small flat of Paul McNulty and his son. Settled on a window ledge he listened to the heartbeats within. The sight of a crucifix pushed him back as he tried to enter, an aura of soft light emanating from the cross clutched tightly in Sean McNulty's sleeping hands. A black and white sheepdog looked up growling.

Awakened, the young man petted the flop-eared animal trying to calm it.

"Here now dog, maybe spending the night wasn't such a good idea. There be rats and such around here."

Rubbing the stiff-backed dog seemed to ease the tension.

"That's okay boy, there'll be no trouble here."

Like a bolt of lightning the spirit left the window pulling back along the coast, retracting into the caravan parked in Mullaghmore. Flynn stiffened then collapsed onto the small table he'd been sitting at. *Damn the beast,* he thought. Sweat beaded on his brow as he tried to rethink his plan. He had to reach that boy, and soon. Twin orbs of darkness continued to glow as he looked out to sea. The rain poured down as he watched the invasive fluid cover the sealed window.

Twenty-one—A meal & old fables unfold

The wind was blowing fiercely as Will headed towards Ballyshannon. He felt rather dashing today in his thick sweater of multi-shades of blue, white Dockers (which he called knockers), and denim tennis shoes. It was cold, the ever-present wind off the Atlantic belied the fact that summer was on its way. Annie was dressed in her granny dress and long brown coat with its hood trimmed in dark fur. They had matching tennis shoes, a sign of affection, he thought.

He looked forward to the day's events with anticipation. Eamonn had invited them to a barbecue and for the world of him he wondered how it would happen outside in this raging blow. The occasional buffeting notwithstanding, he felt quite safe as they drove through Bundoran. In spite of the dismal weather, Annie was in rare form.

His mind seemed lost as reoccurring thoughts hounded him, wondering if life would ever be normal again for his friend. Eamonn's pain and fear was distressing and he wished there was some way he could ease it.

As they climbed the hill, the old brick house looked gloomier than in the past. *Just the clouds,* he wondered.

Annie saw a head peek out the window, "There's Kate," she said happily.

We've become quite close, Will thought. *Kate's a good person. It's nice counting her and Eamonn as friends.*

In a rush of howling wind they entered the house.

"How was your day?" Kate asked as they followed her to the kitchen sitting area.

"It was fun," Annie said smiling, "the cliffs near Bundoran were fascinating to explore."

"Oh, you went to the fairy bridge?" Kate asked, as she spun water out of some lettuce in a special device.

"Yes, we took lots of pictures. Will didn't want one of him on the fairy bridge, but I took it anyway," Annie replied cheerfully.

"Yes, and the great collector found a small starfish and a stick that looks like a shillelagh. Not very big, maybe it belonged to a fairy," Will said, laughing.

It seemed a special occasion as Kate cooked several patties of beef-burger in the broiler. In a grilling pan she added linked sausages. She placed a variety of cooked beans in an open jar, to be served cold.

While they talked, Mollie did her best eleven-month-old imitation of their conversation. She was a true delight, with a wisp of blonde hair turned up on her forehead, a real love. *Eamonn and Kate have surely won the lottery of life,* Will thought.

It must have been near six o'clock when Eamonn came bounding in the door from work. As he greeted them he went into the kitchen to hold his wife for a moment.

"Is there anything you're needing, sweet one?" he said, brushing her cheek with a kiss.

"Yes there is, you could start by opening those bottles of wine on the counter."

The love and affection in the room was intoxicating as everyone bantered back and forth.

"Me brother and his wife are coming," Eamonn said, looking out the kitchen window across the way. "They should be walking through the door any time now."

"Did you see his car come in?" Kate asked, busy with her tasks.

"He should be there, he gets off work right after me."

Listening; Will felt at a loss, as he thought of the importance of a job fading away; retired, that part of his life over.

Talking with Kate's sister, Deidre, was quite fun. She lived one street over from where Will and Annie were staying in Mullaghmore. A strong, feisty woman, she could fence with the best of them. *I'll have a hard time torturing her*, he thought.

Soon it was time to eat and the food was excellent. *Hunger and great cuisine are a perfect match*, Will thought. The red wine was relaxing.

Everyone seemed to click socially. Eamonn's brother, Patrick, and his wife arrived just as the serving was about to begin. Both a little shy, they busied themselves with the hot meal of sausage and burgers. Deidre bit into a green pepper. Her face drained as the hot veggie went down. Laughingly she offered one to Will and Annie. Not one to seem cowardly, Will acquiesced. His throat constricted as he tried to breathe. *Yes, they're hot,* he thought desperately, reaching for a drink. The sound of laughter filled the room as everyone watched the American slowly recover his dignity.

As they were finishing, two neighbors arrived. An older man and his grown son, the former carrying a beautiful German chocolate cake he had made. Eamonn introduced them around the table. A dashing man of seventy-seven years, Hans Richter was an excellent gardener, master chef and investor. Interesting to talk to, he had a wealth of ideas. Will was fascinated as he listened to him speak. His son, Fritz, seemed to be an expert on minerals and mining. The Black Forest cake was a culinary delight with four layers of creams and dark cherries.

Eamonn's mother and father arrived in time for cake and a glass of wine.

"It's a pleasure meetin' visitors to Ballyshannon," Mr. Gallagher said.

"Ireland's a treasure, Sir."

"True, it is that," Eamonn added.

"Here, here," Hans said enthusiastically, sipping his wine.

"How does it feel to live in a small village?" Will asked.

"Vell, quiet vould be a good vord," he said in his accented English.

"With a church right above you, it must seem that God is always near," Annie interjected. "It seems like good times for everyone. After school let out, we saw so many children lining up at the sweets shop."

"Yes, and that historic cemetery around St. Annie's is so picturesque," Will added.

"Not everyone has such good times," Kate said.

"That's the truth," Mr. Gallagher said solemnly. "There was a time when the poor were hidden."

Nodding, Eamonn and his brother listened intently to their father seated in a lounge chair near the door.

"Yes, and they still are," he added. "Which reminds me of a story told to me da."

Everyone grew silent as the old man spoke. "Many, many years ago, so the town wouldn't have to recognize the poor who had died, they had them taken through tunnels up to the church rather than bring them through the village. They were buried in the poverty section of the graveyard."

"Who built the tunnels?" Will asked.

"No one's knowing," Mr. Gallagher replied. "They've been there two, three hundred years, maybe more."

"Before the church was built?"

"That's possible, I'm not sure. You have to know the tales. If it's a good story, the years could be extended for affect," the old man said with a smile.

"Could be the fairies," Will ventured.

No telling why the tunnels were first built, he thought. *Still, three hundred years ago hiding social embarrassments was very possible.*

Time seemed to fly by, and soon everyone was preparing to leave for home. Wonderful hosts and neighbors were a good combination.

"It was great meeting your folks," Will said to Eamonn, standing near the door. "And Kate, the food was delicious."

"I hoped you'd like it, Sir William," she said cheerily.

"Yes, and Mollie, you are getting sleepy," Will said waggling his fingers at her like a hypnotist, "very sleepy."

Yawning, the baby hugged her mother, giggling at the funny-man standing in the doorway with his dark hat pulled down over gray hair, black wool coat hanging to the floor.

"Ah, dear Mollie, see you soon," Will said affectionately. "Take care of the little angel."

Eamonn nodded as he scooped up his little girl and held her close.

"Good visit, Sir W, you get a good night's sleep my friend."

Will waved, then got into the small green car. The drive back to the cottage was silent as Annie contentedly replayed the evening in her head and Will tried to figure out answers to nagging questions. *Was there another reason the tunnels were built? Had the little people constructed roads under their hill? What about the unexplained death of Mary McNulty? Maybe she had angered the fairies. They can be quite dangerous if provoked.* Doubting his own conclusions, he shook his head, *fairies, ridiculous.*

Driving the long narrow road to the cottage seemed to take forever. Finally they reached Barneys Hill. Tired, they gratefully fell into bed. Giving his love a kiss and a hug Will lay awake thinking, the half-light of a summer's eve still peeking around the drapes.

In the early morning he sat in the living-room looking out at the cold gray sky. Unable to sleep, he pondered what he and Annie should do this day. A movement in the garden drew his attention to the small brown bunny with long ears and eyes like saucers. It hopped about, its short white cottontail held high. It didn't notice the man standing at the window watching intently. *You're braver today, little friend,* Will thought as it walked on the cement walkway covered with moss. Unnoticed, or so it thought, it sat on its hind legs eating a long strand of clover it had just pulled from the earth. The small creature seemed surer now as it eyed the man in the window. *Perhaps it's a spirit,* Will thought, *a small clever spirit.* Well fed, the young rabbit padded across the garden, stopping here and there to taste some choice morsel or notice a strange new sight. Though always vigilant, it never looked up. *No fear of menace from above. Maybe there's a lesson here,* Will mused, *perhaps I needn't look up.*

Smiling to himself, it seemed he was losing his mind. The wee folk in the form of a rabbit? Reading excerpts from a book of poems by the Irish poet, W.B. Yeats, Will wondered if the depression Eamonn's neighbors were suffering was contagious, if it had become an accepted way of being, living their lives as though they had a right to feel bad. Thinking of similarities, he tried to match any common thread of those living on the hill. *Maybe it's the food. The soda bread tasted a little odd, something in the grain perhaps. Possibly their creative sides died, the weather's always cloudy and gray. Gads, it rains too much,* he thought looking through the water-streaked window. *Perhaps it's genetic, or alcoholism. There are lots of pubs in Ballyshannon.*

His mind made up, he decided to offer his friend help. Try solving the puzzle of why people were 'offing' themselves and why Mary McNulty may have killed herself in such a bizarre way.

Dialing Eamonn's number he waited for the unfamiliar rarrp-rarrp of the phone ringing to end.

"Hello?"

"Eamonn, it's me, Will."

"Aye, I recognize your voice."

"And well you should," Will said, half laughing. "Listen, I know it's a touchy subject, but I'm thinking I'd like to help you answer a few questions about your friend Mary McNulty's demise."

"Hmm, that would be grand. That is, if there is one."

"For starters, you mentioned she never listened to the radio, didn't like it."

"That's true enough," Eamonn replied softly.

"Maybe her husband suspected her of playing around and decided to end it," Will said, more to himself than to the phone.

"Ah, no, I don't think so," Eamonn groaned. "Pauly isn't the type to kill anyone. Anyway, Mary was true to her man, I'd stake my reputation on that. If she had even mentioned something like that it would have been all over the village. Her being out with another man is not likely, there're no secrets when it comes to being unfaithful. Sure and the whole town would have known," Eamonn replied, his voice fading.

Logically, it seemed the only place to begin their research, as Will liked to think of it, was with Eamonn's friend Pauly. See what he knows, any clues that might point in some new direction.

"I know this isn't pleasant, but what say I come around tomorrow and we go visit your friend. I've got a couple of questions that need answering."

The line went dead for a moment. "Hello, Eamonn? You there?" Will asked, unsure if intruding in matters that weren't his business had upset his friend.

"Aye, I'm here. I was just wondering if it'd be a good idea so soon after the funeral."

"It's up to you. I think your mind would rest a lot easier if you knew Mary's death was truly an accident. No foul play, as they say in the detective stories," Will said with an air of conviction.

"Aye, you may be right," Eamonn replied with a reluctant sigh. "Alright, we'll go, but we must be tactful."

"Tactful it is," Will said, adding, "What say I meet you around eleven-thirty near the corner of Main and Castle Streets outside the chemist's shop?"

"That'd be grand. Then we'll start detecting," Eamonn said half-heartedly.

As the line went dead a chill ran through Will's bones. *I'm tired,* he thought. *Maybe Annie would agree to stay home and rest today. We'll play gin rummy, then after she wins again I'll write and she can read.*

Shaking his head he stared out the window. Rain-swept clouds covered the sun, as a cold wind whistled through the partly opened panes facing the sea.

Twenty-two—A vow taken

Clouds filled the sky, blocking the moon. Above and beyond the slope of the hill no sound could be heard. The cold bite of winter lingered in the air. Only the brave or the lost would venture forth on this night. A ring of trees hid the entrance of a well-worn path covered with ferns. An occasional sheep stood guard, its black face invisible to any passers by.

Rainwater dripped onto the table's edge, slowly moving toward the hand busily writing in a small ledger. The yellow light of a candle revealed the features of a wrinkled face. Deep in thought, the little man whispered a name then checked it off. "Wizards and trolls, slithers and slugs, let the curse be done," he growled over and over as he moved down each line.

No one stirred as the words echoed through the room deep beneath the earth's surface. Cold and damp, the gravel and mud stuck to their shoes. Worn and tattered wool coats hung on tired frames. Frozen in fear they listened, staring at the floor. *If time was a bubble it'd be bustin',* more than one thought tiredly.

The reading went on and on. No one seemed to care save the one. Always the readings, then the wait. Their eyes dark voids, their souls gone, only the voice reciting the names on the list pushed them forward.

One by one they came to the table, each held out his hand and recited along, "With this offering I come to thee, sworn in blood."

The flick of a razor across each palm glistened red, as each paired with another. Bound in a contract with no escape they all said their words until the room fell silent, the faint scribble of the little man screaming out their pain.

Them that takes, pays, the evil one thought flatly. *If it takes two thousand years I'll get me due.*

Twenty-three—A friend's pain

The noisy wipers clacked as fat raindrops covered the windshield. Driving to Paul McNulty's street-side apartment reminded Will of scenes from old black and white Ingemar Bergman movies.

Empty and desolate, it seemed the people had vanished, leaving gray brick edifices of another time. *Perhaps if we clicked our feet together . . .* Will smiled, *I've been in the forest too long. Best keep this stuff to myself,* he thought.

Parking in front of the three-foot brick wall surrounding Paul's flat, he wondered if any good would come of this. Barging in on other people's affairs uninvited was one thing, but barging in uninvited in a town on the West Coast of Ireland was quite another. Maybe if he spoke from the heart, sat with the man, this widower, and explained how Eamonn was his friend, and Mary and Paul were Eamonn's friends. He would just like to see justice done, if for no other reason than peace of mind.

Eamonn forced the rusted knocker against the metal plate, the dull thud barely discernible through the surrounding walls. The Irishman grabbed the knocker again, banging it repeatedly against the door. Putting his hand on Will's shoulder, they started to leave as imperceptible the knob began to turn.

A tired voice whispered through a musty crack, "Who's there?"

"Tis I and me friend, Will Bonner, " Eamonn said. "If you're feeling up to it we'd like to visit for a while." Adding urgently, "It's important, Pauly."

It seemed they stood for hours waiting for a reply as the rain intensified. Without a sound the door opened. Standing to the side, a stooped six-foot man eyed the two men. Dripping wet, they waited, listening to the eternal tick of the clock, before being invited in. Lifelessly he went to a small fireplace and added another piece of peat. Flames flickered around an old kettle hanging on a darkened hook.

"You'll be wantin' a cup of tae," Paul said without emotion.

"That would be grand, old friend," Eamonn replied.

"Here, take a seat by the kettle, it's warmer."

Soon steam poured out of the small hanging pot. Seated at the table, Will looked around at the starkness. Except for a few photos on a corner hutch there was only the kitchen table, four chairs and a rocker near the center of the room. Paul's black wool coat, white shirt covered by a vest and dirty long pants gave testament to the man's hardworking character. Slowly he brought three saucers from the cupboard then three cups from the hooks attached to the shelf. On the mantle, above the kettle, sat a bottle of Old Bushmill. The kettle in one hand and the whiskey in the other, he sat down at the table across from Will.

"Would you care for a spot in your tae?"

"Yes, I would," Will replied shivering.

"And you, mate?" he asked Eamonn.

"Is the Pope Catholic?"

The three men laughed softly as Paul McNulty poured a good measure into each cup, then topped it off with strong steaming tea. Nodding, Paul raised his cup to the other two.

The silence that followed seemed to soothe the men as the hot whiskey lightened their somber mood. After a second helping of tea and Old Bushmill, Will felt his face warming.

When they had relaxed a bit, Eamonn looked into his friend's suffering eyes.

"Pauly, I know this won't be easy, but I need to . . . actually me friend here from America would like to help us find out what happened to Mary. He's a mystery writer and has a knack for finding answers. You remember Will from the funeral?"

Will reached across the table to grasp Paul's outstretched hand. "I'm pleased to see you again, Paul."

"Aye, likewise," he replied, "but I'm not sure I'll be needin' any help with what I'm supposin'. The wee folk took their due."

"Sir, more times than not, things are not as they seem," Will said, his voice a little uneven.

"Pauly, I know Mary never liked the radio, so how'd it get in the tub?" Eamonn asked.

"Aye, and that's a secret," Paul replied, his face filled with pain.

"Could your wife have made an enemy? Someone who hated enough to kill." Will wondered out loud before realizing it was better left unasked.

"Oh, I don't think so. The ones we knows are few except for our boy, Sean. Bad stuff, me best friend died a few days before Mary, bless his soul," Paul said raggedly.

"Aye, Joseph McGowan. Seems they found a knife in his back," Eamonn said.

"Is that the work of fairies? I thought they used magic," Will interjected.

"True enough," Eamonn replied, "but you can never be sure they didn't put a man up to it."

"Aye, and that's the God's truth," Paul added, casting a furtive glance around the room.

"Did your wife love you, Mr. McNulty?" Will asked gently.

Paul's face twisted in anger, then softened when he saw the earnest look in Will's eyes.

"Aye, that she did, and I know what yer asking. No, she didn't have a jealous lover. She might have had an admirer or two but no other luvs."

"I'm sorry for asking," Will said. "Did the Garda find any clues?"

"Ah, that'd be wasting your time, I'm sure they're useless. Better the time spent in the pub with yer mates," Paul said bitterly.

The crackle of the burning peat seemed to add credence to the suffering man seated across from Will. Satisfied that this husband hadn't killed his wife in a jealous rage and there were no lovers, he decided the next stop would be the Garda. If anyone had hard evidence it would be them.

Thanking his friend for the tea and whiskey, Eamonn said his good-byes. As Will shook hands with

Paul he whispered, "Whoever did this to your wife will be brought to justice."

A tear came to Paul McNulty's eyes, "Aye, that'd be grand, Sir."

Twenty-four—Searching for answers

The entrance to the Garda Station was empty except for the bedraggled looking drunk leaving. So many pieces of the puzzle didn't fit. A conspiracy of men and fairies? Will entered the inner sanctum of law and order thoroughly confused. Though it was never too late to find the truth, he wondered if he would ever discover what had happened to the dear lady who had supposedly committed suicide. Obviously it was too late to talk to her, but he prayed that the local Garda would have some answers.

The long corridor to the front desk was lined with images of local dignitaries. A large framed photo of O'Donnell, a descendant of the chieftains of Donegal, hung ominously near that of the President of Ireland. Seated at the desk, a rotund man in a gray uniform was busy writing. It seemed to take forever to be noticed. The whole atmosphere felt quite stifling. The smell of dead skin and controlled anger permeated the air.

Looking up slowly from his busy writing, the officer eyed the silver-haired man standing in front of him. "Ah yes, and what might I do for you, Sir?"

"My name is Will Bonner. I write mysteries. I'm working on a story based on unusual deaths that have occurred in the last twelve months."

"Well, Mr. Bonner, I've not heard of any unusual deaths in Ballyshannon," the officer replied stoically.

"Actually, I was thinking of one particular case," Will replied.

Seated at the worn desk, the bothered man eyed the American. "And what case would that be, Mr. Bonner?"

"Mary McNulty," Will said evenly. "I was curious if there have been any new developments, any new evidence."

"And why would the likes of you be askin'?"

"Paul McNulty is a friend of mine."

"Ah yes, he's yer friend," the Guard repeated, his back stiffening. "We have no new evidence. Mary McNulty died of accidental electric shock."

"It was said she was found with the radio in the tub, even though she never listened to it, didn't like it," Will persisted.

The officer shook his head as he looked through the papers on his desk.

"There's nothin' in the records to indicate Mary disliked the radio. Where might ya be gettin' yer information, Sir?"

"I must be mistaken," Will said.

"Aye, ya must be at that. Our investigation was very thorough," the agitated man replied. "Will there be anything else you'll be needin'?"

"No, no, thank you very much for your time," Will replied as he turned to leave.

"You have a nice visit here in Ireland, Mr. Bonner," the officer said. "A word of advice, it might be better to leave the detectin' to us and concentrate on your writin'," the stern-faced officer added. Will nodded in agreement as he quickly exited the gloomy building.

Twenty-five—Spiritual musing

Afternoon light reflected off the crystal vase, throwing a rainbow across the wood and leather furniture decorating the large study. With an admiring eye, Father Kerrigan looked about his new domain. *The Lord has been most generous,* he thought. The parishioners had agreed to build him a new home, one befitting a servant of the Lord. A shred of insecurity filling his mind, he wondered if the members would be able to pay the seven hundred thousand it cost to build. *A nice home is so expensive these days,* he mused. *Well, I'll prod them a little at Sunday service. They can surely tithe a bit more.*

A bell rang in another room, interrupting his thoughts. The walk to the front door seemed endless as he went down the long hallway towards the foyer. Small brass plaques identifying bedrooms, a parlor, and an office marked closed doors on each side. Finely polished floors and oriental carpets pleased the cleric hurrying to the grand entryway. *The housekeeper should be here every day,* he thought puffing along.

The wind whistled through the hallway as he opened the solid oak door. His priest's gown fluttered out behind him as he stared sternly at the tattered man with hat in hand. "Haven't I told you to be calling at the rear, McIntyre?"

"Aye, yer right Father, I forgot meself for a moment. It won't be happenin' agin," the skinny man said shivering, his worn coat hardly stopping the cold. "Might I come in for a moment, it's freezin' out here and I've got somethin' that might be of interest." His thin lips, curling at the corners, seemed to make his nose protrude.

Eyeing the poorly dressed person standing on his porch, the ruffled priest motioned him to follow. "Close the door firmly, mind you."

Walking down the passageway, Father Kerrigan wondered what McIntyre had for him. *Perhaps a little gossip, probably who's been slighting the offering.* Trying to think of where to take the wretched man, he decided. *The kitchen would be an appropriate place for getting information, give the bugger a bit of bread.*

Quickly he turned down a narrow corridor to an unlit area. Flicking the switch, he turned to stare at the shivering man leaning against the polished aluminum countertop. "All right, McIntyre, what's this thing I might be interested in?"

A chill traveled the slender man's spine as he heard the sound of an old cuckoo clock chiming the noon hour. "Aye, I'll not be wantin' any compensation, Father. I was just thinkin' ya might spare a bite, maybe a potato for me poor ailin' wif."

The priest rolled his eyes tiredly as he nodded impatiently.

"Ya see, I was in the pub, Father. Mind you, I only goes for celebrations and such. But I was speakin' to Thomas Quinn and he was tellin' me on the QT that Eamonn Gallagher was askin' questions about Mary McNulty's recent demise. An American was doin' most of the talkin', seems he thinks poor Mary was done in. Mind ya I just heard this from me mate. It's not for me to question the comin's and goin's of such folks as might be me betters, but the guards didn't find anythin' suspicious like. So I got to wonderin' why Eamonn was nosin' around, unless he's thinkin' the wee folk done poor Mary in."

"That'll be enough of that, McIntyre. There'll be no blasphemy in this house," the cleric said, making the sign of the cross.

"Aye, Father, it's sorry I am. It's just that folks are saying the wee ones are upset with all them that lives on the hill," the frightened man said. "Revenge, Father."

His face clouded, the priest thought on McIntyre revelations. *It's dangerous allowing superstitions to run the good folk of Ballyshannon. It's bad enough without people breaking ranks and openly looking for creatures that never existed. I'll have to see Eamonn, take a look at this American; discourage this investigation before it gets out of hand. Eamonn and his wife haven't attended services in a good while, nor tithed their part for that matter.*

His mind in a muddle, he hurried to the storage bin and grabbed two small potatoes, then a piece of bread from the refrigerator. Handing them to McIntyre he made the sign of the cross, then motioned the nervous man to leave through a side door.

God in heaven, he thought, *I must speak with Eamonn.* Thunder rattled the windows as the priest walked back to his study. An uneasy sensation gnawed at his stomach, as he tried to shrug off feelings of impending doom.

Twenty Six—A gypsy's curse

Seated alone at a table, Flynn looked out at the desolate shore, the occasional sound of sheep baa'ing in the background. Ice cold wind whistled through the cheap plastic windows. *This old caravan needs replacin',* he thought, *soon I'll be getting' a new one. This business is takin' all me time, all me energy, strainin', never knowin' who's next.*

Wisps of sand from the beach blew against the small trailer like a thousand particles of glass.

Almost in a whisper, he chanted, "Goats and lambs, son of man, nature's spirit, come to me and hear my wish, 'tis all I ask, give your life and pay the price." Over and over he repeated the call. Sweat covered his forehead as the cosmic energy was pulled from his mind, his voice straining to speak. Beyond the shore waves rose higher and higher crashing against the rocks near Bundoran. Far and away a small figure appeared. Running towards Donegal bay, a young man glowered with hatred as he bounded into the foaming surf. Driven forward by an unknown force, he started to swim out to sea.

His head arched backwards, the chanter repeated his words. Louder and louder they echoed through the young man's mind. Chilled to the bone, he swam and swam. Far from shore, he looked around suddenly, his strength waning. First deep in a trough, then high on a crest he stared hopelessly towards land. He sank then rose to the surface gasping for air, his muscles fatigued. Again and again he tried to float, to swim towards the light. His resolve weakened with each numbing movement of his arms. Praying, he struggled to live. His mind all but lost, he inhaled the sea, sinking beneath the waves, was gone.

Twenty-seven—A picnic & deductive reasoning

It was a particularly miserable day, but a picnic was in order Eamonn had said. They'd go to a beautiful lough (lake) and relax under a tree. Wearing the insulated denim jacket he'd brought from Maine, Will stared straight ahead at the on-coming traffic towards Sligo. A freezing rain was blowing off the Atlantic. Passing old churches and cemeteries he wondered if the whole of Ireland was one big graveyard.

Ahead, a car heading towards them on the narrow two-lane highway had its signal light on to indicate it was passing. Almost automatically now, Will moved over to the paved shoulder, giving the on-coming car plenty of room.

Since visiting the Garda he had decided to list all the people on the hill that had died the previous year. *Ten so far, eleven including Mary McNulty. Though her death seemed more a crime than the others, and she didn't live on the hill, she was still included. There seems to be a strong belief in the wee folk,* he thought. *Margaret O'Neil had a carving of a tree spirit hanging in her kitchen near the door. That in itself doesn't prove anything, but the fact that she had told others she was being watched, indicated she was either going nuts or really was being watched. By man or beast who could say. She had killed herself and the Garda had deemed it suicide due to depression. Maybe the loss of her man was too much, even though it was ten years ago.*

Having Eamonn as a friend was fortunate. In such a small town as Ballyshannon everyone knew everyone else's business. Most, according to Eamonn, believed with all their hearts that living on the fairy hill was a mistake . . . a big mistake.

Elizabeth Gillespie was only in her forties. A little nosy Eamonn had said, but otherwise harmless, living with her sister all her life. She couldn't have made anyone angry enough to force pills down her throat. Her neighbor had told Kate that small footprints were frequently found outside Elizabeth's living-room window. *Could have been children peeking in,* Will thought. *They might have thought she was a witch or just a little odd. There must be a common denominator in all this,* he mused. *They all lived on the hill and all seemed terribly spooked by the thought of fairies seeking revenge. It does seem strange that each committed suicide,* he reasoned, *unless it's some kind of mind control.* More truth in that than he'd like to admit, he stopped trying to find the answers.

Though on a family picnic enjoying beautiful Glencar Lough, it was difficult to resist drawing off to the side to discuss the dreary happenings in Ballyshannon. Using a small note pad, he listened to Eamonn name off all those who had died thus far. They had decided to investigate each death, see if there were any clues to point them in the right direction. Based on the many murder mysteries Will had seen in the movies, it occurred to him that all these suicides were not merely coincidence. *Where there's smoke there's fire, dear old dad used to say. We must be careful; whatever forces are behind this must be very powerful.* Shivering involuntarily he wrote name after name followed by addresses and surviving relatives.

"Enough already," Annie said. "Let's pretend we're having fun."

"Ah, it's a grand day for a picnic," Eamonn said, trying to change the subject, if not the mood of the gathering, "now the wind's dying down, the sun can come out."

Annie nodded in agreement as she slowly munched a breast of baked chicken.

"It's truly a feast," Will added.

Kate had outdone herself and it was a delight to explore each tasty dish. Fresh carrot-sticks, cucumbers, mushrooms, potato salad, hard-boiled eggs, hard bread and frosted bottles of fruit juice, filled the colorful tablecloth spread on the emerald grass overlooking the lough. Fresh strawberries with sour cream and cookies on the side were so good Will thought he might explode from eating too much.

Twenty-eight—Unanswered questions

Two days had passed since the picnic. Deep in thought, Eamonn took a drink of hot tea as he looked out at the bay. Unsure what to think anymore, he wondered if his friend coming from America was bad luck. The news of Sean McNulty found washed up on the shore in Bundoran was very upsetting. He was only a lad of sixteen, his life still to be lived. It seemed peculiar that a boy raised here all his life would take a swim in Donegal Bay in the dead of night. A death wish would be more like it. Even though his mother had died so bizarrely he seemed strong enough to survive such a catastrophe. It was hard to understand why a basically happy, reasonably intelligent young man would want to die.

The crunch of gravel outside drew the tired Irishman's attention away from his thoughts. Waving as he got out of the car, Will hurried to the open door. Quickly he followed Eamonn to the sitting room overlooking the gray waters below. The Mall Quay looked desolate with the tide out and clouds covering the sky.

"I'm glad you could come. I'm not sure where to begin. Dying seems to be a plague around here these days," Eamonn said with a tired shrug as he told his friend about the boy drowning.

Will sat for a moment trying to organize his thoughts. "Tell me what you've heard about this latest accident. Sean McNulty; isn't he Mary McNulty's son?"

"Aye he is, bless his soul. A nicer lad you'd never find. Minded his da, did his lessons every day," Eamonn replied. "According to Pauly, a tourist found Sean washed up near the Fairy Bridge. He was dressed in seaweed, no clothes on his body."

Thunder rolled overhead, penetrating Will's bones. Cold rain splattered against the window.

"The Fairy Bridge?"

"Aye, I know it's just a place," Eamonn replied. "Legend has it the fairies made the bridge right on the cliffs so they could watch the crashing waves."

"And what do you think?"

"I think the legends are mostly true."

Will watched a sea bird gliding over the bay. "Did Sean like to swim?"

"Not that I'm knowing. Might be better to ask Pauly." Looking at his watch Eamonn indicated they should go. Will had asked if he could go along to the funeral. At the wake someone might volunteer a tidbit that would lead them to a more logical conclusion than Sean committing suicide.

The ride down Market Street then Castle on the R267 was uneventful. Not many cars were on the narrow street crossing the bridge, especially in the middle of the week.

A dismal day, perfect for a funeral, Will thought.

Dark gray clouds covered the sky, adding to the depressing mood. After they parked across the street from Paul's, Will followed Eamonn to the same gated path into the shuttered apartment. As before, it was dark inside save for a few candles placed on the table next to the casket and a hutch in the corner.

Straightaway Eamonn and Will walked to the open pine box holding the waxy remains of Paul McNulty's son. With due reverence Eamonn wiped a tear from his eye as Will looked at the still form of the dead boy, his arms folded across his chest. A sense of fear grabbed at Will's throat as he stared at the deceased child. Following Eamonn's lead he bowed his head in silent prayer for the boy then moved slowly away to a dark corner.

Dressed in black, two old ladies next to a barren wall seemed invisible, lace veils covering their faces. Like a lost spirit one spoke without looking up, "Aye, Eamonn Gallagher, 'tis a sad thing, Sean meeting his demise, him being so young and all."

"Yer right on that account, Fanny Duneon," he replied with equal seriousness.

"And wouldn't you know he left this mortal earth the same as his ma."

"I'm not sure I understand yer meaning, Missus."

"There's a mystery where there's questions," the almost inaudible voice added with conviction.

Wary of offending, and unwilling to get into a conversation that might be seen as gossip, Eamonn excused himself as Will followed him over to where Paul McNulty stood. No appetite, Paul ignored the table filled with plates of cold ham, beef, potato salad, hardboiled eggs and crusty bread, instead choosing to console himself with good Irish whiskey. Together they toasted the deceased, Paul saying a small prayer.

The heavy scent of formaldehyde was inescapable. The numbing drink was welcome as he filled their glasses a second time.

"I'm truly sorry about yer loss, Pauly. I know Sean was a good son and you have ma prayers," Eamonn said to his friend.

Paul looked at the tall man, then over at Will. Smiling weakly he accepted the American's hand. "Sir, if there is any way I can help, please . . ." Will offered.

"Thanks, but it seems the damage has been done. Me wif, then me son, gone. There was no good reason for Mary to die, and now me son, Sean," Paul replied, his voice rising. Almost shouting now, "Why I ask you, when he couldn't swim, would he go out in that damned bay?" Lost in hysterics, he looked wildly around the darkened room, as the reflection of fearful eyes stared back

Putting his hand on Paul's shoulder, Eamonn spoke in a steady, even voice, "Will didn't mean to upset you, Pauly. I swear as God is my witness, we'll find out who's done this to you and yours."

Soothing the distraught man Eamonn kept talking quietly as he looked around the room. "You all know me as one who keeps his word, so there'll be no secrets this day when I say I'll find out who or what evil has come to this house and destroyed this family."

Except for the heavy breathing of the upset man, not a sound could be heard as each mourner held their breath. Though it was none of Will's affair he felt great empathy for the grieving man leaning against the table, his son in the coffin.

Someone proposed a toast to the departed and each gladly refilled their cups and drank. Speaking in whispers, no one wanted to further upset a man who had just lost his last remaining relative.

"Did your son ever give any indication that something was wrong?" Will asked softly. Though he knew this wasn't a time for questions, it seemed as good as any.

"No, I can't say there was anything, except he's been having dreams. Nightmares about something trying to pull him out the window. Him sleeping upstairs it seemed kind of silly, and the dog was with him most nights."

A tear running down his cheek, he stopped. "The night he disappeared the auld mutt was keeping company with me."

"Maybe the dog was keeping him safe," Will said off-handedly.

"From what?" Paul asked.

"Sure now it wasn't the good neighbors," Eamonn ventured.

"There've been stranger things," a small lady in black mumbled.

"Fanny, you been tiddling a bit too much. Don't be spooking everyone now," Eamonn said firmly.

The undertaker knocked at the door, interrupting further conversion. Silently everyone filed out.

As Will reached the door he motioned to Eamonn. "While they're all on the way to the cemetery tell Paul I had to use the toilet and I'll be along shortly. I've got to have a look around for clues."

"Have you lost yer mind? If you get caught it'll be a terrible thing. It'll look like disrespect to the family, it will."

Though in agreement with his friend, Will left him at the door. Moving quickly through the corridor he noted rooms on either side. Looking in one on the right he saw a rickety metal framed bed and a small dresser topped with an oil lantern. Straining to see, he walked over to scan the old dresser. Except for a hairbrush and a picture of Paul, Mary and Sean, it was void of decoration. Looking closer he read the inscription on the picture, "To my loving husband, Mary."

Nothing unusual here, he thought. It seemed this was the master bedroom. Breathing a tired sigh at the starkness and sensing a need to hurry, he rushed into the hallway, then into the room opposite Paul's bedroom. Except for a chest of drawers it was empty. Standing in the doorway he looked down the hallway trying to see. As his eyes adjusted to the darkness he saw something glitter. *A door handle,* he thought, feeling the cold hardness of a glass knob as he reached out. Turning it slowly, the door opened, revealing the shadowed outline of a stairway. The steps creaked as he climbed to an attic area. Walking down the center, he followed the V-shaped ceiling to the opposite end where a sliding window was half opened. Cold from outside filled the small space, taking his breath away with unexpected harshness.

Against one wall stood an old army cot. An orange crate served as an end-table with a candle stuck to the top. Unsure of what he was looking for, Will looked at the bed in disarray. A piece of paper was visible, sticking out from under the orange crate. Picking it up, he saw what looked like a list of names.

Hearing his friend call, he rushed out of the room down the stairs to the looming presence of Eamonn Gallagher.

"Gads man, we best be going before you raise suspicions."

Nodding, Will hurried after the Irishman. Everyone had already gone. They'd have to hurry, waste no more time. It would certainly look bad, unforgivable, if Eamonn wasn't there to see the boy laid to rest.

"Did you find anything, oh, great detective?" Eamonn added with a smile.

"Yes, I did," Will replied, pulling out the tattered piece of paper, "a list of names."

Stopped at the graveyard, Eamonn looked at the water-stained revelation. "It looks like a list of all the people who have died and some who are still among us."

Shaking his head he gave it back to Will as they walked towards the sound of a priest's voice, ". . . to his final resting place we send Sean McNulty, a fine boy, a good son. May God bless his mortal soul and forgive him his sins."

As the priest went on, Will wondered if they'd ever find out what really happened to Sean; or his mother for that matter. A cloud seemed to cover his mind as the chill of a cold wind rushed to find an opening in his wool overcoat. The gray overcast felt like a giant curtain of gloom, adding to the depressing event in this lowland field.

No one noticed the small man in a black top hat watching from behind a distant rock wall. The wind swirled around the diminutive creature, throwing bits of loose grass and pebbles into the air.

Sensing a presence, Will looked back for a second briefly glimpsing the tiny person. Death-like eyes met his gaze. Nudging Eamonn, he pointed towards the fence. The tall man turned to see what his friend was pointing at, but saw only a long, low wall made of rock and gorse. More from neglect, thorny bushes had been allowed to cover most of that side of the cemetery.

"What is it?" Eamonn asked, "I don't see anything."

Whispering, Will looked at the quizzical face. "Over there by the wall is a very small man in a black top hat, just like I saw at Mary's funeral."

"You must be mistaken, I don't see any wee man."

"Well, he was there," Will replied with frustration. "Wee or not, I saw a very small person dressed in black watching Mary, and now Sean, being buried."

Unsure of how to respond, Eamonn patted his friend on the shoulder. They'd talk later.

Confused, Will wondered why he was the only one who saw this man. *Maybe to drive home a point to the blow-in from America? To frighten me away?* Nervously he pulled his coattails together as they made their way back to Eamonn's Jeep Cherokee.

The rain began in earnest and puddles formed quickly. The mourners, used to being damp, ignored the inclement weather as they slowly departed.

Twenty-nine—No one knows why

Seated at the bar of The Thatch, Peter Culmore drank one more pint of Guinness. The trek from Erne, up Main to Bishop, was wet business on this dreary day. It didn't matter, he liked The Thatch. It was busy most days and today especially. Deep in thought he tried to reason why; more to the point, what was an outsider doing, nosing around his village . . . *this Eamonn Gallagher and his American friend messing in private affairs. Sean and his ma were depressed and all, everyone was knowing that. Stirring up problems for the good folk of Ballyshannon. Now Pauly's near his end too.*

Interrupting his angry thoughts, a large man sat down on the next stool. "What's the wizard thinkin' on this fine wet day?" a hoarse voice asked as dazed eyes stared intently at him.

"Never you mind. I don't have to talk to the likes of you, James Creedon. Ain't it enough Eamonn and his mate nosing into local business, now folks meeting their maker a might early?"

"Talk to me or no, makes no difference. What ya say be true, that Eamonn's overstepped his bounds. And you as well for bringin' it up," James replied.

His head pounding with the continual pain he'd had for months, Peter wondered if the large slug would leave him be. Picking up his pint he walked slowly across the narrow dimly lit room to the hallway leading to the back door. No one paid him any mind as he left the noisy pub.

The moon was partially hidden from view. Clumps of gray clouds moved slowly towards the south. A cold wind assaulted his senses as he finished the pint in his shaking right hand. *I'll head home, no sense hanging around here.*

Far off a dog howled at the partly concealed moon. *Oh, tinker's spit, I wish I was free. No more shadows crawling over me dead body,* he thought. *Damn the feelings in ma heart.*

The darkness felt claustrophobic as he walked. At the corner of Bishop and Main he stopped for a moment to button his coat. The faint sound of voices wailing in pain gave him a start. *Jaysus,* he thought, *the fiends are out.* Looking at his watch he realized it was near midnight. Moving faster, he hurried down Main Street past the darkened shops and houses. The clacking of his shoes was disconcerting as he stopped to light a cigarette. Trying vainly to banish morbid thoughts, the few barren trees looked more like sentinels of death.

Though it was cold he was covered with sweat, wiping it from his eyes with a nicotine-stained finger. *Damn this fecking pain, I've got to get something from the chemist. Me mind's going. Sure it's the fairies.* Shadows formed small creatures on the brick wall beside him as the wind strained against a street lamp. Standing still for a moment he looked intently down the deserted street. Except for a few parked cars along the sidewalk, it seemed all living souls were somewhere else. Shaking with fear, Peter wished with all his heart he was home safe in bed. Though he seldom slept anymore, it was better than this.

A dog barked causing him to jump. Slowly he walked down the cobblestone sidewalk; past the solicitor, Joseph Maguire's office; past the painter, Hugh Gillespie's studio; past the carpenter, Samuel Wray's shop.

A flash of lightning caused the frightened man to stop in his tracks. Far up on the hill to the right he saw the steeple of St. Anne's Church. *Oh Jaysus, the fairy hill,* he thought in a panic. *There's evil here for sure.*

Up the narrow alleyway, leading to the cemetery surrounding the old church, a rusted gate clanged. *The wind,* he thought, *only the fecking wind blowing, trying to scare a poor soul like meself.* Rubbing his forehead, he tried to relieve the intense pressure, the feeling of hopelessness. He wished it would stop, if only for one brief moment.

The sound of footsteps approaching from the church alleyway caused him to stop in mid-stride. Straining to see, his eyes widened in fear as a small figure stepped out of the shadows.

"Saints preserve us, Mother of God, I'm sorry. I didn't mean to pass this place."

Slowly at first, then faster, he started backing up. Without thinking he turned and ran down Main Street screaming wildly, "It's Finvana, Finvana!"

From behind he heard the hurried footsteps of small boots growing louder and louder. In desperation he turned into the street. Bright lights blinded him. Throwing his hands up to protect himself he felt the numbing impact of a car register in his terrified brain. His bones broken, he flew through the air. Meat sanding off arms, legs and face brought forth an ungodly scream of primal pain. Flailing for a moment he looked up through blood-filled eyes as he watched the small man approach.

Whispering hoarsely he spoke one word over and over, "Finvana, Finvana."

The driver of the car looked down at Peter Culmore. "I'm sorry mister, I didn't see ya there."

Seeing Peter's lips moving, he placed his ear close to the mutilated man's mouth.

"Finvana."

The driver's companion looked on nervously, "What's he saying?"

Eyes wide with fear, the driver replied quickly, "He said Finvana."

"What's that?"

"The Fairy King," the driver said, looking into the shadows dancing up the narrow street.

"I better fetch the guards, mate, see if you can help the poor sod," the driver's companion said, then started running down the street toward the Garda Station at the bottom.

Slowly the rain fell in blotches of wet on the bloody, nearly faceless man lying in the street, erasing his appearance.

The driver made the sign of the cross several times as he stared in horror at the still form.

The wind, a happy spectator, howled in celebration as everything vibrated from a loud clap of thunder. In the flash of lightning that followed, the dead man seemed to come alive as his eyes snapped open.

Terrified, the driver ran down the street to join his friend. From the shadows yellow teeth reflected a grim smile, then were gone. Ever increasing, the rain poured down washing clean the bony remains.

Thirty—Seeing is believing

It was a fair day driving over to Ballyshannon and Will was looking forward to tea with Eamonn and Kate. Mollie was such a delight at eleven months, a beautiful child in the classic Irish way. The curl of her hair was like a cupid's bow and her ready smile and slightly flushed cheeks seemed purely angelic. Even though she couldn't talk yet, Will was certain she understood every word he said.

Seated across from him, Annie looked out the car window at the pond paralleling the road. Two white swans glided effortlessly along, five babies following obediently.

"It's a wonderful sight, Will. I'll never forget this place."

"Me too," he replied absentmindedly. His mind going a mile a minute, he tried to stop thinking for a moment to enjoy the scenery. Staring at the majestic creatures, Annie's scream brought him back to reality. In front of them an old lady dressed in rags stood directly in their path. With nowhere to turn Will hit the brakes hard as he veered off into the thick brush at the edge of the pond.

"My God, that was close," he said as he looked back for the old woman.

"That was too close," Annie agreed excitedly.

Together they scanned the empty road. Confused, they searched ahead and behind, in the ditch, everywhere, but there was nothing to be found.

The bewildered woman looked at her husband. "Did you see anything?"

"Actually, I did. I saw an old woman who looked more dead than alive." Searching the area thoroughly Will decided it was some kind of shared illusion. Getting into the car, he backed out of the bushes.

"Maybe it was the rasher of bacon we had this morning," Annie said tentatively.

Not replying, Will felt a nervous twinge in his chest as they turned onto the N15 north towards Ballyshannon. *It must be this place,* he thought. Smiling to himself, he thought of a line from a melodrama he'd been in years ago, "s*pooks in the nugget.*"

The traffic was light as they slowed through Bundoran. Mostly deserted during the day, it seemed like a movie set from some Irish drama. *A drama I'm a character in,* he thought. "Gads, I thought when people visited Ireland the only supernatural events were in stories."

"Well, maybe we're getting to live it, like Prince," Annie ventured.

"You know, I could use that in me story. It'd make a great scary scene."

"Me story? You're Irish now?"

"No, but just the same it doesn't seem real. Maybe it was a hologram."

"Will Bonner, a hologram in the middle of the road, in daytime?"

"Okay, but some sort of projection."

Refusing to accept what they had seen as supernatural, he hurried towards Ballyshannon.

Seated in the kitchen of his old house, Eamonn listened to Will tell what they had seen in broad daylight. Kate held Mollie on her lap tightly as she listened intently to the bizarre story.

"Maybe there were shadows from the pond," Kate offered, more to herself than the others.

"Could be yer open to another reality," Eamonn said.

"I told Will it was probably the bacon we'd had for breakfast," Annie interjected

"Could've been the preservatives, causing us to see things that weren't there."

Eamonn stood by the window looking at the bay below. *The whole world's going nuts,* he thought. *Me friend's seeing old hags.* Since he was a lad of six he'd been aware of people leaving God's green earth with some regularity. Now the soft voice of reason was saying, *mind your own business, Eamonn Gallagher,* but in his heart he knew he couldn't sit on the sidelines anymore. If the town objected, he'd deal with that later. Except for baby Mollie making sounds of happiness, all was quiet.

"May I have another cup of tea?" Annie asked softly.

"Oh, where are me manners?" Removing the generations old tea cozy from the pot, Eamonn poured the steaming liquid into her empty cup.

"Thank you. Kate, why don't you show me Mollie's bedroom, I'm dying to see the butterflies and flowers you've painted on the walls."

Kate looked at her husband whispering to Will and nodded tiredly. It was like a never-ending story of fantasy and bad dreams. *If only Eamonn would give this up and stick to the business of selling,* she thought. *There's men enough to chase the evil.* The door to the kitchen closed with a click as Will spoke. "The list of names I found should be checked out. If not by us, then by the Garda."

"Oh, the law doing some detecting, now that'd be a switch. Better the two of us if it's to be done," Eamonn said dejectedly.

"I'm sure in all of Ballyshannon there's not one person wanting an investigation, but I think this list is important. We should start at the top and work our way down, going from friends to relatives of each one that's died. See if there's anything that might explain why." Trying logically to reach some conclusion, Will continued, "and those that are alive, see if they have any idea why they'd be on a list of mostly dead people."

"So that's what yer thinking. That's quite a lot, my fine feathered friend," Eamonn replied half-kidding.

"I know you're used to people meeting their demise, but this has exceeded the norm," Will said, trying to ignore the humor.

"You're right, but it's either smile a little or go off," Eamonn replied. Taking the list he read the names slowly. Finished, he breathed a heavy sigh. "Let's start in the morning; with Margaret O'Neil. I know her neighbor, so that'd be a good place to begin."

"Sounds great, my best Irish friend. As long as we start somewhere," Will said, patting the large man on the shoulder.

"I guess I'll take a few days off from the shop. Me brother can hold down the fort."

More to convince himself than Will, he commented on how he could always trust his older brother to run things while he was gone. If nothing else came from this thing, at least he'd be away from the daily grind of running the business for a few days. Clothing, drapes; there were a million things to attend to when you ran your own enterprise.

"Getting paid for services rendered is harder than pulling scales off fish with yer teeth," Eamonn added tiredly.

The sound of Annie and Kate's soft chatter interrupted further talk. Mollie was in a happy mood as she smiled at the sight of her dad. Holding her in his lap Eamonn spoke in a low voice. Mostly Gaelic, Will couldn't understand the words but the tone was loving and the baby listened attentively.

The day and evening slipped away as Will and Annie said their good-byes.

"It was a nice visit, Eamonn."

"Now don't be going all mushy on me, Sir William."

Kate looked at her tired husband. "You need your rest, Mister. The time for talking is over."

"Aye to that. Maybe time for a little hug and a jug," he replied, giving the lovely young woman a squeeze.

"I'll give you a hug and a jug when you get some rest and take things a little easier, Sir."

Laughing, Will waved goodbye, following Annie out to the small car, the night air clinging to his face. It was time to be a detective and tomorrow he'd keep notes on what they found. A murder mystery was in the making here for sure. Fiction was one thing, but real life suicides and murder were another. No matter what they turned up, he was determined to help his friend. Giving up on life was as alien to him as killing another human being. Through years of life lessons, he had become strong in his beliefs. A lonely night, it was good to be heading towards Mullaghmore.

Thirty-one—A clue

The sky was overcast and rain pelted the windshield as Will followed Eamonn's instructions. Margaret O'Neil had lived on Market Street. Paralleling the Erne River to the mall, Will turned right on Castle past the intersection of College then parked. Like some streets in the U.S., Market was the middle portion of Castle and Back streets. No apartment number visible, Eamonn led the way into a dilapidated, two-story brick building. A faded list of names was stenciled just inside the door in no apparent order. Eamonn ran his finger down the names.

"Ah, here it is, Ellen McPhelim."

"McPhelim?"

"Aye, she was Margaret's friend for most of her life. I wasn't sure, but now it's coming back to me. She's upstairs."

The odor of decayed wood and cooked eggs filled the air as Will followed his friend up the worn stairway. Down the hall the sound of music gave a false sense of gaiety as the Chieftans' played, The Stone.

Will knocked on the battered door. *Amazing, everyone knows where everyone else lives.* Having lived in Los Angeles most of his life and Maine the last two years, Ireland seemed like an alternate universe.

Still, directions in Maine seemed hopeless too. Similar, but off just a bit.

"Go three miles, turn left at the clump of trees, then two hundred yards past the old Mosley barn that burned down awhile back, ayuh."

Smiling to himself he wondered if anyone ever made a mistake. The door creaked slightly as a wrinkled face peered out at the somber men.

"Here now, Eamonn Gallagher, what might you be wantin' from the likes of me?" a voice demanded.

An old prune of a woman became more visible as Ellen McPhelim appeared in the doorway. Beady-eyed, she leaned against the hallway just inside the door.

"Ellen, I've come to talk to you on a serious matter. Me friend here, Will Bonner, is assisting me." Paused for a moment, he smiled at the sprightly woman of seventy-five years.

"Well if it's talk yer wantin', I've got plenty of that. Of course what's said in private can't be aired."

Motioning for them to follow, the elderly lady hobbled down the narrow hall towards a light fanning out into the dark corridor. Pictures, of unknown souls, showing the ravages of time, adorned the water-stained walls. Constant rain and wind had beaten the mortar and stone, seeping in to eat away the interior. One hundred years old, the buildings had seen better days.

A mangy yellow cat lay close to its smelly litter-box, long since needing a change. With a grunt their hostess sat in the only lounge chair, eyeing Will Bonner closely. "I'd offer ya some tae, but I've not been to the market."

"Oh, not to bother with that, Ellen," Eamonn assured her, "I hope all is well. I know how hard it can be."

Leaning forward, he slipped a ten-punt note into her hand resting on the table next to his.

"Yer a grand man, Eamonn, I'll be thankin' ya for yer kindness."

Reaching up she pulled the large man's face close, planting a kiss on his cheek.

A little ruffled, he cleared his throat and straightened up. "I come to ask a couple of questions about Margaret, bless her soul."

"Oh, that's the way it is. Depends on what yer askin'," she hesitated nervously, "I need to know if this man standin' here is from the government or what. I don't recognize his face."

"Oh no, he's just me mate from America come to help, a good man to be trusted."

"Yes ma'am, I'm here to help. You have my word," Will interjected trying to calm the lady's fears.

"Well, ya look straight enough, and I reckon that's what matters," she replied.

The sounds of a fiddle increased from somewhere in the building, seemingly asking its own questions.

"Ya know Margaret O'Neil hung herself," Eamonn said, eyeing the old lady steadily. "It's common knowledge she was depressed, but I'm wondering if you might know of anything peculiar that others weren't aware of."

Thunder rumbled nearby as knick-knacks rattled on a worn bookshelf. A little shaky, Ellen looked out a dirty windowpane and shook her head. Water seeping under the sill, dripped methodically on the dirty hardwood floor.

"I'm thinkin' the last I saw of that poor woman was the day before she died. It was cold as ice and she never used any peat. Bein' so poor she was on the dole, don't ya know. Hardly worth it for some." The knowing look failed to hide the face of fear. "She come to me every day, always the same, 'someone's watchin' me'. A tiny man with eyes of death, she said. Constantly beggin' me to stay with her. I've got me own place I told her, ya should go to the guards. But she never listened. Ya need to go to the chemist for the pain in yer head I said. Some folks never mind their friends."

The room darkened as clouds covered the sun.

"Well, I'm sorry she had to meet her maker that way but I reckon one way's as good as another," Eamonn said sympathetically. "You didn't see anything that would point to this tiny man Margaret was afraid of?"

The old lady pointed to a knitted bag under a small table. "Could ya bring me that? I've somethin' to show ya."

Will walked over and picked up the bag, handing it to the outstretched hand. Slowly the old lady felt around the bag, then pulled out a small shiny object. Eamonn accepted what appeared to be a quartz crystal with a symbol etched in it. Walking over to the window he held it up to the meager light. Quietly he mumbled, "Hy Breasail."

"Hy Breasail?" Will asked, confused.

"Aye, the Phantom Isle."

"Oh, Mother of God, I hope that stone's not possessed," Ellen exclaimed fearfully.

"I don't think so," Eamonn said, trying to reassure the old lady.

"Margaret gave me that in case somethin' was to happen to her. It's better you keep it, Eamonn Gallagher, I don't need any problems with the wee folk."

Not wanting to upset the frightened woman further, Eamonn excused himself while Will assured her, she had been a great help.

Battered by the bitter cold of a storm brewing, Will hurried after Eamonn to the small car parked on the street. Seated for a moment he pondered the name, plus all they had been told. Taking out the list he carefully crossed off Margaret O'Neil.

"What is Hy Breasail, the Phantom Isle?"

"Hy Breasail, it's Gaelic for a place where fairies live. A secret place. Legends say it's an island that doesn't exist for us mortals."

Reluctantly Will looked for the next name on the list. There would be time later to figure out if fairies were killing off residents in the village.

Thirty-two—Visitin'

Almost mechanically now, Will read the next name. "Sean McTeige. Does that name ring a bell?"

"Aye, he passed in the spring of '97. Took too many pills or something." Eamonn thought for a moment. "He lived on Back Street, a quiet sort, minded his own business he did. He's got a surviving cousin, Martha Riley."

"Where does she live?"

"The East Port," Eamonn replied.

The Fiat came to life as Will turned the key in the ignition. Checking the side mirror he pulled out onto the narrow one-way street. "Where's East Port, Mate?" he said with a smile.

"I'll give you, mate," Eamonn said, giving the driver a playful shove. "Stay on this road past the shop, then cross the Erne to the roundabout."

The sky opened up as wet from above blocked their view. Traffic was light and it seemed as though everyone had disappeared. *No humans,* Will thought. *Maybe they're afraid they'll melt.* A sudden headache caused him to squint, the wipers sounding loud and annoying. *Damn this weather, I've got to get home. If they don't stop pelting me with rain I'll kill them.* Surprised by his own thoughts, he tried to focus. Like a magnet he felt a pull, stronger with every breath, a consuming urge to join the others, rest in the quiet place, drive into the Erne and end it all.

Eamonn looked over as the small car increased speed. Barely staying on four wheels, it seemed all but certain they would go off the bridge.

Delirious, Will longed for peace. Swinging the wheel to the right, he felt a vise-like grip opposing him. Riding on the sidewalk, sparks flew backwards off the driver's side fender. With all his strength Eamonn pulled the emergency brake. The back of the car whipped out into the opposite lane, skidding towards an on-coming truck.

The pain in Will's head was intolerable. *Time's up,* he thought. *I've got to be free.*

Like a clap of thunder, Eamonn slammed into his friend as he grabbed the wheel. In the opposite lane a large white truck screeched to a halt. Darkness enveloped Will as he lost control.

Like smelling salts, icy drops of rain hit the confused man lying half out of the green car. Eamonn looked expectantly at his friend. "Jaysus, I'm glad to see you're still breathing. Be a sad thing bringin' you back to Annie in a box."

"I . . . I don't know what happened," Will stammered, "one minute I was driving okay and the next I was hit by this ungodly pain in my head. I thought I was going to explode."

Thunder clapped loudly followed by a searing streak of lightning racing towards the earth.

Standing behind Eamonn, the trucker saw that Will was all right. "Take care, Mate," he said, as he got in his vehicle and drove away.

"You up to visiting Martha Riley?" Eamonn asked. "We could go back to the house if you need to rest or call a doctor."

Rubbing his forehead, Will wondered what in God's name had possessed him. What kind of force was that powerful? Seeing his friend's worried look, Will patted him on the shoulder

"Never mind me, I'm fine, let's just keep on investigating. If the devil wants to end my stay on this earth, resting won't do any good."

"That may be true, Mate, but it's not a bad idea to regroup. We can always start again tomorrow. No sense being hasty."

"I feel fine, Eamonn, honestly. If this car still runs, just give me the directions."

Though shaky, he felt sure the incident was over. Now more than ever, it was apparent they had to keep going. They had to find out who had killed all these folks, and now, true or not, had attempted to kill him and his friend.

Concentrating on driving, he tried to ignore the fierce storm blowing crossways to the road. Though no one seemed to notice them taking Main Street across the bridge, he felt sure they were being watched as they turned left at the roundabout onto East Port. Driving slowly, he followed Eamonn's instructions to the third house from the end, gratefully arriving in a few minutes.

His nerves on edge, Eamonn knocked softly. Prior events had made him apprehensive. Being uninvited, he figured it better to go carefully than barge in. The clunk of a lock releasing went on forever as the door opened slowly.

A tall woman with bright red hair, Martha Riley eyed the two rain-soaked men standing on her doorstep. The robust woman threw back her head and laughed.

"Now there's a sorry sight, if I ever saw one."

Seeing their serious faces, she tried to compose herself, then motioned them inside.

"What might I do for you, gentlemen?" she asked with a gleam in her eye.

Eamonn wiped the rain from his brow. "My name's Gallagher. My friend, Will Bonner, and I are looking into the matter of folks passing before their time."

"Are ya now?"

"Aye, you had a cousin who departed early, Sean McTeige. I was wondering if you might know anything outside the official report"

"Other than he ended his life at the ripe old age of thirty-four, there's nothin' to tell. He was convinced someone was after his mortal soul, and I'm not sure they didn't get it."

"That's a sad state of affairs," Will interjected.

Martha nodded in agreement.

The storm outside raged on as a window shutter banged furiously against the house.

"We're sorry to have bothered you, Martha. I had hoped to get some clue as to why so many folks are doing themselves in on the hill."

"Oh, that place," she said in a whisper. "The fairy hill they built the church on."

Thunder roared through thin walls, announcing jagged streaks of lightning. The Irish woman looked out the window fearfully.

"We'll be taking our leave now," Eamonn said. "I think this storm is trying to tell us something."

"Wait a minute," Martha said, rubbing her brow. "Storm or no, I remember somethin' that might help."

While she disappeared down the hall, Will wondered if they should drop the whole thing. Added to that, it seemed Mother Nature was trying to stop them too.

The boisterous sound of the red-headed lady brought him back to reality. "Sean sent me a post just before he left this earth." Handing an envelope to Eamonn, she went into the kitchen. "You want a cup of tae before getting' wet again?"

"Oh, that'd be grand, dear lady," Eamonn replied.

"Ma'am, that would really hit the spot," Will added cheerfully.

While she busied herself clanging around in the kitchen, Eamonn opened the letter.

"To my dear cousin, Martha,

I'm writin' this note 'cause I've got nowhere else to turn. I don't want you to think I've lost me marbles, but I think someone is after me. Lord knows I've tippled a bit too much now and then, but I'd say if it was the drink. A pint now and then don't usually make me imagine bein' followed or watched. When I look back I see the shadow of somethin' small disappearin'. I'm terrible afraid I won't be around much longer, but I want you to know I love you and give all my worldly belongin's to you if I'm dead.

Your cousin, Sean"

Finished reading, Eamonn looked up as Martha returned with a tray filled with cups, teapot and cookies. After Will read the letter he took a sip of the hot tea she had placed in front of him.

"Would you care for a digestive?" she asked him.

"Digestive?"

"Aye," Eamonn said, "a cookie."

"Oh, thank you, yes."

"He's just come from America," Eamonn explained.

"I knew you weren't from around here," Martha said smiling.

While the storm raged, the investigators sat securely in Martha Riley's living room. *Others have seen the little man,* Will thought nervously. *Whoever he is, he's not from this world.* Worried for his friend and the people of Ballyshannon, he hoped they would solve the mystery before any more folks died.

Thirty-three—Questions

The drive to Mick O'Quin's house, brother of the deceased, Russell, gave Will time to think about what he knew thus far. It seemed that in every case where the deceased had killed themselves, fear of angering the fairies was paramount. *Maybe that man I saw at the funerals of Mary and Sean McNulty was a leprechaun.* Smiling to himself it occurred to him that he might be losing it. *Going nuts, that's it.* Trying to be objective he wondered if Margaret O'Neil and Sean McTeige knew each other. *That would explain why she had a crystal with a fairy rune and Sean was imagining little people following him.*

"Hey, Mr. Detective, stay on Main Street here, then turn right at Martins Row and right again on Back Street." Eamonn looked at the driver deep in thought. "Are you listening, Mr. Bonner?"

'Yes, yes, I'm listening, Mr. Gallagher," Will replied. "Up Main to Martins Row, right? Then right on Back. Is that it? Hmm?"

"Aye, you still got your ears on and that's good. When you're on Back, turn left at Chapel Lane. I'm hoping Mick is there now. It's a little early. But him working less these days, he might have decided to sit and have a drop or two."

Will smiled at the thought of having spirits at two in the afternoon. That had happened a lot lately. As he drove down the lonely streets, his normally talkative friend was especially quiet since leaving Martha's. Except for directions, he was deadpan.

"Listen, Eamonn, if I've offended you in any way, or you think we should stop this investigation, I'll abide by your decision."

"Oh Jaysus no, you haven't offended me, it's just that there's beliefs here that have been around for generations and since we've started nosing around it's sure to upset some who don't want outsiders . . . us poking where we don't belong. They might feel some things are better left unsaid. It won't matter if justice is done or not to most, what matters is that we don't make waves."

"But isn't most of this stuff just superstition?"

"I don't know how much is in the head and how much isn't."

Eamonn sat silent for a moment. "I don't want to stop, Will, I'm just saying we need to be careful we don't offend anyone. It'll be hell to pay if the townspeople decide we've overstepped our bounds."

"All right, Mr. Clarence Darrell, you've won your case," Will said, "Seriously, I concur, the last thing I want is offending anyone or their beliefs."

Turning left on Chapel, Will continued to the front of a two-story brick building Eamonn was pointing to. Together they walked up the few steps to the porch covered with wooden crates. Thankfully the rain had stopped and the clouds were on the move westward, out to sea. Will looked down the cobblestone lane at houses stacked one after another in a never-ending row. Leading to each was a brick path with waist-high brick and mortar walls ending at a porch. No trees and very little greenery held the gloomy atmosphere in place.

The clunk of the door opening behind him reminded Will of why they were here. Eamonn introduced him to the heavyset man at the door. A cheerful soul, Mick O'Quin grabbed Will's hand in a vise-like grip.

"Pleased to make your acquaintance. Come, come in."

Will followed Eamonn and Mick into a smoke-filled room that was the parlor. In the corner was an old wooden rocking chair. Once white drapes now yellowed with nicotine, hung limply on metal rods. Below narrow windows facing the street, filtered light reflected off a potbelly stove and a kettle whistling loudly. The warmth of being inside felt good even though Will had trouble breathing, his lungs long since ruined with twenty-four years of smoking. Forty-nine percent capacity in one lung and fifty-one percent in the other. *No matter,* he thought, *that was nineteen years ago. If I have to, I can stand a few minutes in this smoky place.*

"Sit, sit here by the kettle," Mick said. "How about some tae with a spirit or two to liven up the day?"

"Aye, that'd be grand," Eamonn said with appreciation.

"And you, Sir?" Mick said, looking at Will.

"Yes, thank you, that would be great."

Rubbing his hands together, Will sat watching their host hustle around getting two more cups. Carefully he poured a half-cup of tea, then just as carefully measured out the other half in Irish whiskey.

"To yer health," Mick said as he raised his glass.

"And long life," Will added without thinking. Too late, he noticed the rugged man's cordial face turn serious.

"What brings you here, Eamonn Gallagher?"

"We come on a matter most important, Mick. It would be best if it stayed with the three of us," Eamonn replied, looking tiredly at Will. Even though Will was older, his words had upset their host. Now they had to ask this man about his deceased brother. *A painful topic to be sure,* Eamonn thought, wondering if this whole affair would ever end.

"First, I need to explain that me friend here didn't mean anything by what he said. In America that's a fair good toast."

Interrupting, Will looked steadily at the upset man seated across from him. "I'm terribly sorry, sometimes my brain doesn't kick in until it's too late. Please accept my apology."

Mick's face softened slowly.

"Aye, Mick, we need to talk about something that's most unpleasant. It's your brother's passing. We need to know if there's anything that might have gotten by the guards when they investigated his untimely death."

"Why are you doing this, Eamonn? Why start stirrin' the pot now, after so many years?"

"Mick, too many have died. We aim to find out why. The guards don't know, and could care less."

"Sure and that's the true of it," the deflated Irishman said.

"Did your brother give you anything unusual before he passed?" Will asked.

Mick took a drink of the hot brew he held lightly in his hands. "The only thing he gave me was a stone he had."

While he went into the other room to fetch it, Will took the time to apologize. "I'm sorry, Eamonn, it just slipped out before I had time to think. It won't happen again."

"Aye, just be careful in the future, mate."

Will nodded in agreement as the sound of footsteps heralded Mick's return.

"Russell gave me this the day before his demise."

Eamonn eyed the stone, another crystal like Margaret's with a slightly different inscription. Examining it by the light, he tried to figure out what it meant. *T.D.D.* Unsure what the three letters represented, he looked to Will for an answer.

"I don't recognize them, but we might try to find them on the Internet."

"The Internet?" Mick asked.

"Aye," Eamonn interjected, "it's a place on the computer where there's a lot of information to be had."

Mick nodded absently, not sure what to think.

After a few more civilities and finishing their drinks, the investigators took their leave, assuring Mick if they found anything, they'd let him know. In the meantime, they swore their host to secrecy. Sure that it would go no further, Eamonn felt comfortable now that their visit would remain confidential.

Will read the Garda report Eamonn had gotten from the station. Peter Culmore had died from blunt force trauma. He ran in front of a car on Main Street. While Will studied the document the wind blew with fierce determination, whistling around the rolled up windows.

"Does it always blow this hard?"

"No, only when we get visitors from America," Eamonn replied with a straight face.

"That's what I thought. A grand plan to blow us all away."

"Aye," Eamonn said, "and mores the truth when blow-ins like yourself start pokin' your nose in Irish business."

"Maybe I'll turn into a troll and chase everybody out of town."

"Well now, nobody would notice that," Eamonn said laughing.

Chuckling, Will wondered if they were cracking up.

"Actually, I haven't had this much fun since my pet turtle died."

Trying to be serious, he read the Culmore file out loud. "Witnesses described the victim as suddenly appearing in their headlamps before the driver could take corrective action. The driver of the vehicle did briefly inspect the dying man lying in the street, then immediately had the passenger go for help at the stationhouse on Main Street. Being only two blocks, he went by foot. The driver said the dying man kept saying the word 'Finvana' over and over. An autopsy revealed a blood-alcohol level of 1.0, neither drunk or overtly sober. His mates at The Hatch thought he was a bit off-stride when he disappeared from the pub about midnight. Note: It would seem the victim, being sorely depressed, may have committed suicide."

Will looked out at the afternoon shoppers standing on street corners talking with friends and acquaintances.

"Gads, Eamonn, this is such a small town. Does anyone ever do anything unnoticed?"

"Not much, my friend. You must know, you live in a small town in Maine."

"True enough," Will said, "but right now it's here I'm thinking of and this report seems off the mark for your typical accident. A man runs into the street when there's no traffic, in the middle of the night. Surely the sound of an oncoming car could easily be heard. And the man repeating 'Finvana' with his dying breath, not 'help', not 'call a doctor', but Finvana."

His face screwed up in a question, Will looked at Eamonn. "So what's Finvana, anyway?"

"A fairy king."

"Yeesh," he replied.

Looking at Eamonn, the gray-haired man tried to smile.

"My dear friend, what do we do now? If this problem is related to the wee folk, how are we going to solve it? How do we stop something I'm not sure I believe in? Oh well, as some famous author once said, 'Never judge a book by its cover."

"And outside of that?" Eamonn asked.

"Outside of that, I don't know. If the little people are getting' their revenge, why'd they crank it up now? Folks have been living on that hill for a long time."

Visibly upset, Eamonn shook his head in frustration. *If the fairies are behind this stuff we're all doomed,* he thought. *No sense investigating if all is lost.*

Better to go home and wait my turn to go nuts and do meself in.

"You know, maybe it'd be better to drop this thing. It's too big for us, for me. I don't want to risk me relatives getting hurt. This thing's going into families and destroying them one by one. I don't think anyone's safe."

"You're right about that," Will said, breathing a heavy sigh. "But I think we should at least go on until we find out what is killing all the folks on the hill."

Silently, Eamonn nodded in agreement as he took a swipe at Will's arm.

"Arr, me matey, there'll be none of that," Will said.

"Don't 'arr me matey' me, just get this vehicle going. Me wif and yours are going to be wondering what's happened to us. There's time for hashing this stuff later."

"Yes, yes, later. Anyway we agree, we'll continue investigating for now."

Thirty-four—Thinkin'

Living on Allingham Way overlooking Inis Saimer Island, Eamonn had always enjoyed the view of the ancient boathouse, watching the tides ebb and flow. He thought of his lovely Kate and sweet daughter Molly. If only he could forget looking for clues and get on with his life, loving his family. Exhaling in frustration, the weight of his thoughts seemed less. *I should breathe away all me problems,* he thought. One thing was sure, he knew his neighbors watched him. They watched everyone. *Small towns,* he mused. Staring down the winding road leading to his house, he wondered if Elizabeth Gillespe had spent her last moments watching him. It was a shame, her dying like that. Will had insisted they find out if there was anything odd about her suicide. *Oh no,* he thought, *it's not at all odd to swallow a bottle of pills, folks do it all the time.* Smiling wryly to himself, he watched as the sun tried to show itself. Feeling the warmth of his cup, an overwhelming sense of appreciation for the simple things, especially his morning tea, came over him.

Kate and Mollie were still in bed. They had stayed up late with Will and Annie the night before. Even though the quiet was intoxicating, a time to rest, he continued trying to reason what had happened with his neighbor across the way. Unable to relax, he kept rehashing Elizabeth's suicide. *Her house was paid for. It's common knowledge she had enough put away to live comfortably. Could be she was despondent because her sister disappeared, likely run off with some tinker. The pubs didn't help, and that's the God's truth.* A feeling of uncertainty crept through his mind. Try as he might not to think, he found himself continually trying to resolve why he and Will were looking into everyone's business. It was sure to cause upset in the village. No one wanted an outsider digging into their affairs. Foul play or suicide, murder even, they were still all dead.

Down deep, he knew one basic truth. If he didn't keep investigating, eventually this mess would touch his family. God in heaven, how he feared that. *Will said he'd be over later, then we'll go to the next one on the list and the next one, until every soul on that cursed list is checked out.*

Thirty-five—A priestly visit

A knock at the door startled the daydreaming man. Looking at the clock on the wall he wondered who would be calling at this hour. It wasn't yet eight in the morning. A rush of cold air greeted Eamonn as he opened the door.

Standing there in his long black coat, Father Kerrigan looked solemn.

"Good morning to you, Father," Eamonn said cheerfully.

"Yes, and a good morning to you, Eamonn Gallagher." The flush of cold filled his face as he waited to be invited in. "Might I come in?" he asked sternly.

"Oh yes, where are me manners?" Opening the door wide, Eamonn motioned the priest in with a sweep of the hand and a slight bow. "Come, come into the study and have a cup of tae."

"Yes, that would be fine."

Eamonn waited for Father Kerrigan's coat and scarf before he hurried to the kitchen to heat the kettle. While he prepared a tray of digestives, two fresh cups, and a container of milk, he wondered what sort of business would bring a busy man like Father Kerrigan to see him. *Maybe something to do with Mollie's future schooling. Damn,* he thought, *maybe I'll get the lecture for not attending mass.*

Hearing the wind whistle through the windows, he stopped for a moment. Hurrying to the den he found the priest seated in the large sofa-chair usually reserved for himself. With a determined effort he tried to ignore the intrusiveness of this visit. Handing the cleric a cup of hot tea and plate of digestives, he sat silently waiting to hear the reason for this untimely visit.

"Father, why are you here so early in the morning? Is something wrong?"

Ignoring the questions, Father Kerrigan sipped his tea, then took a bite of a coconut covered cookie. "Tis a fine cup of tae, lad," he said with an ingratiating smile.

"Thank you, Father. I'm glad you like it."

The clouds outside had turned dark. *Feels like a storm brewing,* Eamonn thought. Thunder rumbled up the hill, followed by a streak of searing light.

The portly priest gave a shiver as he put down his cup. "Your shop is doing well, Eamonn?"

"Aye, it's doing okay, Father, for a small business."

"I heard you expanded the men's section."

"Ah, yes, that I did. I had to, expenses being what they are," Eamonn explained, feeling a bit uncomfortable.

"You know God's work can be quite costly too, my son."

"Aye, that it can."

"And I've had it called to my attention that certain of the parish haven't been meeting their spiritual commitments of late," the priest said, staring out the window at the wind blowing the small trees.

"I don't know who that could be, Father. God knows, what with working six days a week, a person could forget."

"Aye, but we wouldn't want to displease our Father in Heaven by not supporting his works, now would we?" the priest said firmly.

Filled with anger, Eamonn wondered why this so-called servant of the Lord had chosen this particular morning to chastise him about tithing.

"Father, I don't have a schedule of my payments to the church; I give what I can and I keep a pure heart for God." Steaming now, the Irishman rose and went to the window, staring out at the sailboats bobbing in the bay below.

"Eamonn Gallagher, don't take that tone with me or you'll be hearing from another."

"All right, Father. Let's cut to the chase, why are you here? What is it you want with me and mine?"

The large priest huffed a couple of unintelligible words, then looked at Eamonn coldly. "I've heard you've been investigating certain serious events occurring on this hill and the town as well. Going into folks' houses with your American friend, asking questions about their dearly departed. No sense of kindness for those poor dears just wanting to mourn in peace."

On the edge of his chair, the priest waited for Eamonn's reply.

"And what if I have, Father? How is that any of your affair?"

Rubbing his round nose vigorously, the priest chose his next words carefully.

"I've got no claim on what you do, it's a free country it is. But some are saying that your evidence points to the wee folk and the church cannot . . . will not, tolerate pagan beliefs being stirred up."

Eamonn took a tired breath. "Father, in all of Ireland everyone follows the example of the ostrich, hiding their heads in the sand, never knowing what happens or why. Like sheep, they follow along, trusting. Well, it's time to change all that and I intend to start right now."

"And how do you propose doin' this fine revelation?"

"I'm going to keep on digging until I've got all the facts. Find out why people on this hill are dying before their time. Then, if I can stop it, I will; no matter if it's man or beast."

"Oh, will ya now," the priest said, looking angrily around the room. "And while we're at it, what might those figures on your mantel be? Fairies?"

"Aye, they were a gift from me mate from America."

"Your American friend?"

"Yes. He and his Mrs. gave them with a true heart, in friendship."

"False idols now, is it?"

"No, Father, presents from a man who didn't think the church would be frightened by two small figurines."

"Eamonn Gallagher, I'm ordering you to stop this insanity right now. Destroy those abominations and we'll pray together for your mortal soul."

"I'm sorry, Father, I can't do that."

"Then I'll be going to the Bishop and he'll excommunicate you and your family. You will be ostracized, shunned in this town forever."

Near his wits end, Eamonn wondered if the priest had lost his mind completely.

Fear of the unknown filled the old cleric's eyes as Eamonn spoke, "If that's all you have to say to me, I'll be asking you to leave my house. I'll not have a priest of the Holy Catholic Church threaten me in my own home."

With that he hurried to fetch Father Kerrigan's coat and scarf.

"Here now, Lad, perhaps I was a bit hasty," the priest said, following Eamonn.

"We'll talk in a few days, after you've had time to reconsider this thing you're doing."

At the door, the priest spoke over his shoulder as he left quickly. "Only an ill wind can blow from this, mark my words."

Eamonn shut the door loudly, hurrying back to the safety of his house. *What right has he coming in here threatening me and my family?* His mind in turmoil, he wondered if Father Kerrigan would follow through on his threat. Rain fell steadily as he stared out at the storm brewing in his own backyard.

Thirty-six—Fairy Revenge

Will and Annie were subdued as they drove up Allingham Way to Eamonn's house. The list had been all consuming, and with the exception of going to the Olympic and Goldfingers to play the slot machines in Bundoran, they hadn't been out much to see the countryside. Still better than Las Vegas, it had been fun, the two pence slots paying more times than not. With all the construction, Will wondered if the west-coast of Ireland was lost to modernization. If it weren't for all the new homes and hotels the whole country would be in the toilet, Eamonn had said.

Parking in front of the old house Will felt a certain sadness. If only he could remove the specter of death from this place, help his friend find peace. Rain came down in frozen drops as he and Annie ran to Eamonn waiting for them with an open door.

"Hurry in or you'll be soaked to the skin and catch your death."

"I need windshield wipers for my glasses," Will replied breathlessly.

"That you do," Kate added, taking their coats to hang in the hall closet.

Sputtering with laughter from the chill, Annie looked at the bright-eyed baby hanging from her father's arm. "Now there's a sight," she said. Mollie watched with interest as the strange lady contorted her face for her amusement, talking words of nonsense.

When they had all settled into the warmth and security of Eamonn's den, Annie gave a sigh of relief. The ever-present hot tea was wonderfully soothing. Small flames flickered as Eamonn walked over to the large fireplace and put on more peat. Quite intoxicating, the aroma was a pleasant blend of dry grass and peppery gorse.

Lost in thought, Eamonn interrupted his own musings, "Dear Annie and Kate, would you mind if me and Will go into the other room to discuss business?" Looking serious he motioned his guest to follow.

"Okay, Mr. Gallagher, if it's business you're needing to discuss, you have our permission," Kate said with a twinkle in her eye.

"I do love you, woman," Eamonn replied. "Come along, Mate, we'll go into the kitchen, it's quiet there."

Laughter from the den followed them down the hall. Seated across the table from Will, Eamonn stared out at the rain hitting the tender shoots of his new garden.

"The parish priest came this morning. He said I should stop investigating or they'll excommunicate me family from the Church."

"I'm sorry." Will said. "How did he know we were snooping around?"

"Someone must have followed us . . . maybe someone spoke up."

"Gads, who would follow us? Everyone we spoke to said they would keep it under their hats."

"Well, someone decided to take off his hat," Eamonn said bitterly.

"I guess this town is too small to expect secrecy."

"Aye, that's true enough. If you're on the side that's wanting to know, there's no secret."

"I hate to quit now, but if the Church wants you to, we can. It's easy for me, I live three thousand miles away. If we uncovered some earth shaking truth, I wouldn't be affected like you."

"I know that, Will, and I know you're just thinking of me when you say it. I appreciate that. But I can't quit now, we're too close. My neighbors are dying and soon it's going to be someone in my family." Eamonn studied his friend's face, then continued. "I think there's great danger if we continue. I'm giving you the option to back out."

The old house creaked and groaned from the gale-force winds blowing outside. Will looked at the Irishman, his face etched with pain.

"I could no more back out now than undo an oath of loyalty."

Reaching into his inner pocket, Will brought out the list.

"I say we continue searching until we find out the truth of the matter. And that is, why these folks are dying in their prime."

With that he reached across the table. Eamonn smiled grimly as he clasped Will's outstretched hand in friendship and commitment, a silent agreement.

"Well faith and begory, now that that's settled let's get on with it."

"I'll faith and begory you. Let's have a cuppa tae."

Will nodded in assent while he scanned the list past the names already checked off. "Have you heard anything about Maggie Gibbons on Back Street?"

"No, the name's not familiar. She must be before me time here. She must have moved or died before I was born."

"How about James McGurran, on Castle?"

"Nope, I don't recall anything," Eamonn said with frustration.

"Okay, John Laughlin on Castle?"

"You know, that name rings a bell. I'm thinkin' that John died about twenty years ago. He had some strange disease. Me da talked about him. Said he was possessed by a demon."

Will stared at the floor as he tried to fit the pieces together. *Why are three people on the list from so long ago? If only we could research them.* "Eamonn, is there any reason why these three would be on this list?"

"I don't know, unless whatever's happening now has been going on for years."

Will listened to the downpour hitting the window. *Timeless,* he thought, *like the rain.*

"That's it! This started before you and I were born. Maybe it's a vendetta. Maybe this list is one of many and wherever people have built on fairy hills, lists like this have been created."

The Irishman's expression turned from stoic to a forced smile. "Aye, that's it, Will Bonner, the fairies are killing the people of Ballyshannon for building on their land."

Giving Will a friendly shove, he added, "Coming from America has affected your brain. The whole of Ireland isn't overrun with little people you know."

"Okay, okay, but I think it's interesting that this list covers a broad span of years. Actually, at this point we don't even know how far back it goes."

"You're right about that. There's a library in Donegal that has reference books on names and family origins." Eamonn thought for a moment. "Let me talk to Kate, then we can take a run over there."

As Eamonn left the kitchen, Will wondered whose list they had found. *Why would all these people with no relation to each other be on it?* He discounted the fairy theory. *Good for fictional stories,* he thought tiredly, *but not a reality.*

Thirty-seven—A store of knowledge

Thankfully, traffic was light during the drive to the small village of Donegal. Sheep stared at the small car passing on the N15. Like sentinels, they held effortlessly to the sides of steep hills, boulders and gorse bordering the green expanse making up garden walls to fence them in. Far beyond the curious four-legged creatures, it felt as though a thousand disapproving eyes were watching. Will tried to clear his mind as he wondered if he had been in the forest too long, as his friend in Maine always said. Maybe he was caving in to the pressure of the unknown.

Neither talked very much as they slowed near the town proper. With a park-like setting in the center, a circular road divided the town in two. Placing a parking permit on the dashboard Will followed Eamonn through the rain, crossing the street.

The library was quiet during the week. *Easy to concentrate,* Will thought. Eamonn quickly found the reference books on family origins in Ballyshannon. While he scanned for Maggie Gibbons, James McGurran and John Laughlin, Will reviewed the list, looking in a book dated 1880 through1930.

Scanning the professions, he searched for familiar names. *Shoemaker, rag merchant; wool draper; gads,* he mused, *a tallow chandler? No names from the list,* he thought. *Could be some died before the turn of the century.* Comparing them he found two, John Morrow, a trim shop proprietor and Peter Kelly, a clothes broker. *Strange, both died on the same day, June 24, 1900.*

Showing what he'd found to Eamonn, there was nothing to indicate the cause of death. For many, the date they departed this world, was missing too.

Eamonn nudged Will. "Here's one, Maggie Gibbons, born 1938, deceased 1974. Thirty-six years old."

"That's a bit early for natural causes," Will replied.

The pages in the old book were stiff and faded, and it seemed to take forever leafing through them. James McGurran's name appeared close to John Laughlin's. They had died within a couple of weeks of each other in 1963. Will marked the list as he tried to figure out why they were on it.

Footsteps in the next aisle drew his gaze through the rows of shelves. The momentary sight of a pair of black orbs staring through one of the lower shelves sent a wave of fear to his stomach. Blinking for a second, he gasped, "Eamonn, look there!" pointing across the table.

Eamonn turned quickly, straining to see, noticing nothing out of the ordinary.

"I must be cracking up," Will said, rubbing his eyes.

"What are ya saying?"

"I heard footsteps, I saw something staring through those books," Will said with a bewildered look.

Moving quickly around the table, Eamonn went to the end of the first row. Seeing nothing there, he moved from row to row. In his quickening search he heard retreating footsteps become fainter, as though scurrying away, then stopping altogether as the front door clicked shut.

Running now, Eamonn yanked the door open. The sidewalk was empty except for a young girl in a school uniform. Startled, the red-haired child jumped back from the tall man glaring down at her.

"Here now, lass, don't be frightened," Eamonn said breathlessly.

Behind him now, Will looked down the street, across the narrow road, then at the tops of buildings outlined in the gray half-light. Not really expecting to see anything, he wondered if he was losing his mind altogether. *At sixty, maybe my brain is fading. This place has such an aura of make-believe, it's probably just my over-active imagination.* Following Eamonn, he returned to the library.

"Eamonn, did you take the list when you ran out?" he asked worriedly.

"No, I didn't."

"Damn," Will said, looking under the table. Picking up the notepad, his spirits fell. The two men's eyes met in frustration.

"It's the old decoy trick," Will said disgustly.

Seated across from him, Eamonn motioned for him to sit as he recited names from memory. Without speaking Will wrote them down one after the other, recreating the ominous mystery. The Irishman's brow beaded in concentration as he kept on. Amazed, Will continued until they reached the last one. Except for the notes on those they had already researched it seemed complete. Together they added bits of information alongside names already visited.

"Now that's a fair bit of memory, Mr. Gallagher," Will said, beaming at his friend.

"If that was intended to stop us, they didn't know about you."

"Aye, you've got that right."

"Total recall, that's amazing!" Will said enviously.

Eamonn nodded, "They'll not stop us, but I'm afraid something else has me a might nervous. I heard footsteps too, then someone ran out the door, sure enough."

"I think we're dealing with a clever trickster, maybe more than one. Are there any other doors in the library behind the rows? Could be there's sound equipment near the front," Will said thoughtfully. "Of course that wouldn't explain the eyes I saw."

"I believe you saw what you say, but I'm thinkin' there's a villainous plot here to drive us nuts in order to invalidate our investigation. If I were to say we saw eyes, they'd claim I was scuttered," Eamonn replied, "you know, fluttered, drunk."

Unable to resolve the questions after searching the bookshelves, Will folded the new list and put it in his coat pocket. He would make a copy for Eamonn later. Rain poured down as they headed back to Ballyshannon.

Thirty-eight—Love & Fear

The day's troubling events had more than unnerved Eamonn. A hot shower would ease the tension. Rinsing suds from his black hair, the large man felt a rush of cold air as the shower curtain was pulled aside slightly. The flow of water was interrupted as soft hands caressed the small of his muscular back.

"Oh my, Luv, that feels grand," he said.

Kate sighed, "Eamonn Gallagher, you have a wonderful body. I love yer tight buns."

Laughing, he turned to look at the smiling upturned face. Married six years, her graceful beauty still took his breath away. With long dark hair to her waist, her slender body was well developed, full breasts rising with each breath. *Mounds of light ending in dark delight . . .* strong desire interrupted poetic thoughts.

Standing inches away from the tall man, Kate kissed him softly on the chest, working her way to his taut nipples. With all her heart she wanted to please him, her tongue caressing him in a needful way.

Water raining down his face, Eamonn stood with his eyes closed, the vision of loveliness filling his mind. Rubbing his back with both hands, she pulled him close.

His excitement growing, he reached down to kiss her ready lips. Her right hand slid down the small of his back as the other made its way to the extension of his desire now standing erect. Slowly she rubbed his quivering sex.

He lifted her as she wrapped her legs around his body. She slid easily to meet him, opening to his desire. Moving her hips slowly she lowered herself until he was fully enclosed. Meeting his body, Kate pushed down. Taut with excitement, she was filled with waves of ecstasy. Moaning with pleasure, she moved her hips more rapidly.

Raising her up he filled his mouth with a dark areola, sucking hard as he went deeper inside. With each stroke he felt his pleasure build. Her mouth on his, he shuddered and moaned in climax, his control gone. Their mingled cries of joy filled the air. Their pleasure unending, the warm water beat down on their entwined bodies. Slowly he lowered her to her feet as they gazed at each other in shared love and passion.

Gusts of wind rattled the shutters, blowing in from the bay.

"I love you," Eamonn said, his face flushed. "You're beautiful, Mrs. Gallagher." Caressing her, he whispered 'thank you' in Gaelic.

Lightning shook the house as they kissed. Secure in their bed, Kate smiled at her man. "I'm glad I met you, mister. If I hadn't, I'd have been a nun."

"Aye, a nun," Eamonn replied, giving the playful woman a hug.

As they snuggled close, Kate drifted off to sleep, secure in her love's arms. The house creaked as the wind blew harder. Thunder boomed and lightning lit the sky. Dark eyes watched from outside the second story sill, grim beacons of death; they blinked and were gone.

An uneasy feeling crept over Eamonn as he watched the storm thrashing about. *I've got to find the answer before it's too late,* he thought. Endorphins filled his being as he held fast to his Kate, slipping into a deep sleep.

Thirty-nine—God's servant

Saying his prayers, Father Kerrigan sat in his study overlooking the garden. Filled to the ceiling with books of every possible subject necessary to answer questions of faith, he wondered if there was a book that would answer the nagging questions popping up now. His sources had said Eamonn Gallagher and his friend had not stopped their search. *God in heaven,* he thought, *is the man an atheist? Does he not fear being excommunicated? Most disturbing, the rumors and pagan beliefs that are surfacing. I must stop this search. What if they turn up something that proves . . . no, it's not possible,* he thought frantically. *Fairies don't exist.*

Ringing the small bell on the table next to his lounge, he'd call for a cup of tea to calm his frayed nerves. *Have the parishioners gone mad? I've spent a lifetime devoting every waking moment to my flock. If Eamonn uncovers anything that points to the fair folk, I'll be finished. The Bishop will take my church, this house.* He looked around with true affection at the paneled wood, the oak shelves ornately carved to his exact specifications. *Damn the heathens, I'll not have anyone take my house away. I'm God's servant.*

An old lady in a plain dress interrupted his worries. "Here now, Father, what might you be needin'?"

Looking out the window at the gray sky, he replied by rote, "I'll have a cup of tae please, and mind you, I want fresh milk."

"Yes, Father, right away," she responded, hurrying out the door.

It's difficult finding decent help, he thought self-righteously. That bit of complaining done, he tried to think logically, formulate a plan. *I must keep an eye on the comings and goings of Mr. Eamonn Gallagher. I'll have him watched from this day forward. What he sees, I'll see. If he finds some untruth, I'll be right there. Perhaps he could have an accident slow him down. With all the deaths it wouldn't be a surprise if he were to drown.*

The creaking of the door stopped his dark thoughts as the housekeeper returned with the tea tray. Pouring a cup, he waved the old lady away.

Eamonn must be stopped. He can't be allowed to continue. It only encourages the masses. His mind made up; he took a piece of paper and ink pen from his desk.

To David McCann:

Your presence is hereby requested by me, your parish priest. Your immediate attention is required in a private matter. You shall come to my house at the Presbytery, post haste. May your sins be forgiven and may you find peace in His eternal grace.

PP Peter Kerrigan

Laying the pen aside, he folded the note neatly and placed it in an envelope, sealing it with great care. *No one must know God's business, least ways no one in Ballyshannon.* Feeling better, he thought about the man he had selected to do God's work. *He'll do as I say in this ghastly affair, he owes the church favors for all that food and shelter. Yes, it would bode well for Mr. McCann to do my bidding.* Drinking his tea, the priest said a prayer of thanks for guidance in his venture.

Forty—Dreams in Mullaghmore

Will sat in the small living room in Mullaghmore, looking out the large window at the nightlights down by the bay. The burning peat was comforting, if not warming. The pad of paper he held in his hand had many doodles of stick-people. He smiled, his artistic ability was surely limited.

If only I could figure out what's cooking in Ballyshannon. Nothing like this has ever happened in Steep Falls. Not even in the whole state of Maine. The media would be up in arms, there'd be newspapers from around the U.S. snooping everywhere. Rag-sheets would be looking for a clue, some explanation why so many people had died in a small village. It's like town-wide acceptance of 'that's the way it is', he thought tiredly. *One thing's sure, I saw a little man at Mary McNulty's funeral and again at Sean's. There's no doubt about it, then those eyes in the library, someone was watching,* he thought, trying to find a rational answer. *If size is any indication, the type of being involved in this mystery definitely points to fairies. The crystals Eamonn had been given, Peter Culmore's dying words, Finvana – the fairy king. If I didn't know better, I'd say the evidence is almost too convincing.*

One by one he ran over all the details and clues he and Eamonn had uncovered. Sometimes the obvious was really the truth of the matter. There was no getting away from the fact that most of the deceased had lived on the hill, except for Mrs. McNulty and her son. Their deaths may be related to some other matter. *They're just similar in that they died,* he reasoned, putting his thoughts on paper.

Laying back for a moment, he closed his eyes. Annie had long since gone to bed, neither of them used to staying up late. The wind whistled through some open crevice near the overhead window vents. The fire crackled softly as he fell into a deep sleep. *Visions of steep mountains appeared abruptly as he flew silently through the night sky. Below, colored lights distorted by fog and distance could be seen at the center of large plots of land. Slowly he descended to the tops of passing trees. In the distance, the flat dull surface of a large body of water appeared. A yellow light glowed at the far edge.*

Suddenly faces appeared, white, lifeless heads. To avoid the morbid sight he tried to pull up into the dark sky, to escape the stares of hunger that looked at him. Small bony hands grabbed at his ankles. Uncontrollably jerking in fear, his pad of paper fell to the floor. Trembling, he looked out the large picture window for a sign. Seeing nothing amiss was a relief. *Just a bad dream*, he decided.

The fire had burned to ashes. *It's time to go to bed.* He checked the doors before heading down the hall. *I'll be safe in Annie's arms,* he thought. *Ghosts never attack when you're under the covers with your mate.* Will smiled to himself as he went to bed.

Early the next day he drove to Ballyshannon to pick up Eamonn. They planned to visit the four survivors on the list, if for no other reason than to see why they were on a list of people who were already dead.

"Aye, top o' the morning, Mr. Bonner," Eamonn said, greeting him in a jovial voice.

"Good mornings aren't always welcome," Will replied dryly.

"Now what side of the bed did you get up on?"

"The left side, like I have for sixty years," Will said, pulling the list out of his pocket, ignoring further civilities.

"All right, Mate, we'll go see Horace McBride," Eamonn said, pausing for a moment, "he's not a pauper, a might difficult to talk to, maybe. He lives on College."

"Good, where is College?"

"Arrg, me matey, I forgot you don't know the village. Go down Back, which turns into Market, then left on College Street. He lives at the end."

Will listened as he started the rental car. "So this guy lives more in town than on the hill."

"Tis the truth of the matter, but I'm thinkin' he lived here when he was a wee lad," Eamonn said.

Leaving Allingham Way, Will made the turn down narrow streets leading to Market. They all seemed the same as he drove down Back, a one-way thoroughfare. Adding to his frustration cars were parked out in the middle, blocking traffic again. Too early in the morning to complain, he hoped they would find Mr. McBride at home and that he would have all the answers they were seeking.

Horace McBride's house was dreary and depressing, neglect in paint and repairs evident. It reminded Will of a forgotten child. Like all the other streets they had visited, this one was deserted too. The metal knocker, shaped like the head of a fish, registered loud and clear.

The silence is deafening, Will thought, *no one's home.* Rusty beyond its years, an ornate knob creaked as it turned, the door opening. A face stared out at the two men. A tired looking woman in a paint-stained dress stood motionless, waiting for them to state their business.

"My name is Eamonn Gallagher, and I'd like to see Mr. McBride please."

"Well now, so would I but he's gone."

"When would you be expecting him back?" Will asked.

"No tellin', he went away day before yesterday and that's the last I've seen of him," the woman said.

"I know you don't know me and my friend here, but we're trying to find some missing folks. Find out why they left without tellin' anyone," Eamonn said, looking at the wrinkled face listening more out of curiosity than anything else.

"What's yer interest in Mr. McBride then? Someone payin' you to find him? Owes you a few quid, does he?"

"No, no, he doesn't owe me a pence," Eamonn said, rubbing his arms against the chill. "Might we come in and explain in private?"

Looking up and down the street, she turned quickly, leaving the door open behind her. Will followed Eamonn as the old woman led them to a room painted white many years ago. The only furniture was three aged wooden chairs around a scratched, table. Offering the two men a seat, the beady-eyed woman waited for Eamonn to speak his mind.

"Ma'am, me friend and I are on a mission. A confidential investigation. We're trying to find out why so many people on the hill are dying early, disappearing for no apparent reason."

"And how could I be of help, just bein' the Mister's housekeeper?"

"Aye, I was wondering if we might have a look around his personal room. You could watch, of course, see that we don't bother anything."

"I guess it'd be all right. If you were crooked I'd be knowin'," she said, eyeing Eamonn closely. "Don't be makin' a mess or his nibs will be upset for sure when he returns."

Eamonn nodded, then he and Will went down a short hall to a bedroom at the end. The room was filled with furniture. There was barely enough space to walk around the bed past a glassed in hutch in the corner. Porcelain dolls dressed in elegant gowns from another time were posed in various positions facing the bed. Portraits of handsome women and dapper gentlemen filled the walls. End tables flanking the bed were cluttered with men's jewelry, cuff links and coins. It didn't appear that Horace McBride had planned a trip.

Turning on a small bedside lamp, a sparkle caught Will's eye. Bending closer, he picked up a crystal stone. Turning it slowly in his hand, he felt a small crevice.

"Eamonn, look at this." Handing it to the Irishman, he waited for a reaction.

"Aye, it's the same as the others, only this one has an 'F' inscribed on it."

"Finvana?" Will asked.

"I reckon. That's the third one so far," Eamonn replied, replacing it on the bed stand.

Wondering out loud, Will continued opening dresser drawers. "Are those good luck charms?"

"I don't know, could be," Eamonn said as he stared at an old book. "Haven't worked so far."

Will smiled at the morbid humor as each continued looking. The only clue of obvious value, the stone seemed redundant. Thanking the housekeeper they left, retracing their steps to the one-way road down the hill to Mall Street near the bottom.

Next on the list, Frances Murray lived in a stone-faced apartment. Will knocked loudly on the old door, not really expecting a response. A whoosh of air pulled at their coattails as a girl with red pigtails stood in the doorway, her hip cocked to one side.

"Hmm, a couple of fancy Dans," she mumbled under her breath. "What would you two be wantin'?"

Eamonn smiled at the expectant face. "My name's Eamonn Gallagher, I live on Allingham Way. I'd like to speak with Frances Murray."

"Who's yer mate?" the gum-chewing girl asked.

"Oh, this here's me friend, Will Bonner, from Maine."

"Where's Maine?"

"The U.S.A." Will replied.

"Well, okay, yer welcome to come in, but it won't do no good 'cause Frances went to our sister's house in Cork."

"Can I get the number there?"

"No tele," the young girl replied.

His face filled with frustration, Eamonn turned to Will. "Best we go on to see Patrick . . . "

"Here now, Mister," the red-headed kid said, interrupting him, 'me sister left a package for Eamonn Gallagher."

Running into another room, she soon returned with a small parcel wrapped in plain brown paper.

"Take it," she said as the Irishman hesitated.

"Thank you for helpin'. You're a bonny lass for sure," Eamonn replied, giving the young lady a pat on the shoulder. Blushing, she ushered them out quickly.

Clustered together, clouds, hurried westward on their journey to the coast. Unable to ignore the cold air, Will pulled up his collar, covering his ears. Seated in the car, Eamonn opened the small box the girl had given them.

"A crystal," he said. "I have no idea why Frances Murray would leave a stone like this unless she felt threatened."

"Could be that's why she took off for her sister's place," Will added thoughtfully.

Eamonn handed him a long rectangular stone with a Gaelic symbol on one of its sides.

"What's this mark?" Will asked as he returned it.

"It's a symbol of the Fairy King."

"Just like all the others?"

"No, but still fairies," Eamonn replied.

"Gads, is everyone thinking about little people?"

"So far," Eamonn replied. The smooth surface felt cold to the touch as he studied it. "This one's different, it comes from Connemara, down the coast."

"Well, that could be significant," Will said. "You know, this all seems too simple. If I didn't know better I'd say these crystals were planted. It's just too convenient."

Rolling the stone in his hand, Eamonn studied the clouds moving across the sky.

"Will, you have to understand that certain beliefs in this country are not easily removed. Call them superstitions, but most folks here still believe in some form of little people. Whether it's leprechauns or fairies, makes no difference."

Will looked in the rearview mirror as the wind buffeted the small car. Shaking his head, he started the four-cylinder engine. "Where to next?"

"Aye, me fine feathered friend, you have to go back up the hill and around."

"Your fine feathered friend? Do I look like a rooster?"

"No, more like a duc'"

"A duc'," Will said, imitating Eamonn.

"You're going to have to duc' if you keep funnin' the self."

The lady at the door was slender, her black hair pulled tightly back in a bun. Her hands quivered slightly as she pushed loose bangs from her eyes.

"Good afternoon, Ma'am, my name is Eamonn Gallagher and this is me mate, Will Bonner. May we come in and speak to you in private?"

"You can as long as you mean no harm to ma family," she replied nervously.

"Oh no, Ma'am, you're safe with us."

Stepping inside, the darkened hallway cluttered with wooden boxes marked Spirits', felt more like a pub storage room.

He must be in the import business, Will thought. Led off to a dimly lit room to the right, they sat on a small leather couch that creaked from their weight. The smell of stale tobacco filled the air. Seeing the woman's uneasy look, Eamonn got right to the point, asking if they could speak to Patrick McDermott about a personal matter.

"I'm afraid that won't be possible, me husband has taken to his bed and won't come out."

While Eamonn asked Mrs. McDermott questions, Will looked about the small room. *This coffee table has seen better days,* he thought idly. Even though it was worn with age, he noticed some letters freshly etched into the surface. *Gads, those are the same words we saw at Russell O'Quin's and he died a year ago. Maybe these guys were in a club. That's it, a death club.*

Eamonn rose to leave, interrupting Will's frightening revelations.

"Thank you, Ma'am," he said as they were going out the door.

The last rays of sunlight cast an eerie glow on the street as they went to the small car.

"What's Tuatha De Danann mean?" Will asked.

"That's Gaelic, where'd you see it?"

"It was scratched into the table back there."

"By itself it means nothing, but this fella's not wanting to see us might put things in a different light," Eamonn replied.

"So what do the words mean?"

Eamonn didn't reply for a long minute. "It's the name of a powerful group of fairies."

"Oh great, another fairy clue," Will replied, then thought aloud, "maybe not a clue, but a symptom. Maybe these folks are infected with a disease called the little people syndrome.

"That may be as close as we get. More times than not, those dying were in good health."

While they sat on the narrow street, thunder echoed in the distance, the half-light of evening placing a protective blanket of darkness over the fears and insecurities running through their heads. For Patrick McDermott to be so afraid he didn't want to talk, seemed logical to Will. He probably wouldn't want two strangers barging into his house asking questions that surely touched the very center of his being. *No,* Will understood. Tomorrow they would continue their search, see the last person on the list.

Forty-one—Lost in fear

Coming out of Sean Og's Pub on Castle Street, a biting wind crept into every available opening in Michael McGinty's coat. The pub was empty tonight, no one to pick a fight with unless he counted the dilapidated sot sleeping at the table near the wall. Hating the thought of going home to his lonely room, he decided to take a walk up Market to Back Street, then around Martins Row, then down Main. *I'll go the long way,* he thought. At the top of Back he looked up at the cloudless sky. The moon was out and shadows from buildings across the street made images of stretched walls and flat windows. There was no sound except for his footsteps. It was the same as before, no friends, no job and not two-pence to his name. Michael was upset and angry.

Crossing to Martin's Row he didn't bother to look for cars, he'd hear the engine or tires crunching the road. *Damn me feckin' brain,* he thought, *can't quit thinkin'.* Six pints had dulled his senses, but not enough as he automatically ran the tapes in his head again. *No woman, no work and no pay all adds up to shite. Huge piles of shite.* Bitterly he walked along Martin's Row, a short street at the top of the hill, then headed over to Main.

Enough exercising the legs, time to go home. Stopping to catch his breath, the muscular man adjusted his collar closer to his neck. At the single streetlight he watched a scraggly tree over on Martin's Row bending slightly from the breeze. Just for a second he thought he saw someone duck behind a parked car. *Me eyes are playin' tricks,* he thought tiredly. Clomping loudly down the narrow street a foreboding feeling of being watched pressed in on his mind. *If someone wants a piece of me, well . . .* Stopped at Main and Church Lane, an alley leading to St. Anne's Church, he looked back. Thirty yards away a small man in a black top hat and a coat with tails stood smiling wickedly at the hunched over Irishman.

"Here little feller, you better get on home before I decide to make mush of yer face," Michael said angrily.

Punching his right fist into his left palm, like a hardball hitting leather, he watched the diminutive figure. The little man ran towards him, stopping ten meters away.

"Arr, if it's a fight you want I'll give it to ya," Michael said, a touch of fear in his voice.

Without speaking, the evil-faced creature came flying at the inebriated Irishman. Michael's anger turned to fear as the small fiend moved towards him. A strong man, Michael stepped sideways running up Church Lane. Never looking back, he dodged around an old Peugeot and headed towards a large rusted gate leading to St. Anne's Church. Yanking on the lever, the gate creaked open. A cold wind blew with such force, it momentarily stopped him. Looking back towards Main Street, he thought he saw a top hat bobbing up and down as it came rapidly up the lane.

His head filled with images of gremlins and trolls, Michael ran wildly up the path through the graveyard to the church. Trying a side door, he thought he heard footsteps coming up behind. Quickly he went around to the back where he found a small entryway. With all his strength he slammed into it hard. The smell of incense and old wood filled his nostrils as he fell threw the open doorway. Terrified, he ran up a stairwell, round and round. At the top, he found the door to a room.

The exertion of running had circulated the alcohol in his blood to every cell in his body. Tingling, he wondered if fairy-folk would enter the sanctity of a church.

"Holy Ojes," he whispered, "please keep this evil from me."

His mind filled with thoughts of darkness, he looked at his shadow on the wall. *Have I changed? An angel,* he thought with amazement, *I'm blessed with wings of an angel. I can fly.* Opening the door to the bell-tower he walked to the edge and climbed up. To the west the lights of Bundoran glittered. All around, the town of Ballyshannon glowed softly. Down below, dark eyes watched from the shadows.

Raising his arms like a bird in flight, Michael flew. His piercing scream was interrupted abruptly by the sudden impact of the concrete path below. Walking up to the disjointed body, the little man smiled then went on his way.

Grimly Eamonn opened the door for Will and Annie. The news of Michael McGinty's unusual passing had upset him greatly. It seemed that everyone had lost their minds. The Garda said the drink had caused Michael to fall out of the bell-tower at St. Anne's. What madness would make a man break into a church, a Protestant church at that. Seeking refuge? So, what makes him decide to jump? The bell-tower had a waist-high railing. He'd have had to deliberately climb over it. What had frightened him?

Settled in the den overlooking the bay, they all sat deep in thought as the wall clock ticked loudly. Meanwhile Mollie played with her talking doll, oblivious to the outside world.

Pressing its finger, an animated voice gushed, "Turn loose of me finger".

Laughing, she pressed its foot and the recording continued cheerfully, "Me foot."

Will smiled at the happy child. Waggling his fingers like a hypnotist, he whispered, "You are getting sleepy," repeating the mantra over and over as he moved his hands back and forth. Thoroughly amused, Mollie thought the strange man quite funny.

Distracted by his own thoughts, Eamonn stood up and walked to the window overlooking Donegal Bay, the clouds ever present in a sky destined for darkness.

"I don't know how to stop the dying on this hill," he said stoically.

"Well, three crystals engraved with symbols were found indicating a strong belief in fairies." Will said emphatically.

"That it does, me friend," Eamonn replied.

Annie held onto Will's hand as she asked Eamonn a nagging question, "What does Tuatha de Danann mean? Outside of you and Will, the only other place I've heard that phrase is in an American movie called 'Willow'. I didn't know it was from Irish folklore."

"Aye, Annie, folklore it is and true to most with roots here." Eamonn said reluctantly. Atlantic winds whistled through the tiny cracks in the windowsills, causing him to shiver.

Turning, he spoke in a whisper, "The most powerful fairies were the Trooping, or Herdie. They had organized courts. They were the Daoine Sidhe tribe of Ireland. They spent their time followin' grand pursuits, like Fairy Rades."

"Fairy Rades?" Will wondered.

"Riding horses in solemn processions," he replied. Pausing, Eamonn looked at his two visitors. "The Tuatha de Danann once ruled Ireland, but were conquered by the Milesians. They were forced underground and legends say they went to a fairy island called Tir Nan Og, the land of the young. This place gave them all they needs; feasts, hunting, lots of love and music. It was a fairy paradise. Their king was Finvana."

A relentless foe, the wind blew through the house as it creaked and moaned in protest.

"How does being on this hill make fairies the villain in all this?" Will asked. "So far all we know for sure is that everyone thinks the fairies are intent on killing all the folks up here."

"That's true enough," Eamonn replied, "but how do you explain the little man in the top hat you saw on two occasions?"

"I don't, unless someone has a hologram as I've said before."

"Not in broad daylight," Annie interjected.

"Ah, that's true, my brain must be fading again," he replied. "We've been here before."

Forty-two—Paying his respects

Will wondered if coming to Michael McGinty's funeral was a good idea. This being his third in as many weeks; to some he was surely a jinx. Having the service at St. Anne's was strange enough, Michael being Catholic. However, his brother had insisted on it. He died here, James had said, his funeral will be here.

There weren't many folks in attendance, not more than twenty-five. Will thought that maybe some were witnessing this man's demise to validate their own beliefs. If a tough guy like Michael jumped from the bell-tower, it was evident mighty powerful forces were at work.

The droning voice of the priest issued a failed prayer from high on the pulpit.

"Heavenly Father, we pray you treat this man, Michael McGinty, with forgiveness; have mercy on his soul; give him peace. In Jesus' name we pray." Raising his head he continued, "Please turn to hymn 134 in your books."

An organ began playing a soulful melody over a woman's mournful sobbing. Standing next to Eamonn, Will wondered if there was a serial killer in their midst. *Man or woman, they could be killing for the pure joy of seeing these folks suffer. There'd be no way to tell. Maybe that creature, that character I saw at Mary and Sean McNulty's funerals, is the killer.*

Unconsciously, Will scanned the side pews before he realized that Eamonn was looking at him with a questioning eye.

Near the doors a small figure watched intently. No one noticed him standing near the last row of seats.

Eamonn placed his hand on Will's shoulder just as he followed his friend's stare. Surprised and angry he went around Will, walking quickly towards the back of the church. Hearing footsteps behind him, Eamonn turned motioning Will to stop. In that instant, as he looked back, the small man was gone.

Unaware, everyone continued singing a little off key, adding to the despair and loneliness that filled the church. On display in the front, near the empty choir-box, the stiff body of Michael McGinty lay stretched out, his eyes closed.

Temporarily re-seated in the back, Eamonn felt like a guard against evil. Now he had seen the same apparition as Will. His friend wasn't delusional. He wasn't going nuts from reading too many stories about little people. *Damn,* he thought, *why is this happening here? Why did I have to see that face after all these years?* A morbid feeling filled his heart as he watched the proceedings. *Am I next? Maybe the both of us?*

Nudging Will, he left the sanctuary. He had always thought the wee folk couldn't come into the house of God when there were prayers. *Even though this is a Protestant Church, it's still a place of worship. Maybe that little bugger isn't a fairy; maybe it's a man, a midget. A small magician who's playing tricks on the likes of us. Sure and it would convince most, especially if it were done on the sly.* His mind racing through all the possibilities he had no doubt that he needed to talk to Will in private, away from inquisitive ears.

In the car, Will listened to Eamonn explain his theory about the little man and the mysterious deaths. It seemed plausible, in fact it made sense. Even if they didn't have a clue how to find this devilish character, they'd just hash it over till they found a lead telling them where to look next. Right now they'd head back to Eamonn's house to rerun everything they knew so far.

Kate was busy explaining her recipe to Annie as she prepared an old-fashioned Irish salad.

"See, first I cook some potatoes, carrots, onions and asparagus." Draining the boiled vegetables, she cut up some Romaine lettuce and hardboiled eggs. Throwing it all in a large bowl, Kate sprinkled bits of cheddar cheese on top.

"My that looks scrumptious," Annie exclaimed.

"Oh, I'm sure you could throw something together just as good," Kate said. "I love cooking for company."

Taking a container of shrimp from the refrigerator she sprinkled them over the growing mound of food. A little salt, a dash of black pepper and dill weed, it was ready. Gathering around the table, they joined hands while Annie said a prayer of thanks for the food, their safety, and for having such a great cook. Eamonn opened a bottle of white wine. Feeling festive, Kate turned on a music radio station. The soft sound of flutes rendering a folk ballet penetrated Will's consciousness, etching in his mind as one of his nicest experiences.

No one noticed the knock at the door. Much louder the second time, Eamonn gave Will a concerned look as he excused himself to answer. Though the sound of Eamonn's words seemed void of emotion, Will tried to hear what was being said. The outside door shut with a clunk then footsteps came their way.

Coming into the dining room, Eamonn held up a large brown envelope. Ignoring the object of interest, Kate motioned for her husband to return to the table.

"Whatever's in that post can wait until we're finished," she said in a patient voice.

If there's to be any upset coming into this house it can wait until my husband's eaten his meal, she thought tiredly. No one inquired as to the large envelope lying next to Eamonn's cup of tea, but it seemed to grow with each passing moment.

"Well, Mr. Gallagher, what do you suppose is in the envelope?" Will asked, using an official tone. "Fairy dust?"

Eamonn ignored the patter as he slowly opened the brown missal. Taking out a neatly folded paper, a key fell onto the table. While the others looked on, Kate picked up the ornate object.

"What's in the letter?" Annie inquired softly.

"Yes," Will chimed in.

"Okay, I need some light on the subject. Moving closer to the hanging lamp, Eamonn began:

Dear Sir,

I have taken pen in hand to share a bit of information on subjects you seem to be strongly interested in. I had a friend die a few years back. She had some relations who died the same as them that's dying now, so I was informed. I'm thinking that if you take this key to my friend, Lucy O'Sheeran's house, you might find something related to your present course of research.

Respectfully,

A friend

Will rubbed the back of his head, trying to think. "Maybe it's somebody's idea of a joke. Or maybe this is the first real break we've had."

"Aye, I think it's a break," Eamonn replied optimistically.

Turning the heavy instrument, Kate looked at her husband expectantly hoping to find an answer. "Where did this come from?"

"I don't know," Eamonn replied, "it doesn't say anything except 'a friend'."

"A friend isn't much of a name," Kate said, a worried look on her face.

"Aye, that's true enough luv, but the letter's a good lead."

"To what? If you don't know who sent it, how do you know you're not in some real danger?"

"I'll just have to be careful," he replied defensively.

"Sir, I want you to know I love you, Mollie loves you, and I'm sure Will and Annie love you. But I don't care how much love there is in the world, if something's out to get you it might be time to end this investigation and concentrate on your family." Pausing, Kate looked out the window at the trees straining, bending with the force of the wind.

"I think you should give up this madness before some harm comes to us."

"Maybe Kate's right," Will said. "Maybe you're putting your family in danger."

"I appreciate what's being said, but me feeling is that whether I quit or no, harm has all ready come to this family."

"Well, to coin a phrase, it looks like the die is cast," Will said evenly.

Forty-three—Night & day

Lying in bed, Eamonn tried to sleep. His friends had gone to the cottage at Mullaghmore and he wanted to rest, stop thinking about the Tuatha De Danann. Half dreaming, half thinking, it seemed locked in his brain. Trying to reason with himself, he ran over what had been passed down; the legends that some of mother's blessings had not gone to the Island of the Young. How defeated, some had stayed in Ireland where they made their homes in hills. That was where they had become the Daoine Sidhe. He knew. *In the beginning they were many . . . time has a way of gnawing away at things. Legends said t*hey *couldn't handle the Church. It made them shrink.* His mind went to those that had the sign of Finvana on their stones . . . *My God,* he thought, *he's the high king of the fairies. Them that's dead worship him.*

A moonlight night, Eamonn looked at the high ceiling filled with ghostly shapes. *He might still be holding court under the hills of Knockma. If the wee ones are behind these foul deeds we're all doomed,* he thought, more depressed than he'd like to admit. Wind rattled the bedroom window. Frost had formed around the glass. Getting up quietly he went to look out. One thing he knew, the Irish Sidhe have a great love of beauty and wealth. *They despise thrift and people who budget every pence.* Confused by his own reasoning, the same question kept surfacing. *Why are innocent people dying?*

No reply to his question was forthcoming from the void below. Down in the yard everything lay in dark shadows. Tired of thinking, he took an antidepressant his doctor had prescribed two months earlier. *Damn,* he thought, *I didn't take them, now me chest is tight. Moods more down than up. Heavenly Father,* he prayed, *please don't let me be one that goes early, I must take care of me family.* The wind blew harder, sending a chill through the old house. His eyes heavy, the troubled man fell asleep.

It was nearly eleven when Will arrived at Eamonn's house. Neither talked as they turned onto Chapel Lane. Lucy O'Sheeran had lived alone, a spinster Eamonn said. The house was like all the others, a gray brick front. A row house, it was situated near the corner of Chapel and Back Street.

"I'll be checking the neighbor next door, see if someone's here," Eamonn said as he got out of the car.

It had started to rain, the cold causing him to pull his coat up around his ears for warmth. Knocking on a nondescript door he waited in the wet entryway.

A small lady with a large head of white hair peered out at the tall man.

"Yes, and what's your business with me?" She asked in a voice cracking with age.

"Aye, Mum, I need to find someone who can give me permission to go into Lucy O'Sheeran's house."

"I'm the one what says who can or can't. Then too, it depends," she said with a slight twinkle in her eye.

"On what, Mum?"

"On whether or not you be the one who's got the key."

Lightning followed thunder, adding to the old crone's statement.

Ah, tis the "me" in my secret letter, he thought. Reaching into his pocket he produced the key. The old lady eyed Eamonn for a second, then motioned him next door. As he began to thank her, the door shut in his face.

Eamonn hunched forward as he ran back to the curb. The street was deserted except for Will's rented car. *Still, you can never be too careful,* he thought as he started up the steps to Lucy O'Sheeran's.

Silently the two searchers entered the gloomy building. Will shut the door behind him as he adjusted to the dim half-light filtering through curtains gray with age. In the small living room were two lounge chairs, a table piled high with books and a coal stove near the wall.

Eamonn looked around as he entered the bedroom. *Nothin' left of a personal nature,* he thought. The room looked bare, no bedding or lamps. He turned on the overhead light hanging on its own electric cord. Will stepped into the room just as his friend was pounding his foot on the floor.

"So you want to dance, do you?" Will said with a smile. "I don't know that jig, but if you care to show me."

"Aye, it's a dance on a hollow floor," Eamonn said.

With both hands he began to pry up a board. The shadows from the swinging light appeared and disappeared, making it difficult for him to see what he was doing. On his knees now, Eamonn reached in and pulled out a small box. Will watched with rapt attention while Eamonn forced open the lid. A few quid, some coins and a folded piece of paper was all he found. Will unfolded the paper, seeing some form of writing foreign to him.

Handing it to Eamonn, he said, "Can you read this?"

"Aye, that I can, it's Gaelic."

The old script was still legible even though dampness had long since crept into the box. Holding the paper up to the light, Eamonn translated, "A tinker was found guilty of murderin' Jacob O'Sheeran, June 24, 1899. He was hanged by the neck 'til his wretched body gave up the ghost."

"What's a tinker," asked Will.

"A traveler, a gypsy."

Will rubbed his forehead, trying to think. "What has this to do with folks dying on the hill?"

"I honestly don't know," Eamonn replied.

Will looked at the note. "Why would you receive a letter and key to this house from someone named "me", who then hoped you'd be lucky enough to step on a hollow board and be curious enough to wonder what's under it? Unless "me" just wanted to help and didn't really know anything. If she did know about the box, why not give it to you directly?"

"I don't know the answer, but I suspect the letter is telling us more than we realize."

"On the other hand," Will added, "this may be completely unrelated. It seems the whole town knows what we're doing. Maybe they're secretly trying to help."

Unsure of what to think, Will followed Eamonn out the door. They had put the box back in the floor cubby, replacing the board. No use letting anything fall into the wrong hands and start bad feelings between the villagers and the gypsies.

It was late and the skies didn't look friendly as Will dropped Eamonn at his house.

"I'll be seeing you tomorrow, mate, I need time to think on this."

Lightning flashed across the sky as rain pelted the serious face looking at Will.

"I agree, tomorrow's another day."

Saying their good-byes, Will turned on the wipers and headed down the narrow road. The day's events were unsettling, more so because going to Lucy O'Sheeran's seemed contrived. *Like lambs led to slaughter,* he thought tiredly.

Forty-four—The enemy revealed

The bedroom window flew open with a bang, startling Kate as she prepared for bed. Insecure and a little nervous, the young woman had waited up for her husband. They had never been apart in the evenings. Since Eamonn had been investigating this depressing neighborhood business, she had worried that something horrible would happen. The book she was reading, an American novel called The Wedding Day, had made her feel more protective of her man. *I need to learn kick-boxing,* she thought, laughing to herself.

The rickety windows rattled as cold sea air whistled through the cracks. Living high on a hill, the wind blew with some force up from Donegal Bay. *I need a cup of tae,* she decided. The old stairs creaked as she hurried down to the kitchen. Putting on the kettle she waited by the counter for the familiar sound of the steaming whistle, then put a teabag in for five minutes. The amber fluid would be relaxing.

Rain hammered the kitchen window causing her to look up in alarm. A crash echoed through the house just as a rush of cold air came down the hall. Fearfully, she walked into the hallway. The front door stood wide open, rain pouring in. A small figure caught her eye as she started towards the door, his coat and top hat glistening in the light. Frozen in place, he stood there with an arrogant stance.

"Were you worried about the wet, me dear?" He asked in a frog-like voice.

"Here, let me help you."

Frightened, Kate turned and ran back to the kitchen. Seated at the table, the small man watched her approach. Breathless, she stared at the wrinkled skin and long pointy fingers. *How'd he get in here?* She wondered. *I was between him and the doorway, running in . . . nobody passed me. The evil has surely come, I know it now,* she thought desperately.

"What are you wanting in my house, you foul creature?" She said, trying to hide her growing fear.

Studying his hairy fingers, eyes of hatred moved slowly to the frightened woman.

"I've been thinkin' I need a woman, a bosom on which to comfort meself. Legs to wrap around . . . "

Kate's primal scream interrupted the croaking voice as she ran from the room to get her baby. We *must flee this creature from hell,* she thought frantically.

Blocking the stairs now, he appeared in front of her with a lecherous smile. Everywhere she turned, he was there. *There's more than one,* she thought in a panic. Swinging her arm with all her might, she aimed at the ugly thing in front of her. From behind she felt something slam into her back. As she fell, hands quickly grabbed her arms, pulling them behind; tying them so tightly pain shot through her shoulders. Before she could scream out again, a foul tasting cloth was jammed into her mouth. Slowly, large hands rolled her over onto her back.

Like a giant, a large man with beady eyes looked down at the terrified woman.

"Here now, 'tis a fine catch it is. Yes, Mum, you'll do nicely."

Flynn felt a tug at his loins as he stared at Kate's heaving breasts, her dress hiked up to her hips. Thunder shook the house as he made a hasty decision.

"Bring her along now, quickly. There'll be plenty of time later for breakin' this one in."

In the blink of an eye they were gone, the door slamming shut. The only sound echoing through the empty house was a baby's cry.

The rain poured down, hastening Eamonn's run to the house. *It will be good giving Kate a grand hug,* he thought. Mollie's lonely cry greeted him as he came through the door. Light shining into the hallway from the kitchen seemed peculiar at this hour. A sliver of fear pierced his heart as he walked into the room. The kettle was still hot on the stove.

Listening for a second, he called out, "You here, luv?"

Walking quickly back to the stairs, he double-stepped up to Mollie's bedroom. Sitting in the middle of her crib, tears ran down her baby cheeks.

"Where's yer mum, darlin'?" he whispered.

Carrying her, he went into the master bedroom, then to the bathroom beyond. Finding nothing he went downstairs, his dread building. Something was very wrong, he felt it in his bones. Kate was nowhere to be seen and she would never leave the baby unattended. *Something evil has occurred this night.* Frustrated, he wanted to scream out.

Holding Mollie to his chest, he ran to the telephone. *I must call the guards; they'll find her.* Fear turned to anger as he realized what must have happened. Looking out at the stormy sky he cursed the fiends that had taken his wife. Tears of pain filled his eyes as he lovingly changed the frightened child. In the morning he'd ask his mum to mind Mollie, keep her safe where no one would find her, then he and Will would look for his Katie.

The flashing lights of a police car stained his house as a serious looking officer approached the door. Wiping the rain from his face, a man in uniform eyed Eamonn.

"It's a miserable night out. I hope it's not a waste."

He brushed past the visibly upset father holding his baby close. Thunder shook the house as Eamonn closed the door and led the officer to the kitchen. Removing his soaked hat and raincoat, Officer Shanklin looked around the dining room.

"Nice old house you got here," he said, taking a pad of paper and pencil from his pocket. "Alright now, I'll have the facts as you know them."

Eamonn held Mollie tightly as he thought about the officer's comments.

"Aye, it's a grand old house," he said aloud. "My wife was here this morning when I left, and when I returned home she was gone. That's the sum of it, and she would never leave our daughter alone. Something's surely wrong, officer."

"'Tis true enough, sir. Are you Eamonn Gallagher?"

"Aye, it's me. And this is my baby, Mollie. My wife Katherine has dark hair, rosy cheeks, a trim figure . . . "

"What business were you about that you left your wife alone this night?"

Eamonn shot a cold look at the man sitting at his table. "I don't see what that has to do with my wife's disappearance."

"I'll be the judge of that, Sir," the stone-faced officer replied.

"I was with my mate from America. He's helping me with an investigation."

"Investigation?"

"Aye, there's been too much death on this hill."

"And how might that be your business, Mr. Gallagher?"

"I felt my family was in danger."

"Don't you think that kind of investigation might best be left to us? It appears you've went and done it now."

Eamonn looked the defiant man in the eye. "Like it or no, I did what I thought best."

"Best. I'm not sure of that. Now, if you'll be so kind as to tell me what you've uncovered, it could give us clues as to where your wife might be."

Unsure as to whether the local guards could be of any help, Eamonn decided to reveal what was now, probably common knowledge in the village anyway.

"We've been looking into the deaths that have occurred around here, including my friend's wife and son, Mary and Sean McNulty."

"I see, you've been busy."

"Aye, in many cases, clues have pointed to the wee folk."

"The wee folk, is it? And how did you arrive at that conclusion, scientific study?"

"No, most who died were in possession of a stone with markings of Tuatha de Danann, the fairy kingdom and Finvana, its king."

Lightning struck outside, making the lamplight dim. Nervously Eamonn continued. "There have been too many unexplained deaths, unless all my neighbors are going nuts."

Officer Shanklin wrote something on his notepad, then rose from the table.

"One thing's sure, your wife's missin' and I can't report she was taken by fairies now can I?"

"No, I guess you can't," Eamonn said dejectedly.

"Until I know more, I'm orderin' you to stop this dangerous foolishness, this investigation. You've got an enemy now who knows how to get in your house."

"Aye, that's true enough, but I've got to look for my wife and that's that," Eamonn declared emphatically.

"Nobody broke in here did they?"

"True enough."

"There was no forced entry?"

"No."

Officer Shanklin looked around. "Then the alleged kidnapper had access to yer house?"

"Aye, that makes it all the more true that some evil force is working its powers on this hill and will continue until we're all in our graves."

"I'm thinkin' you'd better see the chemist and get somethin' for that imagination of yours. I'll send someone in the mornin' with fingerprint equipment. You might check with your friends, maybe your wife ran off. She might have gotten tired of her husband chasin' the boogyman."

Letting himself out, the guard left. After putting Mollie to bed Eamonn called his mother, explaining as much as he could that Kate was gone and he needed to find her. Would she please take Mollie to her house where she'd be safe. *Me mum will guard Mollie with her life,* he thought, *she'll be safe there. I've got to make a plan for tomorrow, there's no turning back now,* he thought desperately. *When Will comes over, we'll find Katie.*

Forty-five—Finvana & a missing wife

The officer dusting for prints had left, saying he could find nothing definitive. There were no fingerprints on the front or back doors. Nothing, like they never existed. He said he'd report his findings to Officer Shanklin at the stationhouse.

Disgusted and tired, Eamonn sat in his favorite chair. The loneliness seemed overbearing with Mollie away at his mother's. A light rain was falling and he wished it would stop, if only for a day. A loud knock jolted him from his thoughts. The house felt cold and lonely with Kate and Mollie gone. Hopefully it was Kate saying everything was okay. She had just been up to her sister's in Belfast. They'd get Mollie from his mum and everything would be back to normal. Will would come over with Annie and they'd have a pot of Tea.

He swung the door open with a great flourish. Standing in a puddle, Father Kerrigan flinched at the sudden movement. "Here now Eamonn Gallagher, don't be playing any pranks."

"Oh, I'm sorry, Father. I thought you were someone else. Honestly, I never meant to scare you."

Ignoring the apology the priest walked stiffly down the hall to the study. "I've come to ask you to stop your investigation."

"I'm afraid it's a little late for that, Father, me wif has disappeared and I think it's Finvana."

"Finvana?" Father Kerrigan said nervously, "Isn't that the heathen king of the fairies?"

"Aye, and the dead."

Seated in Eamonn's favorite chair the priest rubbed his hands together anxiously, then looked sternly at the distraught man standing by the window.

"As God is my witness, you have got to stop this madness before you end up in hell. Your wife is gone and now you think the fairies did it."

"It would seem so, Father. All the signs point to them. I'm not sure, but the reasons are becoming increasingly clear that all who lived on this fairy hill are being punished in the most severe way."

Thunder rumbled as the rain continued to fall. Father Kerrigan shook his head slowly

"Eamonn Gallagher, I'm pleading with you to stop this. Denounce this thinking and pray for forgiveness. If you don't do this right now, you'll be excommunicated from the Mother Church now and forever. And that's me last word on the subject."

Eyeing Eamonn steadily, he stood up straight.

"I see you've made up your mind. Remember, the Church only wants what's best for your soul and the souls of your family. May God protect your wife wherever she is."

Stalking down the hall, the angry priest paused, "My worst fears are being realized. You're bringing the devil himself to this place and I hope you realize it before it's too late."

He made the sign of the cross.

"God be with you," he said, then left with a loud bang of the door.

Damn that priest, Eamonn repeated, banging his fist on the wall. Frustrated, the pain felt good; better than feeling the loss of his Katie, not knowing if she was dead or alive. There was precious little time now, he'd be looking for her right this minute if he wasn't waiting for Will. A thought occurred to him as he went upstairs; *maybe she left me a sign.* Her brush and comb were on the dresser; a pair of his pants still draped over a chair. The bathroom countertop was neatly ordered, a bar of hand soap and towels all in place. Seeing nothing unusual he went downstairs to the front door. A coat-rack and a metal wastebasket in the shape of a small boy with his hands out, sat in the corner. A piece of paper on the floor caught his eye. Crudely written words read:

"Pale is the water on a blue sea, burnt red the forests and the trees. Hard as stone thy feelings be. Cast out the fair folk and pay will thee."

What manner of rhyme is this, a threat? Eamonn wondered angrily. The sound of Will's voice interrupted his misery. Composing himself, Eamonn greeted his friends.

"It's good seeing you," he said, trying to hide his mood.

"What's cooking?" Will asked cheerfully.

"It's a sad day indeed, my wife has disappeared, she's gone, she is. Mollie was left alone and Katie would never do that."

"Oh my, this is terrible," Annie said.

"Did you notify the police?" Will asked.

Aye, I did, but I don't know what good it'll do. I looked everywhere for a clue , a message from Kate, but all I found was this."

Will read the barely legible note then took a deep breath.

"Well, it looks like we've got our experiment now, don't we," he said, more to himself than his friend. "That note, in itself, could be from anyone trying to spook you. But that plus the stones and the nine people who have died, under other than normal circumstances, sure points to the wee folk."

Thinking, Will studied the piece of paper. "Taking your wife may be revenge for butting into their business."

He didn't want to hurt Eamonn as he tried to think of a way to tell him his thoughts without dashing all hope.

"If we make a plan, one where we methodically go step by step through the evidence, then check out each lead we've listed, we should be able to figure out how to get Kate back," pausing, he looked at his troubled friend.

"I know fairies aren't entirely receptive to humans, but maybe they're willing to negotiate."

Neither man spoke for awhile as the rain continued unabated. *The fates are against me,* Eamonn thought.

Annie looked at the bedraggled man, "You know, if someone had a desire to remove people and didn't want to be found out it would be a perfect ploy to leave stones marked with fairy symbols."

"I know you're right, but . . . "

Interrupting Eamonn, she continued, "Knowing how the local villagers believe in earth spirits, it wouldn't take a whole lot to push someone over the edge . . . just food for thought."

Will wondered if they would ever find Kate.

"I've decided to go on, Sir William. If you don't want to continue with the investigation, I won't think less of you. There's danger for sure."

"We've come this far, buddy, we may as well finish it," Will said firmly. "I think it would be a good idea if Annie stayed here by the phone, in case anything new develops from the police."

"Aye, I agree with that. I don't have a cell-phone so that would probably be a good idea. Is that alright with you, Annie?"

Sighing, she reluctantly nodded in agreement.

"I've been thinking," Eamonn continued, "we could go to Connemara, Lough Doo. There's a fairy ring there that might be a good spot to meet the Tuatha de Nanann. If not, it'll be a good trip for you to see what some believe is sacred."

Will closed his eyes as he gave Annie a hug. "I love you," he said softly. "We'll be back soon, I swear."

Annie kissed him, then went into the kitchen to make some tea. They would leave immediately. Eamonn had already made arrangements for his brother to run the shop.

Maybe taking Will's green Fiat would be lucky. Certainly it got excellent mileage. Passing all the ancient artifacts; the castles and ruins, the burial site of W.B. Yeats, Will thought how driving through Ireland was like touring a great museum. Traffic on the N15 towards Sligo was nonexistent. Following the signs at the roundabout, they veered right onto the N4 through rolling hills and valleys toward Westport. The miles seemed to melt away as they followed the narrow two-lane highway to the N17 south, slowing occasionally as tractors from the turn of the century chugged along the lonely road.

"I really appreciate your coming, Mate."

"I've got to help find Kate. If we meet fairies, it'd be the adventure of a lifetime," Will said almost enthusiastically.

More serious than he'd like to admit, Eamonn looked over briefly at the sixty-year-old driver. "Meeting fairies can be fatal, my friend. Even if they don't exist, whatever evil fiend has my wife may still want us dead. I don't want to frighten you, but . . . "

"Enough said," Will interjected, readily agreeing.

Clouds covered the sky as they turned onto N57 toward Westport. Minutes became hours before they arrived in the old village. An Irish version of Carmel, California; shops were filled with wood-sprites and folklore, jewelry, wool sweaters, shillelaghs and blarney-stones. It was a tourist delight. Will was glad Annie wasn't with them, there would be no time for shopping today.

Old buildings of brick and mortar were fast losing ground to flourishing new construction. It sounded familiar. *No matter, it's all very quaint and Irish,* he thought.

Stopping for lunch, Will ordered two eggs over easy, a rasher of bacon, which tasted more like pieces of fried pork, and chips. In a somber mood, Eamonn ate very little. Other than to thank the waitress, he didn't talk very much either.

Once more winding through the crowded streets, Will thought how European it all seemed. *But then Ireland is in Europe,* he thought with amusement.

Continuing on to Clew Bay, a mudflat when the tide was out, Eamonn pointed to a sign near a tree-covered lane leading to the Rosbeg Country House. They'd stay here for the night. Built over one hundred and fifty years ago overlooking the bay; it held onto the Irish aristocratic ambience of old. The proprietors, the Kelly's, were a friendly couple. The missus ran about barefoot and it all seemed perfectly natural.

Will had his own room and it was much like he had imagined a rich man's house would be. It was decided to forego the evening meal, instead retiring early. They wanted to be sharp in the morning. By the next afternoon they should be in the Connemara region.

Lying in bed, the only sound he heard was the squawk of an errant seagull who had forgotten to go to bed. *I'll make a note of that, he* thought, laughing to himself. The firm mattress was relaxing and he drifted off almost immediately.

Dreaming, *he saw himself standing in a hazy forest of old trees with gnarled roots. A small glow appeared as a tiny figure floated towards him. Transparent, it had the body of a ballerina. At eye level, long delicate fingers reached out to touch his face. Colder than ice, the pain traveled quickly through his body. Paralyzed, he was unable to move as it smiled, revealing small jagged teeth. He tried to scream as it bit into his nose, blood splattering everywhere as he struggled to breathe.*

His arms flailing, he knocked over a glass of water, waking himself. *Must have been all that talk,* he thought nervously, drying himself and the blanket. With a sigh of relief he noted everything was as it should be. Taking a sleeping pill to help him forget, he returned to his slumbers.

Forty-six—Distrustful servants

Father Kerrigan pulled out onto Allingham Way as Will's green car passed him. *I'll let him go a ways then follow, I can't risk being discovered by the likes of him.* Angry and bitter, the portly cleric pondered where they were off to. *Sure and that American's got Eamonn all riled up, fairy this and fairy that. If I don't stop them, we're all doomed. My position in the Church, the Church itself . . . God forbid. Whatever foolishness they uncover it's better if I nip it in the bud.*

Driving past Sligo, he closed the distance between the two vehicles. He didn't want to chance losing them. It certainly seemed that Eamonn was out of control, willing to be excommunicated, damned to an eternity of hellfire. That frightening thought gave the priest a chill. *There must be no more thinking like this*, he thought as he followed the Fiat down the N15 to the N4 toward Westport. Close behind, he followed them into the small village then waited as they went into a restaurant.

His stomach grumbled as the aroma of hot beef and fried bacon wafted through the air. Determined not to lose them, he decided to abstain until they arrived at their final destination. It seemed to take forever as the priest waited. The sidewalk was filled with school children released for the day. In their matching blue uniforms, young boys and girls talked excitedly about the cutest lad or lassie in the their class and other equally fascinating subjects. Listening to their chatter, the old priest felt tired. *Sins of the flesh,* he thought, *I shall pray for them.*

Lost in his daydream, he almost missed the two men exiting the Four Leaf Clover Restaurant. The familiar sound of his new Mercedes coming to life was reassuring. Slowly he followed them around the narrow streets parallel to Clew Bay. Watching them pull in at an inn on the shore, he stopped nearby. It appeared they had stopped for the night. He'd find a place, somewhere close and get up early in the morning. Upset that he had to wait to eat, that he had to follow these men to God knows where, he tried to compose himself. *Surely it's a test of me faith,* he thought. *I can't take the loss that will surely result from this investigation; me house, me annual stipend, everything will be gone.* Bitterly he rehashed ways to stop Eamonn in less than priestly ways. Sitting in a dimly lit pub Father Kerrigan finished his pint, then went to a public phone. He waited for the housekeeper to answer as the phone rang and rang. *It's difficult gettin' good help,* he thought.

Finally, a voice on the other end answered, "Who's there?"

"It's Father Kerrigan and I'll thank you not to take so long answering the tele next time. I've got more important things to do than waiting to chat with you."

Hurriedly, he explained how he would be gone for a few days on God's business if the Bishop called. *It's important his Holyness not find out about this horrible situation until I have corrected it.*

Tired and hardly able to sleep, Eamonn woke Will early. Seated in the inn's dining room, it seemed that others had the same idea. There were only four tables. At one, an English couple sat drinking tea from old china cups, while a friend of the proprietor, Amish McDuff, a slightly built man, sat at another reading his newspaper discussing events with Mr. Kelly, the owner of the inn.

As Will and Eamonn drank their fresh juice and hot tea, the old Englishman sitting with his wife, looked over and made eye-contact with the American. "Good morning, Sir. I hope you're feeling well," he said in proper English.

"Yes, thank you, it's a beautiful day," Will replied.

"Oh, that's a bit dashed," he said, sounding a little more familiar. "It rains a lot, you know, never stops."

His wife looked at him with glowing eyes as he spoke. Laughing, they continued talking to one another. Mrs. Kelly came to take their order of eggs, two rashers of bacon, white and dark blood sausage, chips and wheat soda bread toast. It seemed a lot, but Eamonn assured Will it wasn't.

Thinking about their journey, he ventured, "How far until we get to Connemara?"

"I'm not sure," Eamonn replied.

"Maybe I can be of help," said the man with the paper. "Depends on where you're off to, but I'd say Connemara is roughly eighty kilometers. Just a guess, though." Smiling broadly, he continued, "You from America?"

"Yes, I am," Will said. "I'm writing a story about fairies and my friend here is taking me to likely spots they might live.

Unsure what Will was going to say, Eamonn breathed a sigh of relief at the story. No sense telling the world they were both nuts looking for Katie in a fairy ring.

"Well now, that's a pleasant bit of business," the Englishman added.

"Aye, 'tis that," Eamonn said smiling.

"Where might you be looking in Connemara?" Amish McDuff asked. "There are only a few special places to see the fair folk and even they can be dangerous business."

"Aye, that it can," Mr. Kelly said with a twinkle in his eye. "And when's the last time you saw a fairy, Amish McDuff?"

In for a long story, Eamonn was glad to see their breakfast arrive. The slices of fresh tomatoes garnishing each plate looked inviting, *excellent,* Will thought, as he tried a bit of sausage dipped in egg yolk.

Eamonn whispered, "Don't be talking too much about the wee folk. It'll only get everyone in a dither."

"I'm sorry, I thought the writer routine would keep it silly."

"Aye, that it did, but I don't want anyone knowing my business, especially regarding the loss of me dear Katie," Eamonn said, reminded of the seriousness of their quest.

Looking around the quaint dining room, he wished she was there to enjoy this lovely place of old furnishings and rare antiques.

Forty-seven—Payin' his just deserts

Thank God the days are passin'. That Eamonn Gallagher's got no right pokin' around asking about the self, Patrick McDermot thought angrily. *Jaysus, now it's gettin' him too, his wife gone. There be no secrets in Ballyshannon,* he mused, *none worth knowin' anyway. Him and his mate have no right lookin' for me, I've done nothin' to them.* Staring out the window he watched the clouds rushing to fill the morning sky. Thunder rumbled in the distance, as it had a thousand times before. The wind whistled through the cracks around the old sills. *The feckin' sky's fallin',* he thought as he watched raindrops hitting the glass. The time was he felt safe in his house. His wife was a good woman, she always kept a stiff upper lip when the moods came. Now the distance. The last months had changed her too. *No lovin', no hot tae in the evenin',* he thought bitterly.

Trying to erase the futile thoughts, tired of the same old stuff, he put the kettle on. *A nice hot cup . . . ,* he thought. The shingles rattled as the wind blew up the side of the house. In his head, demons ran wild. Like a mirror of hell on earth he felt the depraved cravings of the damned; urges to use women then kill them off slowly, cut off an intimate part and eat it raw.

Sweat beaded on his brow as he thought how unlike him, all this was. Still, it was getting stronger every day. *God in heaven,* he prayed, *please save me. Remove this foulness.* Quiet for a few moments, he breathed a sigh of relief, followed by still worse imaginings filled with visions of decayed beings.

Home alone, he took the steaming kettle and poured some tea. The hot fluid was calming as he sat in his chair looking out at the fierce storm building.

Time was when me and the wif would sit when I wasn't workin', smilin' and holdin' hands. Those were grand days. Maybe I shoulda' kissed the Blarney Stone, then my luck woulda' changed and my head would be clear and them damned wee sorts would stop interferin' with ma life.

A flash of lightning blinded Patrick as he tried to shield his eyes. *I need some spirits,* he thought, walking over to a cabinet door worn with age. A half empty bottle of whiskey glowed in the half-light. Pouring some into his tea, he set the bottle on the floor. Using his finger as a stirrer, he swirled the brew a couple of times. The burning sensation of the hot liquid hitting his stomach was reassuring, temporarily deadening the nervous twinge in his gut.

Unable to stop, his thoughts continued unabated, *them that butts into business that don't concern them, gets it back. Eamonn's messin' where he shouldn't, now he pays. That's the way it goes. First she's there then she's gone. Lost from this miserable earth. Lose a wife then your life.*

Taking another drink of the strong brew, he wondered why he had to suffer through this hideous torture. For what seemed an eternity his family had lived a peaceful, normal life. *Could be,* he mused tiredly, *they didn't keep the secrets. Damn, always have'n to swear somethin'.*

Hearing footsteps down the hall he wondered who was in the house. His wife had gone to the grocers and he was quite alone. Taking another drink to calm his nerves, another bolt of lightning jolted him upright in his seat. Looking towards the door he thought he spied a small man in black top hat and a coat with tails leaning against the doorjamb. The burning sensation in his stomach increased, as adrenaline began to flow. Rubbing his eyes, he looked again. The apparition closer now, he saw dark eyes filled with hatred and fingers flexing to form fists of hairy, knotted skin.

"Here now," Patrick exclaimed, his voice rising, "what do ye want with the likes o' me? I'm already payin' ya wee slug."

"Oh, I don't think so, Patrick. You haven't paid near enough," a froggy voice replied.

His mind nearly bursting with fear, he ran to the kitchen stove and turned on the burner. The hiss of natural gas was loud as his brain got fuzzy. Croaking laughter came from the twisted face staring up at him, drawing closer for a moment, then disappeared as Patrick lost consciousness.

The small figure moved quickly from room to room, checking that all the windows were closed, then was gone as quickly as he had appeared.

Winds screamed down from the heavens as Patrick gave up the ghost, a small bit of drool escaping his blue, lifeless lips.

Forty-eight—Anxious moments

Eamonn was anxious to get going. The small road paralleling Clew Bay was empty as they drove by an occasional solitary stone house hugging the cliffs.

Feeling melancholy, Will watched the scene unfolding in front of them. "This is really beautiful, cloudy but beautiful," he said, trying to elevate the mood. ""I love this rugged coastline stuff."

"Aye, Mr. Bonner, but you might not like it after a year or two, the everlasting rain could drag you down."

Will thought about what his friend had said. Almost tiredly, a revelation dawned, *maybe folks on the hill were so depressed by the rain they decided to end it all.* Thinking back a few days, it seemed he had reached this same conclusion before.

Interrupting the quiet, he spoke to the increasingly morose man seated next to him. "I know I've said this before, but maybe the inclement weather is causing depression, making people want to die."

Eamonn didn't reply as they went through Killagangon, a town in name only. Passing the small cluster of houses facing the sea, his silent friend finally answered his observation. "It's possible some went that way, but if it's true, it still wouldn't explain Mary and Sean's deaths. And it wouldn't explain Katie's disappearance, or why Michael McGinty decided to jump from St. Anne's bell tower. That was too deliberate. Then there was Sean McTeige's note saying he was being followed."

At a loss for words, they listened to the sound of the wipers clacking methodically against the windshield. Ten kilometers down the narrow road the passage of time went unnoticed as Will slowed through Leckanny. The streets void of people only added to his bleak mood as he looked briefly at the empty town.

Nine kilometers more and they passed Kilsallagh, a grayish group of dwellings. A desperate feeling came over him as he looked for a public phone to call Annie. *The Garda may have found Kate. Maybe she was hiding somewhere out of fear of the fairies. Gads,* he thought, *she would really have to be terrified to leave Mollie unattended.* Adding to the increasingly unclear picture in his head, visibility became poorer as he drove. *The coast of the undead* he thought, trying to lift his mood with sick humor. Heaviness had settled on his heart and no matter how hard he tried to think of something happy, it all made him sad.

Entering Louisburgh, Eamonn pointed to a sign indicating they should turn left, south towards Cregganbaun on Highway N59.

"Aye, there's a tele," Eamonn said, pointing to a small convenience store. While he went to the bathroom, Will got on the phone. Checking his watch, it was 10:30. *Annie should be up,* he thought.

"Hello, the Gallagher residence."

"Hi, Annie, it's me," Will said, trying to sound happy.

"Where are you?"

Will looked out at a sign post. "We're in the town of Louisburgh, we've still got a ways to go. Any news there?"

"Nothing on Kate," Annie said, somewhat subdued, "but I got a call from a Mrs. McDermott. She said to tell Eamonn her husband Patrick died. He was asphyxiated by natural gas. He'd been drinking and must have turned on the kitchen stove without lighting the burner."

"Sounds like an accident."

"You're probably right, except Mrs. McDermott thought her husband had been acting strangely the last few months; hiding in his room, wouldn't talk to anyone."

"That's true," Will said, "he wouldn't talk to Eamonn and me a few days ago."

"I love you, Will," Annie said, worriedly, "you must be careful. We're in a foreign country you know."

Sighing tiredly, he responded softly, "I know. One thing's for sure, whatever's causing these ghastly deaths, it's not simple depression."

"It's true dear husband, so watch your step," Annie said with some affection.

The operator interrupted further conversation, "That'll be one and twenty pence to continue."

"I've got to go, love," Will said, "I'll call you . . . "

Disconnected, he hung up the phone. Explaining to Eamonn what had happened to Patrick only depressed the Irishman more. The fog and constant drizzle added to the grim mood. Groves of trees clung to the side of the mountain as the road followed the valley floor. New to the American, it was a beautiful scene of high peaks and fresh water loughs. With small streams cascading down the hills like sparkling soda, Will had a hard time watching the road.

Suddenly, out of the corner of his eye he saw movement just as Eamonn yelled, "Look out, bloody sheep ahead!"

An abrupt turn in the road, neither had noticed the four-legged creatures appearing in front of them. Will yanked the wheel hard to the right, slamming on the brakes. Gravel flew as wheels locked.

Staring out at an empty void, neither could see anything as the road disappeared. Jerking to a stop, the smell of burnt rubber filled the air. Will swung open the door, almost falling from the car. Inches from the edge of a thirty-foot drop to the rocky shore below, he ran around back to see if the rear tires were still on solid ground.

Eamonn stood staring at the car dangerously close to the bank. He shook his head, then looked back at the road filled with sheep staring blankly at the two men. "It's a strange day, my friend. That was too close."

"You're right about that. It never occurred to me sheep would walk in front of a moving vehicle."

"Aye, that they will. They don't have a brain for safety, that's for sure," Eamonn replied.

"Let's just be off and try to forget this little episode."

While Eamonn stood outside the car, Will backed up ever so slowly onto the N59, very cautious now, they continued towards their destination of Lough Doo. What signs there were, indicated it was before the town of Delpi in Connemara.

Forty-nine—Sibling love

In Cobh, County Cork, overlooking Cork Harbor, the sun had not yet risen. The lights from the Swansea, the car ferry, shined brightly as it passed the narrows of Roche's Point. Frances Murray wondered if this was far enough away, to hide, to be safe. From Ballyshannon in the north to Cobh on the southern coast seemed a long way. Whatever evil had befallen her, it shouldn't find her here. *My sister Angelina has been very good to me. The devil has been cheated this time,* she thought, *the good Lord has blessed me.*

On the horizon the faint flicker of pinks and blues blended in a kaleidoscope of color. In many ways it reminded her of everyone she had ever known who had died on the hill, had known personally. The hill had seemed a safe place for her, sad at times from all the deaths. Now friends, close friends at that, had left this good earth to join their ancestors.

Frances tried to turn off her mind, remove any morbid thoughts. *Maybe Angelina and I could go on a picnic near the shore.* Going into the kitchen she looked in the refrigerator. *I'll make a lunch basket,* she thought. Looking at the neatly packaged foods she decided on a cooked chicken, a jar of pickles, tomatoes, lettuce and a tray of raw eggs. *Good, I'll boil some eggs and make chicken sandwiches.*

The water heated quickly as she took four eggs and dropped them into the boiling liquid. Her mind on her work, she didn't hear her sister come into the room.

"Mornin', you're up early," Angelina said, brushing the hair from her face.

"It's a fine morning, don't you think?" Frances said over her shoulder.

"Could be, if you weren't so chipper," Angelina replied.

"I thought it would be good if we went to the shore, bring some food for the soul."

"Oh sister, it's a wee bit early to be thinking such things."

Angelina's head had been aching for days now, and she desperately wished it would stop. Her sister had come and so had the pain. Time was when they were close, but now her head was filled with fiendish thoughts. *Me sister's a hex,* she thought.

Drawn by an inner desire stronger than she'd ever known, Angelina felt like harming her sibling. *Me dear young sister.* Clutching the meat cleaver that Frances had given her, she whacked away at the cooked chicken.

"No need to be killing it again," Frances said cheerfully.

Angelina stared at the mutilated fowl on the cutting board. Her head ached as words repeated themselves in her brain – *dead's dead, slice and cut me sister's head.*

Clouds covered the sky as the rain started.

"Oh my," Frances said, staring out at nature's rage, "me picnic's ruined, it is." *That's odd,* she thought, the sky had been clear a few minutes ago.

Behind her she heard the clunk, clunk chopping sound of her sister cutting chicken, grow louder and louder. Lightning flashed across the sky. Frances felt a twinge of fear as she turned to her sister. Their eyes met briefly, the glazed stare of a lifeless being watching her.

"Ar' you okay?" Frances asked softly, hoping all was well, that she had just imagined the apparition in front of her. She said a quick prayer as the wind outside blew harder, whistling through the cracks.

"Frances," a froggy voice said.

Frightened, Frances stepped back from the source. A cold hand reached out, grabbing her wrist.

"Angelina, you're scaring me."

"Oh, I'll do more than scare you, me wonderful sister," Angelina replied, drool creeping from the corner of her mouth.

Trying to muster anger over fear, Frances yelled at the deranged creature pinning her hand to the counter. "Let go of me or I'll bust your chops!"

"Oh, I think not, little sister. I'll shorten yer complainin' soon enough. I may even shorten yer hand a bit."

Swinging the meat cleaver over her head, Angelina brought it down hard. The crunch-thud of the sharp tool cutting through meat, gristle and bone registered dully in Frances' brain. Screaming, she yanked her bleeding hand from the table. Shortened fingers wiggled wildly, blood spurting from the ends.

"Have you lost yer mind?" she screamed.

More animated than before, Angelina reached for the other hand flailing about defensively. Unable to withdraw it from her sister's vise-like grip, Frances watched in horror as the cleaver descended once more. She felt the dull pain of metal cutting through her arm. Alarm signals raced to her brain, as she fell across the cutting board. Blood flowed freely across the red stained surface, chicken flying everywhere. Angelina pulled her further onto the wooden table. Turning Frances quickly, her weapon fell relentlessly, blood staining her flowered dress. Pools of warm goo spread quickly. Unable to stop, she swung again and again until large swaths of blood outlined her ribs.

Her mind in shock, Frances screamed continuously.

Angelina felt the sexual excitement of an adrenaline rush as she watched her sister jerk and shake in the throes of death. Eyeing the squirming bloody mess coldly she raised her arm high, red fluid dripping from her blade. Frances tried feebly to stop the downward movement of her sister's arm, tiny remnants of fingers grabbing at the air. Faster than light, the blade bit into the exposed throat.

Frances was dimly aware of the crunch of cartilage and bone; she gasped futilely trying to suck air into her tortured lungs, her mouth opened wide. Blackness descended as her head rolled slowly off the bloody table. Her body convulsed, then went limp.

Thunder and lightning filled the heavens as small dark eyes looked at the brutalized remains. Suddenly aware, Angelina stared at the horrible spectacle then clutched her throat as she fell dead.

Fifty—On a quest

       While Will went into a shop to get a map, Eamonn closed his eyes. Tired from lack of sleep and frantic feelings of hopelessness, he quickly slipped into the alpha state. *A small cave appeared. Light from torches set into the walls cast a yellow glow over everything it touched. A young woman cried out for help. Eamonn recognized his Katie, her hands bound behind as she gazed desperately at a small exit. His feet felt heavy as he tried to reach her. Whispering his name, she strained towards him. Slowly wiggling her body, she pushed herself forward; her dress in tatters, her scratched and bruised legs aching with pain.*

       Suddenly a small figure blocked her path. In his hand he held a short walking stick. Slowly he walked around the tethered woman, stopping near her rear. Lustful eyes stared at the full curve of her bottom as he slowly raised her skirt with his stick. Rage filled Eamonn's eyes. With every ounce of strength he pushed forward. Harder and harder his legs pumped until he was running across the short space to the object of his love, the fearful look on Kate's face pleading silently for help. In a flash he grabbed the small hairy hand holding the stick and yanked it away.

       Will yelled in pain as Eamonn suddenly jerked his arm against the headliner of the small car. Startled awake, the Irishman quickly released his vice-like grip.

"God, buddy, it's me, your friend," Will said nervously.

"I'm sorry, I was dreaming. More a nightmare I reckon. I saw me Katie tied up and a wee troll in a black hat and coat was . . . " Eamonn stopped, his face flushed with anger. "I swear, I'll kill anyone who touches her."

"You've convinced me," Will replied earnestly. "It seems that troll is a key to this whole mystery. I've seen him twice and now you've seen him."

"Actually, I saw that foul creature last week as well," Eamonn said tiredly.

Will looked at his friend. "Could be we're both projecting our fears, now you've dreamt about this character too. One thing's sure, he's involved in this whole sordid business. Could be he's a fairy of some kind, maybe a leprechaun."

Neither man spoke as the reality of what Will surmised finally hit home. His heart heavy with sadness, Eamonn wondered what to do. *If this black rot is a fairy, how will we fight him? Will the protections I know work against the wee folk?* Running through the list he couldn't remember anyone using bells or iron, or the bible for that matter. Even bread and a crucifix were just hearsay. *Maybe, as* he thought about it, *we'd better stop and get some salt and St. John's Wort.* He'd heard somewhere that burning thorns on top of a fairy hill would release captive children. *They might not know the difference,* he thought soulfully.

His mind racing from thing to thing, he wondered if holy prayers and ancient churchyard mold would work. He could pray, if he knew a prayer good enough. He'd have Will stop at the next store. If he had to sell his soul to free Katie, he would.

At some distance behind, a dark Mercedes followed the unsuspecting pair.

Fifty-one—The counting

The stench of decayed animals filled the air. No one complained or spoke; all attention focused on the diminutive figure seated at a small round table. An oil lamp reflected two glowing eyes staring at a piece of parchment long past its prime. Water dripped from the cavernous ceiling forming miniature stalactites. A bony thumb and index finger held an old quill firmly as he made a note next to the last name on one of two lists. "Them thats done wrong must pay," he said, then in order he recited,

"One, Margaret Mary O'Neil, deceased;

Two, Maggie Gibbons, deceased;

Three, James McGurran, deceased;

Four, John Laughlin, deceased;

Five, Sean McTeige, deceased;

Six, Russel O'Quinn, deceased;

Seven, Elizabeth Gillespie, deceased;

Eight, Horace McBride, deceased;

Nine, Frances Murray, deceased;

Ten, Patrick McDermott, deceased;

Eleven, Michael McGinty, deceased;

Twelve, Eamonn Gallagher. . ." He stopped for a moment as he turned a page, moving to the second list he continued, "And folks who meddled in business not their own:

One, Lucy O'Sheeran, deceased;

Two, John Morrow, deceased;

Three, Peter Kelly, deceased;

Four, Mary McNulty, deceased;

Five, Sean McNulty, deceased;

Six, Eamonn Gallagher, alive."

The dripping water was louder as the wrinkled hand lay down the pen.

"The last of six, Eamonn Gallagher is mindin' other good folk's affairs."

Raising an eyebrow he stared coldly into the darkness.

"A double reason he should be on both lists, he's drawing attention to our quest. He must be eliminated."

Heads nodded in agreement as they watched in fear. "He'll be the twelfth," they said in unison.

A voice at the back, thick with hatred, echoed through the chamber. "Not so easily accomplished it would seem, Mr. Gallagher is still investigatin'."

"Who questions what's being said?" wide stained lips asked.

"Aye, it's Flynn, me little friend. Case in point, Eamonn's wife is here, nonetheless for wear I might add and he's not come runnin'. I'm thinkin' it's time to begin her trainin.'"

"Keep your britches on a while longer you horny pig, unless you want to release me."

"Try and pay the price," Flynn shot back, moving into the light.

"Yes, yes it would seem a deal is a deal," the froggy-voice croaked.

Staring at the motley Irishman standing in the back, the little man moved closer.

"You'll still do it my way, or know the reason why."

An evil grin spread across his face.

"I know what yer friend is up to, Flynny. I know where to finish the game."

"Aye, 'tis your job," Flynn replied.

"Yes and soon this will end our deal." Dark beady eyes stared at Flynn with the malice of a thousand years.

"Tis true, a deal is a deal," Flynn said, the sentence escaping his lips in a final grasp for control.

Fifty-two—Being followed

At Eamonn's request they stopped at a petrol/convenience store. While he went inside to buy some fairy frightening stuff, as he had put it, Will called the Garda station in Ballyshannon.

After several rings a voice came on the line. "Officer Shanklin here."

"Yes, this is Will Bonner, Eamonn Gallagher's friend. He asked me to call in regards to any news of his wife Katherine's disappearance."

"Ah, Mr. Bonner. Still detectin' are we?"

"It's in my blood I guess, comes naturally."

"Yes, well to answer yer question, there are no new developments. We still don't know the whereabouts of Mrs. Gallagher. Let's hope she fares better than Frances Murray, bless her soul."

Almost afraid to ask, Will posed the next question. "She's gone the way of all things?"

"If what yer asking is whether she's dead, the answer's yes. And I would have to say there are better ways to go."

"How did she die?"

"She was cut to pieces. Lost her head, she did, cut clean off." Officer Shanklin explained what they thought had happened, a brutal murder/suicide by her sister.

Frances had left just before they had tried to talk to her. *Nothing makes sense anymore. Why would Frances Murray's sister suddenly decide to do her in?* Will stared at rain trickling down the glass of the bright red booth, unable to find an answer. *Her sister's house was her refuge.*

Explaining the news to Eamonn, he was overwhelmed with the futility of it all. The insanity that was rampant in Ballyshannon was spreading. Giving his friend a comforting pat, Will continued down the road.

Being a priest had always been rewarding, but now Father Kerrigan wasn't at all sure. Following these men was a desperate move, but these were desperate times. In this mystical valley with steep slopes on the left and misty bodies of water on the right, it all seemed too strange. The mountaintops fading into the clouds made him uneasy, an emotion he was unfamiliar with.

Sure, it isn't the wee folk, he thought. Feeling better for that revelation, convinced it was just a mood, he relaxed a bit. This atmosphere, this setting, had always been associated with the unknown and, in fact, was just that, a setting. *If Eamonn Gallagher chooses to pursue this dangerous path then he must surely accept the consequences.* Yet he wondered. A crack in his faith? Only God in heaven knew. Saying a prayer, he asked forgiveness for even a shred of doubt.

A sunless day, rain continued to drum his windshield. Father Kerrigan had watched Eamonn's car swerve abruptly. The sudden appearance of sheep in the road was unexpected, but everything seemed strange since Eamonn had started this ridiculous investigation. Perhaps when he found out what these men were looking for he could reason with them, reach a rational solution. *When Eamonn stops this nonsense everything will get back to normal; me sitting in my study overlooking the garden with me best cup of tae.* The loneliness he felt grew stronger the further they went. *God help me,* he thought. The ever-present pressure pushing against his chest had become painful. *Why me,* he thought, *why must I go to this ungodly place?*

Filled with bitterness and fear, the priest took a deep breath, shuddering. It seemed to be this or nothing. Angry for this twist of fate, he watched the Fiat disappear over a hill. Following at a safe distance, questions still probed his mind. *Where are they going? Eamonn seems to have a destination in mind.* The more he thought about it, the more convinced he became that Eamonn had been taken in by his friend. *It wouldn't be the first time,* he thought wearily, *and that's for sure. Maybe he's joined a cult. It would appear he's taken up with the devil himself.* Confused by his own frustrating questions, the portly priest accelerated to the top of the hill. Breathing a sigh of relief, Father Kerrigan watched the miniature outline of the green vehicle moving slowly along the narrow road ahead of him.

Fifty-three—A fairy circle

Maybe it was Will's imagination, but the further they drove the narrower the roadway seemed. An ominous feeling filled his heart as they wound their way through the enchanted valley. The lough to the right now covered the entire valley floor. Beautiful and unknown, bright yellow flowers appeared in clumps near the rocky shore. More and more trees covered the mountainside to the left, fog-like mist hovering just above the ground.

Rounding a bend in the road, Eamonn saw several giant trees in a circle at the base of the mountain. He signaled Will to pull over. The air felt heavy and oppressive as Eamonn rolled down the passenger-side window.

"Will, you don't have to go with me," he said staring resolutely at the fifty-foot circle of trees across the highway.

"Where you go, I go," Will replied flatly.

"Aye, then keep to me back. That way no one will sneak up."

Will nodded as he got out of the car and waited for Eamonn to take the lead. Walking into the circle the sky became void of sound, the cawing of a passing crow abruptly ended, the chirping of a cricket stopped, as the chatter of insects in the bush quit. The unnatural quiet proved more nerve-wracking than they were willing to admit. Well-worn paths led under gnarled roots. Ferns thinly veiled oval openings at the base of one old giant. Though soft and wet, it seemed peaceful to Will. *Legends have a way of getting out of hand,* he mused.

Great trees reached for the heavens, vainly searching for the sun. Standing in the center of the circle, the plush green carpet of moss seemed never ending as bushes and plants crowded inconspicuous places.

Eamonn scanned the circle hoping for a clue to their next move.

"Well, I reckon we've come on a wild goose chase. We must be looking in the wrong place."

The approach of a slow moving vehicle could not be ignored, hearing it stop at the side of the road, the door open, followed by footsteps crunching gravel, Will thought his heart would jump out of his chest. Abruptly the footsteps stopped close to the two men.

Heart beating with fear of the unknown, Eamonn jumped out ready to fight the enemy.

His face pale, Father Kerrigan fell back on his long coat with a thud.

"Oh Father, I didn't expect to see you out here," Eamonn said, relieved.

"That could be true except for all the sneaking going on around here. You scared the wits out of me, you blooming fool."

Reaching down, Will and Eamonn helped the shaken priest to his feet.

The old cleric leaned against a tree trunk covered with knotholes, trying to catch his breath. He stared with growing apprehension at the fairy ring where they stood.

"So you've done it, you've finally gone off. You're in this place looking for the wee folk. You've finally snapped your cap."

Eamonn looked hard at Father Kerrigan. "I'm looking for my wife, Father, not anything small or mysterious. I'll not chase legends."

Bristling with rage the old priest sneered at Eamonn.

"I've asked you to stop this nonsense time and time again, but did you listen? No! Did anyone listen?" He fairly shouted, "No! You and your American friend had to keep poking around, getting' everyone to talking, questioning their Christian faith. Believing all this pagan rubbish."

Dusting the dirt from his pants the portly priest took a breath.

"Now you've got the Bishop in an uproar, afraid the parish will turn into a bunch of heathens. In point of fact it doesn't matter what you do, as long as you don't find anything relatin' to those foul little creatures."

"Father, it was never my intent to show anything. I just wanted me neighbors to stop dying before their time." Eamonn paused as he looked around the circle just below where they were standing. "Now all I want is to find my Katie and I'll stop this investigation for sure."

Patting Will on the shoulder he took a step down into the fairy ring, walking to the center.

"Sorry Father," Will said, following Eamonn onto the damp moss covering the circle. *The pathways under the tree-trunks seem larger from here,* he thought curiously.

"You must leave this place of eternal damnation before it's too late," Father Kerrigan said, putting his hands together in prayer.

While the priest stood on the slight bank surrounding the trees mumbling a litany of prayers for the damned, Eamonn walked carefully over to a path leading under the tree roots. It appeared to have been used as some sort of cover by the many bedraggled sheep passing through. *None smarter than a stone,* Eamonn thought wearily.

The priest's piercing scream caused Eamonn to whip around just in time to see him fall on his face at the edge of the circle.

His muffled voice kept repeating, "It's me imagination, it's me imagination."

Above, thunder shook the mountain, as cold wind cut through the trees. Will went to help the priest once more, only to have his hand pushed violently away. The white-haired clergyman lay on the wet ground trembling, both hands covering his face.

Before Will or Eamonn could do anything, a man appeared at the edge of the trees. Dressed in baggy red pants, a dirty jacket and hat of some stature he looked coldly at the priest lying on the ground. "It's too late for prayin', Father."

The tap of an errant branch slapping another as the wind blew with some force was the only sound they heard. The old priest stared up at the grim face.

"I demand you let me go, you devil. It'll be on your soul forever if you don't release me." As if to convince himself as well as his tormentor he went on, "The Bishop will see you excommunicated from the Church. Do you wish to end up like Mr. Gallagher here?"

"Oh, I don't think I'll be endin' up like Mr. Gallagher," the tall man said.

Feeling braver Father Kerrigan rose to his knees, studying the mustached face for a sign. "I could make it worth your while, Sir, if you could but help me get to my car."

"I'm sure you can," the tall man replied, "and under different circumstances we might have made an arrangement, but now . . .," " his voice drifted off.

The priest clutched at his throat as though having difficulty breathing. Eamonn stepped forward, raising his hand in anger. "I don't know who you are, but it'll do no good to put a spell on the priest. He doesn't live on the hill."

"Oh, livin' on the hill or not, he knows too much. Just like your friend here."

Will felt a tightening in his chest. "Don't bug him, Eamonn, he's choking me."

"Who are you?   Me friend's not your enemy," Eamonn fairly yelled as he edged towards the stranger.

"Me name is Flynn, and me clan's before Red Hugh O'Donnell, before Ui Neill. We went our ways until you made us criminals, making us pay for all yer crimes. Innocent or no, it made no difference to yer hangin' ways. Well, no more. The injustice is ended, as I hold the stone."

Lightning lit up the sky, striking the ground. Will looked up at the crazed spectacle talking to Eamonn, his hair blowing wildly about. Unsure what he was facing,

Eamonn thought hard before speaking. This man was human, but he seemed to have powers not of this world. In a panic his mind tried to reason, *I've got to stop him quickly.* Looking at Will crumpled on the wet moss he could see he was still breathing. In his peripheral vision others appeared at the outer rim of the circle. Silently they came into the fairy ring.

Thinking quickly, he yelled, "Have you not noticed you're in the wee folk's front yard?"

"Could be you and yours should do the worryin'," Flynn replied with a laugh.

Struggling to breathe, Father Kerrigan grabbed at Flynn's coattails. From behind a tree a small man dressed in a black coat with tails appeared, an oversized top hat placed lopsidedly on his head. The failing priest looked up at glowing red eyes and made the sign of the cross. The little man bent down, putting his hand on the priest's chest. Speaking like a hoarse frog he mumbled in Gaelic, "Damn the Church," chanting it over and over. In a gesture of power he pulled his hand upward, tearing at Father Kerrigan's heart. A choking rattle emanated from the cowering figure lying face up, eyes staring dully into the void.

Fear filled Eamonn's heart as he looked at the small figure of a man standing over the struggling priest. The half-light outlining his animal-like features looked distorted with his pointed hat. Stove-piped at the center it rested on large ears. Beady eyes, perched above a reddish nose, burned with fire, his mouth wide like a monkey's. Spindly arms poking out of a coat with gold buttons and scraggly hair failed to hide his features.

My defenses, Eamonn thought, *I must keep him occupied until I think of something.* "So we finally meet. It would seem that you are in league with this foul man. He must have powerful magic to make a fine shoemaker like yerself do his bidding."

Interested, the little man took a few quick steps closer, an evil smile on his face. Undaunted, the Irishman continued, "Unless you are pretending to be one of the wee folk, a leprechaun maybe?"

"Aye maybe a leprechaun, Mr. Smarty Two-Shoes," the froggy voice replied, small hairy fists beating together.

"And just why would you do his bidding?"

Ignoring the questions, the spry little man spoke coldly to Eamonn. "Me presence was needed here," he said, jumping around the circle.

"And why is that?" Eamonn asked, his voice rising in anger.

"You have come to me home, Master Eamonn, you have come to yer doom."

Lightning flashed, hitting an old giant, racing down the trunk in a fiery rage.

"You and yer friend here with the words must pay the final installment, then me job is finished."

Rain filtered down through the umbrella of green, forming small rivulets. In desperation Eamonn clinched his fists, ready to fight for his life. "And why are you looking to me for payment? For what?"

The leprechaun stared at the fiery man and his friend, one ready to fight, the other gasping for air. On the moss-covered ground the priest was mumbling prayers, lost in hushed laughter. A crafty smile slowly covered the fairy's face as he stepped closer, his hands on his hips. "Not that I'll be owing you anything, but answers won't hurt them that's doomed. All them that met their demise knew at the end, so shall you." Eyeing the Irishman he muttered softly, "It was a hanging in the village nigh a hundred years ago, in 1899. It were one of yer ancestors passed sentence on Flynn's. Twelve men sittin' in judgment."

A piece of the hellish puzzle fell into place, but it still didn't make sense that one of the wee folk, a cobbler, was involved in this foul business. If only he could distract him long enough to gain the upper hand. *Questions, I must keep up the questions.*

"I don't understand. You came from under the hill and you don't like tinkers."

"Aye, that's true enough," the froggy voice croaked, "but I was caught by them that's got the power."

"The gypsies?" Will whispered.

"Aye, could be. And you must pay like them that done the deed," the little creature said with finality.

The wind blew harder, joining the tiny man in a quick jig.

"And now," he said, his voice rising, "me wishes have been granted. The earth has opened up and swallowed all that's been too hasty and them that's dead as well. That's good fortune, I'd say. First was John Marrow, for bossin' the jury, then Peter Kelly for sittin' in judgment."

Lost in the hatred, he screamed to the heavens, pointing a bony finger at Eamonn. "Both meetin' their end in 1900. The others took them. Now all are dead."

A harsh laugh came from the weathered mouth; hairy hands clapping in delight, "and them that's dying now are all from me. And yer the last of the lot."

Dreading the answer, Eamonn still asked the question. "Who did the tinker kill?"

Waiting for an answer, his head pounded from the rapidly building pressure.

Pumping his fists together the little man spoke, his voice getting shrill, "He kilt Jacob O'Sheeran, that's how it was. Then nothin' 'til I had the misfortune of getting' caught under me rock. Hummin' to me self I was. But that's all over this day. All twelve, plus a few others, decidin' to leave this earth."

No one spoke as the wind swirled about. The buzzing grew louder in Eamonn's head until it felt like it would burst. Searching for Will, he saw his old friend moving slowly towards the glowering leprechaun.

Seemingly oblivious to Will, the dancing shoemaker suddenly turned to the old man reaching out for him. "And now I'll be takin' me final payment, Will Bonner, as well as yers, Eamonn Gallagher. You will make the twelfth, and yer friend for knowin' too much."

"And yer wife will be a bonus," Flynn added with a gleam in his eye. "She'll be earning her keep, supportin' me house."

A woman's cry was heard as he signaled one of the watchers.

"She'll be as good as me other ladies doing favors for them that pays. A bit of nipple and the place between her legs."

Dragging Kate, her arms held behind her back, he had her brought forward.

"So you see, it's a woman's purpose in this world. Give us men a feckin' good time."

Eamonn saw his terrified wife, hair in tangles, her dress torn, shoes gone. Anger such as he had never known welled in his heart. He lunged forward determined to kill Flynn, choke him to death with his bare hands, and any other slimes who had touched her. Only twenty feet away, he charged. From somewhere a blade flickered in the half-light as it flew through the air, finding refuge in Eamonn's chest. Kate screamed from the bottom of her heart as she watched him gasp, then fall to the ground. His eyes fluttered then went still, blood spreading in a dark pool around his body.

Breaking free from her captors the raging woman grabbed a hatpin from an old hag's hair and ran at Flynn with the precision of an executioner. Quickly she plunged it into his chest, penetrating his evil heart. Thunder shook the earth as he looked at her in surprise, then fell to the ground at her feet. Dying, his features changed. Hands became distorted with knotted joints, his nose longer and hairy, eyes bigger as the hatred burning in them quickly faded. Legs that were strong and straight, became spindly and bent. Finished, the deadly beast lay still.

Like a giant funnel the wind blew with gale force.

Jubilantly the leprechaun jumped around the dead fiend that had enslaved him, laughing and singing, "I'm free, I'm free at last. I'll no longer do your bidding."

The travelers shrank back as he went faster and faster around the circle.

Will rushed to Kate kneeling by her dying husband. He felt the futility of lost love and friendship.

"You'll die in hell before this is over, Mr. Leprechaun," Will said angrily to the small hairy creature walking towards him. "With my dying breath I'll see you, and them, pay for this," he added, waving his arm at the stone-faced audience.

"Well now, maybe I'll finish the job with you and the good woman here."

Before they could move the travelers tied them up and dragged them under a large branch.

"Aye, it'll be a hangin' to end all hangin's," the wide hairy mouth cried with glee.

Eyes filled with hatred stared at Will and Kate. Tying ropes around each of their necks, silent men threw the other end over thick tree limbs.

"A double hangin', that'll be dandy. Seein' them twitch, it'll be a grand party."

Nobody laughed or spoke. Revenge was one thing, but dealing with a crazed fairy was quite another. The travelers watched fearfully. The leprechaun licked his lips as he stood there, intoxicated by the fear around him. *Maybe I'll kill them all,* the twisted mind thought, *one at a time so it'll last longer.*

"Yes, that's it!" he said gleefully. "You'll all meet yer makers this fine day. First I'll hang the old man, then the woman." Pausing he looked at the frightened faces staring obediently, "Then one of you," he said, pointing to a scar-faced old man near the bank.

Time stood still as the wind blew harder; the heavens lit up with lightning flashing in deadly arcs.

Kate felt the rope around her neck, all the while keeping her eyes glued to the silent form lying on the damp moss. If she must die, better to have a last look at her love. She prayed with all her heart that Eamonn's passing had been painless and that baby Mollie was safe.

Will nudged Kate, comforting her as best he could. *Hell on earth,* he thought, *the whole of Ireland's lost to this demon. Vengeance is mine sayeth the Lord,* he rationalized, but with all his heart he wanted an eye for an eye. *One tinker for each dead villager. More even, kill them all,* he thought wildly. *Destroy every dark-coated leprechaun. Use every method Eamonn knew to push the fairies away forever, bells, iron, the bible, bread, St. John's Wort, anything to stop this insanity.*

The little man looked at Will muttering angrily to himself. *It's time,* he thought, motioning to the four men. They pulled hard on the ropes slung over the large limb, yanking the hapless pair skyward. Blinding light filled the circle of trees. Will blinked trying to see. *Am I dying?* He seemed to be lying flat on the moss, Kate beside him. The surreal look of the travelers' frozen faces added to his confusion as he watched a procession of small finely dressed men and women exit one of the tree stumps. Many armed with spears marched to the outer parameter of trees. Others, with regal coats and dresses, filled the circle to overflowing. As the last came out, they made way for him. A crown atop his head and a staff held firmly in his hand, he walked in a stately fashion to where the leprechaun stood frozen, a surprised look on his face. Angry eyes surveyed the troubling scene. On the moss lay a man with a knife in his chest; a pool of dark crimson surrounding his body. A second man and woman lay at his feet, ropes around their necks, while a clergyman lay facedown with his hands pulled up over his head. Many men stood in what appeared to be a circle of judgment. Waving his staff, all were able to move and speak.

"Aye, it's me lucky day," the leprechaun exclaimed, bowing to the king in a slow deliberate way. "I was just finishing some business for yer excellence . . . "

"Save your words," the fairy nearest him ordered.

Nervously, the shoemaker stepped back. The others moved aside as the regal fairy with long silvery hair walked past each traveler. "You have all trespassed on this land. You have deceived others, using us as your villainy; pretending we had taken revenge on those living on our hill. You are murderous thieves, one and all." Carefully, he turned to the leprechaun, "And you, shoemaker, you have added an even greater sin. You have used our powers to kill."

Fearfully, everyone watched as thunder shook the mountain.

"Aye, I did use the powers. You see, the man Flynn had the stone. He wouldn't release me until I did his bidding," the leprechaun said patiently, eyeing the stately fairy king.

Pointing his staff at Flynn's grotesque form, the hatpin sticking through his bloody shirt, he spoke harshly, "Were you not released by his death?"

"Tis true, but I thought I'd finish doing his bidding anyway. A matter of principle, you see."

"His bidding was not yours to obey, you should have been willing to die rather than fulfill his request."

"Die, is it," the leprechaun; said, a sly smile covering his ugly face, "perhaps this is better suited to you."

Reaching behind his waistband he withdrew a small dagger.

Will watched, listening in disbelief to the conversation, saw the hairy hand bring the knife from under its coat. Rising, he ran quickly closing the distance between them, hitting the hateful leprechaun as hard as he could, knocking him sideways. The sharp blade, raised to strike, fell to the ground. The leprechaun groaned, his back straightening, then slumped over dead with a fairy spear wedged in his black heart.

The remaining travelers rushed towards the fairy king in a fit of rage. With a wave of his staff each stood frozen. Grimly he walked over to where the leprechaun lay and waved his hand. Fairy dust sprinkled from his palm fell on the lifeless form. Cold winds blew like the breath of a demon as the tiny remnant of a man faded, turned to dust and blew away.

The fairy king looked at the travelers in various stages of attack.

"You will pay for all eternity," he said, motioning to the guards. "Take them to the mines."

Animated again they struggled to get free, crying and screaming. Fairy guards grabbed them one at a time and took them into the small opening under the tree. Each shrank in stature until they were the size of the guards leading them. Soon all had left save the king and a small group of attendants. Will feared for their lives as the stern-faced king turned to him.

"You have trespassed on our land," he said, studying the frightened old man's face.

"I'm truly sorry," Will said in a shaky voice, "We meant you no harm. My friend here and I were just trying to stop the dying on the hill."

Yes, I'm sure you were, but the law is strict, no one enters our domain without permission."

Huddled together, the king seemed to be talking to his advisors. A heated conversion with no apparent winners, he stared at the old man standing in front of him.

"You are a good man, Will Bonner. I'm sure you meant us no harm."

Rubbing his forehead for a moment, he spoke softly, "You saved my life this day and I am eternally grateful," he said, bowing low. "What evilness has passed can never be undone," he added as he looked at Eamonn lying quite still, Kate huddled by his side weeping. "Perhaps I might do one small thing."

Walking over to the Irishman, he placed his hand on Eamonn's chest and pulled out the knife. Bright light glowed around the wound. Kate held her breath in disbelief as she watched the wound slowly disappear. The stately little man bent over Eamonn once more and lightly touched his brow.

As though someone had blown air into his lungs, Eamonn took a deep breath. His eyes fluttered, then opened.

Seeing Katie, he smiled at her with such love Will was moved to tears.

"Thank you, kind sir . . . I mean your highness," he said with true affection.

The king smiled as he turned to leave. "You are welcome to return here, Will Bonner," he said, following the others into the opening under the giant tree.

Eamonn looked up at his wife and friend. It all seemed like a dream. The travelers were gone, Flynn was gone, the demon leprechaun was nowhere to be seen. The only sound, mumbled prayers, caused all three to turn. Still lying face down, Father Kerrigan seemed quite lost. Together, they helped the portly cleric to his feet and back to his car. It was agreed Will would drive Father Kerrigan, who was now sitting there uttering unintelligent words of wisdom to the floor.

"I'll follow," Will said, getting into the priest's car. "If we take him back to the church they can decide what to do with him."

Eamonn nodded in agreement. It would be best if he and Kate got home as soon as possible. She was anxious about Mollie and he missed her too. Mollie had always been with her mother till now. Added to that, so much had happened that was impossible to talk about it.

Will looked up at the non-changing sky, still the same cloudy gray. With one last glance at the fairy circle, he wondered if anyone would believe such a story. Little people? Another world? Better kept a secret. He thought about the king in his grand robe. *Finvana? Oh well, maybe next time I'll ask. After all, I have been invited to return.* Looking in the rearview mirror he saw the deranged priest in the backseat, a smile covering his face. Words of a language long gone escaped his lips as he communicated with an unknown being.

The trip home went quickly as they drove through the night. No one wanted to stop on the way. Occasional oncoming vehicles blinded Will with bright lights, but thankfully those were few and far between.

Arriving at the Presbytery, Kate knocked on the door of the massive house while Eamonn and Will assisted Father Kerrigan. Soon a light came on, followed by a jangling of chains and locks.

"Here now, who's out there?" a frightened voice inquired.

"Aye, it's Eamonn Gallagher and me wif and friend bringing the good father home."

"Bringing the father home?" the housekeeper said as she opened the door.

A silly grin on his face, Father Kerrigan was led in and put to bed.

"You might want to call the Bishop and tell him the father has gone off a bit," Eamonn said tiredly. "He was following us and it proved to be too much for him."

"That it was," Will piped in with a smile.

"You're right about that, he was havin' bad thoughts about the two of you," the housekeeper said with a knowing smile. "Come to think of it, the whole town was havin' bad thoughts."

"Well, maybe, we can put that to rest now," Will said. "It was more a tourist's curiosity in the legends of Ireland, than anything else Ma'am."

Nodding she smiled at the three bedraggled visitors, then said her good-byes. *Folks dyin' on the hill, more since these two started their sleuthin',* she knew the truth. They had stirred up a big mess, angered the little folk they had.

No matter, I'll mind me own business. Even the priest has paid, lost his sanity he has. Hurrying down the hall she went to her room and locked the door. The creak of straining timbers from the wind made her shiver as she turned out the light and went to bed.

Fifty-four--Reminiscing

Unable to sleep after the nightmarish events, Kate prepared a hot cup of tea. She and Annie listened to Will tell Eamonn what had happened in the fairy circle after he had been stabbed. How the fairy king had disposed of the evil leprechaun and saved Eamonn's life.

"I can't tell you how hard it is believin' what you say, but I saw it with my own eyes too, that damned leprechaun was real."

"He was that," Will agreed. "He was evil incarnate. You know, if Kate hadn't stopped Flynn this could have turned out much worse."

"That's the God's truth," Eamonn said, looking at his wife with pride. "You were very brave, Luv."

Seated next to her, he hugged her for a long time.

"I got so angry," Kate whispered. "Seeing you lying in yer own blood and that foul man standing there with his mighty smirk . . . I wished him dead. I'm sorry for that, but I did." Tears flowed down her cheeks.

"Well, you're safe now and no more harm will befall you," Eamonn replied.

"That's true, with the fairies on our side," Will added. "That fairy king said I was welcome to come back."

Annie rolled her eyes as she listened. "One meeting in a lifetime with fairy kings, okay?"

"Okay, but it's nice to know I have a friend in the fairy world."

"Oh, now that's grand, it is," Eamonn said, "next thing you know you'll be lording it over me on account of you've got an inside track with the wee folk."

"I'll wee folk the both of you if you ever go off on another wild goose chase," Kate said, laughing and crying at the same time.

"Aye, but the killing's done," Eamonn said more seriously. "Those damned tinkers are gone, and I say good riddance to the murdering thieves."

"So a lot of good was done for the folks on the hill," Will said softly. "Mullagh Na Sidhe is just that, the Hill of the Fairies. They live under it and the good villagers of Ballyshannon live on top."

No one spoke as they sat looking out at the dark sky, rain softly pelting the earth.

Fifty-five—Poems & stories

Irrespective of being late in the evening, Will welcomed going to bed.

"That's enough excitement for one lifetime," Annie muttered as she got under the covers beside him. They hadn't stayed in Mullaghmore in over a week, but right now it felt more like home than anyplace else.

Next morning Annie cooked a rasher of bacon and eggs with soda bread toast. Everything tasting so good, plus the elimination of murderous fiends demanded a celebration, a small one maybe, but still, exploring the seashore seemed a fitting reward.

"What say we take a brisk walk down by the bay?"

"It's a little too brisk for me, Mr. Bonner," Annie said, as reading by a warm fire seemed more appealing.

The cold air invigorated him and for the first time since they had arrived he felt that he was truly on holiday. The gravel road down to the bay was deserted except for an old woman standing by the seawall.

"Good mornin' to you, Sir," she said, a slight cackle in her voice.

"Good morning to you," Will said cheerfully.

"American?" she asked inquisitively.

"Yes, I'm here on holiday visiting my friend."

"And who might that be?"

"Eamonn Gallagher, we're staying in his cottage on the hill."

"Nice view from there, I reckon?"

"Oh, it's a beautiful sight overlooking the bay."

"Yes," the old lady said in agreement, pulling a ragged shawl over her white hair. "It's a fine place to visit." Her frail fingers held tightly to her throat, she mumbled, "You have a good day now," then hobbled away past the shops, toward the cliffs.

A little disconcerted, Will felt a chill penetrate his long coat. More cautious than usual, he wondered if he'd ever completely trust strangers again. *Maybe it's the price one pays for being an adventurer,* he thought halfheartedly as he walked along the seawall. The clear green of the sea was inviting as he looked to the bottom hoping to catch sight of a fish or some other creature from the deep. *Maybe an Irish crab,* he thought. Laughing to himself for thinking like a tourist, he felt on a roll, *maybe* a *crab with a shillelagh.*

Enough humor, he decided to return to the cottage. The beauty of Ireland was never more evident as the sun gave one of its rare visits to the western coastline. In the distance he saw several cows standing knee-deep in the surf, staring out to sea. Though he had seen this sight before, it was still fascinating.

As though to end his musings, the penetrating sea breeze seemed to push him up the hill. Walking briskly up the rocky road he couldn't help noticing how stone walls sheltered long-eared brown rabbits busy foraging for food. Maybe he was imagining it, but he felt they were staring as he walked by. Could be they knew he wasn't Irish. Shaking his head at his own foolish thoughts he hurried home.

This afternoon he and Annie were joining Eamonn and his family for a picnic. *Quite overdue,* he thought. *A bit of quiet by the lough.* He smiled. *I must be turning Irish. Well, when it comes to loughs I am.*

The afternoon was blissfully quiet and it was almost fun driving to Ballyshannon. The drive past Bundoran, on N15 north, was uneventful. Passing Finner Military Camp, Annie pointed at hundreds of brown and gray rabbits in various stages of repose. Some watched the passers by while others the sea to the west. The Donegal Parian China factory seemed to beckon Annie. She had wanted to buy some small treasure to take home to Maine.

She needs her "buy fix", Will thought with some amusement. "Would you like to stop for a few minutes? Maybe find some rare treasure?"

"No, no, I'll tell you when," she said firmly, her nose a little to the side.

Laughing, he gave her a gentle pat. They still had a few days before they had to leave.

The picnic was a delight and the sun appeared in all its glory. Will finally knew what the term Emerald Isle meant. The landscape was breathtakingly beautiful, many shades of green, abundant moss and ferns, flowers blooming everywhere. It was everything the brochures had said it would be.

"Kate, I've written a poem for Mollie," Will said softly. "I thought she needed something to remember the visitors from Maine."

"That was very sweet, why don't you read it," Annie urged.

"Oh, I don't know if I'm up to that. Fighting Leprechauns is more my speed."

"Aye, Will, I'd like to hear it too," Eamonn said seriously. "Anything that's written for my daughter needs to be read. Besides, look at her, she's dying to know what this American has said in the written word."

Sitting on her mother's lap, Mollie eyed her admirer with an expectant smile.

Okay," he replied, "Here goes:

Child of life, Rise up! Rise up!

Fair damsel be, delight with simple vices

For out of love has come your song

Never mind the winds so fair, for out of love has come your peace.

With cheer and song to the sky, be free, my love, to always be."

There was silence as Will handed Kate the piece of paper. Mollie laughed, giving her impressions in her own language. *She's very impressed for a wee one,* Will thought happily.

"That was nice, Mr. Bonner," Eamonn said with true affection. "you'll be famous before you know it and I'll say I knew him when."

Seated on a blanket, Eamonn leaned against a tree looking more relaxed than Will had ever known him to be.

"Now that you are on such good terms with the wee folk, it might be a good idea to warn you of those to steer clear of."

"As long as you and Will don't start another investigation," Annie said, feigning being bothered.

"Yes, Eamonn, as long as nothing wants to bite me or have us for lunch, charge on," Will added.

"Aye, it'll bite you alright," he said, rubbing his chin as he looked off into the forest. The sound of water rushing over the rocks lulled Will into a listening mood as Eamonn continued. "All me life I've believed in the wee ones, but I never met one until that damned leprechaun so I reckon it's wise to tell you about the others, just in case."

"In case what?" Will asked.

"In case you meet up with one," Eamonn said quietly. "Hear that stream there, the gurgle of the water? Well, there's legends that ghosts of women washing the clothes of those about to die haunt those places. Women who've died in childbirth and must wash until they normally would have died, linger near streams where no good folks live."

"My goodness," Annie said with a shiver, "I hope we don't run into any old women."

"Oh, don't worry about that," Kate said reassuringly, "they don't come out where there's a group anyway."

Not sure what to believe, Annie thought it best if no one went off by themselves.

"Forget all that," Will said motioning Eamonn to continue.

"You see the tufts of grass in that field, well those are fairy tufts and if you step on one a spell comes over you."

"What happens then?" Will asked suspiciously.

"You might see things that aren't there." Pointing to a stile exit across the field, Eamonn explained, "that might disappear. You might become lost, where nothin' looks familiar."

"How do you remove the spell?" Annie wondered out loud.

"You turn your coat inside out, then put it on and wear it that way," Eamonn said solemnly, "It's called pixie-led."

Kate put down her plate of cold chicken, pointing at some animals grazing in the field nearby. "See that horse there? Well, that could be a phooka."

"Phooka?" Will asked.

"Aye," Eamonn said, "an Irish goblin that takes the shape of a horse or a dog. Some say even a bull."

"A shape changer," Will said with a laugh. "They morph?"

"True enough, they morph," Eamonn said dryly. "Anyway, it can look like that old horse there until you climb up on his back, then take you for a wild ride through the thorny bushes." Eamonn indicated the peaceful lake in the distance. "If an Each-Uisge (ech-oosh kya) or Aughis Ky (agh-iski) were in there, you best stay away. They carry their victims on their back to the deep and then eat them, leaving only their liver."

"What does that creature look like," Will asked nervously.

"They look like horses with a second set of eyes by their nose."

Thoroughly frightened, Annie snuggled up to Will as a cold wind started to blow.

The sun hidden behind the clouds, Eamonn seemed to follow the lost mood and recited some old verse; "There was a time, long ago, when searching in vain, looking this way and that, a wraith so small, never lost its bite, while unknown hatred lurks nearby, for evil thrives on reasons why."

All was silent. No one spoke, no bird warbled, no sounds of the brook; everything had gone quiet. Finally Eamonn whispered, "Goblins are small, evil creatures. Some say malicious."

"Dirty thieves and villains of the fairy world," Kate added. "Companions of the dead, I reckon," she said with conviction.

Will took a deep breath just as the sound of rushing water, birdsong and wind blowing in the treetops filled his ears once more. "Eamonn, that was quite a spell you put us under. That poem . . . "

Interrupting, the dazed Irishman interjected, "Aye, some old sage wrote that. It's not from me memories."

Annie laughed nervously as she helped Kate pack up the leftover chicken and salads.

That poem was strong magic, Will thought, trying to understand. *Now there's more dangerous fairies to worry about. God, I hope we haven't started something.* Fervently, he hoped not. *Damn, just damn. I won't ask any more questions. I won't even think about fairies.*

The wind pushed against them as they walked. "Leave this place now," it seemed to say. *Gads, the whole of Ireland can't be haunted,* he thought. Hurrying to get in the car, Will pulled the door shut with a loud thunk. None too soon, the windshield filled with rain. Damp from the rush to the car he thought how nice it would be to sit in front of a warm fire.

Fifty-six--Goodbyes

Leaving for home in five days, Will wanted to take his friends out for an evening of fine dining. At Eamonn's suggestion, they went to a place overlooking the rocky cliffs in Rossnowlagh called Smuggler's Creek Inn. Only ten kilometers from Ballyshannon, it was a nice ride. Heavy with exposed timbers over a low ceiling it was the perfect place to sit and talk, eat a good meal and drink a bit of Irish whiskey.

Warmed from the drink, mellowed by the spirits, Will felt like hugging the world. Raising his cup in toast he spoke with affection. "To good friends and good visits."

"Amen to that. It's been more than interesting," Eamonn said. "It's changed me life. When I see a Fairy ring, I'll always think of how we scared Father Kerrigan. Him falling on his pride like that. And I'm swearin' I'll never investigate' anythin' again."

"Eamonn, if ever there was a saint in heaven . . . you'd do it all again because you have a good heart," Kate said, feeling very warm towards her husband.

"It's true," Annie added. "I don't think Will will ever be quite the same. After all, how many men fight leprechauns to save a fairy king?"

"None, I'd imagine," Will answered.

"Aye, none that lived to tell the tale, that's for darn sure," Eamonn added.

"Well, buddy, I did live and I thank my lucky stars, that fairy king and your wife for being so brave."

"Yeah, yeah, enough with the thanks, just drink your brew."

Laughter filled the cozy inn as the blue half-light of evening painted the sky. For all their time in Mullaghmore with its grand views of Donegal Bay, this scene of rocky cliffs, sandy beach stretching for miles to the north, was food for the soul.

An old man had taken up the flute as their dinner was being served. The haunting melody was more than atmosphere, reminding Will that Irish culture was steeped in tradition, thousands of years in the making.

"That's good stuff," Eamonn said wistfully. The look in his eye held fast to times long past. "I love that tune."

"It's beautiful," Annie agreed.

Lost in a daydream, Eamonn spoke of memories, "I remember going with me Da to the sea when I was a wee lad. He and his friend took me to the other side of Bloody Foreland before droppin' anchor. The sky was lit up with a million stars and I always thought there were strange creatures looking down, watching things movin' in the rocks."

"When I was a kid I had strange occurrences too," Will said.

"Your mind lives in strange occurrences," Annie said laughing.

"It must run in their genes," Kate said smiling.

"That's the real truth," Annie added.

Seated across from her, Will gave her a playful pat on the hand. "You're right about that. I've always thought there was a troll under the bridge at home."

"Aye, a troll that eats writers," Eamonn said.

"Okay, I know it sounds strange, but unless you know for sure . . . "

"Will Bonner, there is no troll under our bridge," Annie exclaimed. "Don't listen to him, he's just trying to go native."

"So you're thinkin' you can come to Ireland and be tellin' tall tales to the self, the master of legends?"

Ignoring Eamonn's question, Will stared out at the lights twinkling along the distant shoreline.

"There was a time folks around our neighborhood were afraid to come out on certain nights. Especially in the early fall, just before Halloween. It wasn't that they were afraid of the little spooks and goblins trick-or-treating, it was the time of year when spirits supposedly left their graves in the cemetery on the end of our lane to search for a new body to occupy."

"No one was ever afraid of any such thing," Annie said indignantly. "He's such a storyteller, I swear."

Will waited until Annie was through, then continued. "Years past a certain man lived at the end of our lane right next to the graveyard. He was strong, not easily given to superstition. One night the wind was blowing hard and one of his bedroom shutters was banging. Getting his boots on he went outside to reattach it. The wind was whistling through the clapboard on that side of the house something fierce. Unafraid by nature, he went to the bedroom window facing the old cemetery. Mostly from the early eighteen hundreds, the headstones were faded and cracked. While he was fixing the shutter to its clamps, he felt a cold hand grab his shoulder. Angry, he whipped around to beat off whatever was holding him. He tried warding off the shadowy figure coming towards him. Like slightly visible silk, he felt it enter his body. His face changed from anger to a cynical smile."

"Who saw his face change?" Annie asked, totally frustrated. "Nobody was there, were they?"

Will gave Annie a fiendy look. "Some said it was the original owner of our house."

No one spoke for a long minute as Annie shook her head.

"It may be just a folk tale, but I'm not sure," Will said somberly. "I've always been afraid of things that go bump in the night. When I was little, noises under the bed really pulled my whiskers."

"Right, spooks in the nugget," Annie said, giving her husband a hug. "Don't you worry, I'll protect you," she added.

"Aye, and me too," Eamonn said in mock sympathy.

Kate stared thoughtfully into her glass. "I can see where you might have been hidin' under the covers. When I was a young lass I thought there was a monster in the chimney and the only thing that kept it there was the fire."

"Well, there's no need to fear anything with me here to protect you," Eamonn said affectionately.

Annie took a sip of hot coffee and Bailey's. "Except for this fairy stuff . . ."

"Aye, in all me life I never saw the likes of that," Eamonn agreed.

"If I never see fiends like that again, it'll be too soon," Kate added.

Food for thought, the conversation faded. The sky was clouding over as they sat listening to the flutist play his worn instrument near the large open fireplace.

Out of the blue, Eamonn said, "You don't have to chew your cabbage twice on that."

"Gads, I didn't know you were a vegetarian," Will said.

"Aye, I've just begun."

"Yes," Kate said, giving Eamonn a shove, "he's tired of eating meat, he is."

"I'll be giving the both of you a knuckle sandwich if you're wanting to try me food."

Laughing, they held their glasses high as Will gave a toast. "To my best friends, to my only friends in Ireland, may you always be blessed."

Each said amen to that as they enjoyed the warm ambiance of the small cliff-top retreat.

"It's been a total evening," Annie said softly to Kate. "My baked chicken was excellent, the coffee and Bailey's was excellent and the view is . . . "

"Yes, yes," Will said, interrupting his wife, "don't get carried away."

"Aye, don't get carried away or we'll be making toasts all night," Eamonn added.

Really the first time they had been alone, the foursome talked and laughed about everything.

Annie watched their friends, both very down to earth, not given to flights of fancy, yet they lived in this place of fantasy and dreams. On the other hand, she lived in a very down to earth place and Will lived in a fantasy world all his own. Consumed with her thoughts, time flew by.

Finishing their drinks, everyone agreed it was time to go. Mollie had never been left with a babysitter before and, even though it was Eamonn's mother, Kate was anxious to get home. Will and Annie followed in their rented car. They had had so much fun it seemed a pot of tea would be the perfect ending to a wonderful evening.

"They are such dear people," Annie said as their headlights outlined the sports utility in front. "I don't know when I've enjoyed myself so much."

"Well, I'm glad," Will said, genuinely touched. "This trip really hasn't been much of a holiday for you."

"Oh, it has. Not exactly what I'd pictured. But one thing's for sure, there's the makings of a great story here."

"You're right about that. Maybe if I kiss the blarney stone it'll be better."

"Maybe if you kiss me it'll be even better," Annie said smiling.

Patting her hand, Will felt the security of their years of love fill his heart. Through all they had endured, the ups and downs, she had always been there to encourage and comfort him. The years had flown bye since they met, and now they were here in this land of magic.

The sound of thunder rumbling across the sky brought Will out of his daydream. A light rain speckled the windshield. Ahead of them Eamonn and Kate pulled into their driveway as Will parked on the narrow, dead-end street overlooking the bay. While Kate hurried to get Mollie, Eamonn stayed to talk.

Will's heart skipped a beat as Kate's scream filled the air. Eamonn spun around, heading for his mother's house next door. Together, Will and Annie followed right behind. Eamonn stared at his tearful wife, then his mother, seeking answers.

"She's gone," Mrs. Gallagher said sobbing. "Mollie's been taken from her grandmother's bosom."

"What happened, Mum?" Eamonn asked, his voice thick with pain.

The old woman glanced at the wall filled with photographs of generations of Gallaghers. "I went to the kitchen to get the wee one a bite of applesauce and digestive for meself."

Mrs. Gallagher's eyes welled with tears.

"When I come back there was no sign of her. Her blanket, coat, all gone. I'm terrible sorry, I am."

"Oh Mum, you didn't do anything wrong. If someone was intent on stealing our daughter there'd be no stopping them."

While Eamonn consoled his mother, Kate, Annie and Will looked for clues, anything that wasn't as it should be. Using a flashlight Will searched outside for signs of tire tracks or footprints in the wet dirt near the door. With their mad rush into the house any prints other than theirs would be hard to distinguish without a forensic expert. And that was unlikely, in a town this small.

Searching the living room, they found nothing out of order. Nothing around the coffee table or end tables near the door. Deep in thought, Annie went to sit down in a lounge facing the couch. Her ankle buckled as she stepped on something hard and fell backwards into the chair.

Hearing Annie's moan, Eamonn reached down to comfort her. Kneeling, Will inspected her ankle. "Are you okay?" he asked worriedly?

"I think I've sprained my ankle on a rock," she said stifling the pain.

"A rock?" he repeated, running his hand along the carpet, suddenly feeling a cold stone. Bringing it into the light, he gasped in disbelief. "It's a fairy rune."

Eamonn came over quickly.

"Mum, is this yours?"

"Oh Lord! Have ya lost yer mind, I don't keep evil in me house."

Studying the half-inch stone, Eamonn read the finely etched letters, M N S.

Kate studied the small quartz crystal.

"I don't think that belonged to fairies, the symbols are too finely cut."

"Aye, I agree with that," Eamonn said, thoroughly puzzled.

"Could those be initials?" Annie asked.

"Yes," Will said, his face lighting up with an idea, "they could stand for Mullagh Na Sidhe, M N S."

"Aye, Hill of the Fairies," Eamonn said fearfully. "Damn, I thought it was over. You said the tinkers were all taken, Will."

"They were, I swear. Kate and I saw every one of those hateful creatures shrunk and taken inside that tree."

"Then what's this? Someone or something under that damned hill has grabbed my daughter. From all I know it's only fairies that take babies. Maybe that leprechaun has friends we don't know about."

Thunder rolled, rattling the windows. A flash of lightning stabbed the darkness, adding an eerie hue to the shadows cast by the streetlight.

"God," Will said, "we saw them disappear."

"It's the truth," Kate said in a pleading voice.

Eamonn finally nodded. He knew deep down Kate and Will saw what they saw. His mind in a muddle, he sat down next to his mother and tried to think. Of them that were there, all were taken. Maybe there were more fairies in cahoots with tinkers who weren't in Connemara.

Will patted his shoulder, "I think we've got more investigating to do."

"Aye, that we have, Mate," Eamonn said firmly.

"What about the guards?" Mrs. Gallagher asked. "Should I ring them?"

"No sense," Eamonn replied.

"More's the pity, if you do. They don't pay no mind," Kate said bitterly.

"One thing has become increasingly clear, whatever the problem, it's right here on the hill," Will said emphatically. "We've got to get inside this thing, to the tunnels your dad was talking about, and get to the bottom of this once and for all."

"More importantly," Annie interjected, "we've got to find Mollie."

"Aye, that's the God's truth," Eamonn said grimly, getting to his feet.

"Eamonn Gallagher, you're not going anywhere without me. I damn near died in that fairy ring. This nightmare is as much mine as yours," Kate said moving towards the door.

"No woman of mine will be fighting me battles," Eamonn began.

"If it's fighting you want, Mister . . . "

"Listen you two," Annie said softly, "take a deep breath. Perhaps if we make a plan . . . "

"Annie's right," Will said, "whoever's behind this is awfully dangerous."

Eamonn looked at his determined wife and smiled slowly.

"I reckon I agree with Annie. We've got to make a plan so we don't do more harm than good for our Mollie."

While the others discussed what to do next, Annie went into the kitchen to put the kettle on. Eamonn knew of an entrance into the hill used years ago. It might be more fable than true, he wasn't sure. First they'd try some antidotes, try to find out what they were dealing with, fairies or men. Kate suggested they burn thorns at the top of the hill. If they were dealing with fairies, they would have to release any captive children. If Mollie wasn't released they'd know fairies weren't involved. Or, as Will pointed out, she might not be under the hill at all. Maybe someone had kidnapped her looking for ransom.

"You should check your answering machine," Annie suggested.

"We don't have one," Eamonn said reluctantly. "Here in Ireland . . . "

"Here in Ireland if you aren't at home you don't answer," Kate offered with a smile.

"I think we should be at your house nonetheless," Will said. "In case it's a kidnapper, it would sure be sick if we were out chasing fairies and weren't there to take the call."

"Aye," Eamonn agreed, hugging his mother and heading for the door.

The rain continued steadily as they sat in the den talking in whispers. It had been over an hour and no one had tried to reach them. Annie helped Kate gather torches, (flashlights), to use if they had to go into the hill. Who would go and who would stay still hadn't been settled. One thing was sure, the phone had not rung since they had arrived back at the house.

Eamonn stood near the large plate-glass window looking out across the steep incline of the hill. *Not many folks awake this time of night*, he thought. In the distance only an occasional house was lit. *Someone else unable to sleep*. Finally he spoke, "In all me thoughts, I keep coming to one conclusion. I've got to go alone. It's too dangerous to drag anyone else along."

Kate stared at her husband, her mind a jumble of fears. "And I've got to go with you, Eamonn Gallagher. I'll not have you risking your life and me not being there. You're too precious to me. My love of life would die if I didn't try to save my daughter right along side you."

Finished, Kate sat there stiffly lost in thought. Will stood and walked over to where Eamonn was standing.

"I know you both feel strongly about this, but it might be better putting our heads together to outfox the enemy. First we should decide who will stay to answer the phone, then who will go to the hill. Someone's got to burn some thorns to see if Mollie's released. If not, you really need to decide on a practical basis who will go into that hill to look for her."

Kate looked at her tall, physically fit, thirty-five year old husband. Grudgingly, she knew in her heart, it would be best if he went. When it came to fighting men he would be hardest to beat. Will was a good planner, a good lookout, but in truth she and Annie should really stay behind. Reluctantly, she voiced that opinion.

That settled, the men got ready to go. Bundled in their overcoats, Will carried a lantern while Eamonn carried a torch. Using the list Will had made, they brought a large ball of twine, a knife for a weapon, and chalk to mark their way out.

Ready to leave, Will gave Annie some last minute instructions, "If we're not back by daylight you had better call the Garda."

She nodded, giving him a big hug. With Kate's prayers for their safety, they left quickly. It was bitter cold outside and an offshore wind was blowing up the hill as they made their way down the deserted street towards the bay. Will wondered if this was more madness added to the insanity that had already taken place so far. It would still be better to call the Garda after they knew something for sure. *Most likely they'd think we're nuts,* he thought tiredly.

At the bottom of the hill Eamonn led Will through an open stretch of land leading up to the graveyard at St. Anne's Church, the very place Michael McGinty had jumped from the bell tower. The smell of wet earth permeated the air.

"Reminds me of a freshly dug grave," Eamonn muttered.

In fair shape for his age, Will kept up with the younger man leading the way. No stopping him now, Eamonn was ready to go into hell if necessary. The line had been drawn when Mollie was taken. Tinkers or leprechauns it made no difference, they'd give her up or pay with their lives. Anger filled his heart as they neared the top of the hill. Standing near the rock wall that separated the field from the cemetery, Eamonn made the sign of the cross and set his torch on the wall.

"I've got to try burning thorns like Kate said."

Looking around in the half-light of Will's lantern he gathered some gorse. Breaking off a bush-like branch he crushed it with his boot and took the twigs over to where Will was standing. The small pile of thorns burned brightly, their musky scent filling the air. Eamonn looked at Will as it flared into flames. Dancing about, it seemed hundreds of eyes were watching, reflecting off unknown surfaces.

With all his heart Will hoped they'd hear the baby's cry, Mollie's voice coming closer. Minutes passed as the pile of gorse became red embers, then dark ashes, smoldering spirals of smoke rising lazily into the darkness.

Eamonn looked at his friend, an almost evil glint in his eye. Both knew the truth now, it was men they were dealing with. No fairy had stolen his baby. It had to be tinkers bent on revenge, sick-minded filth set on one thing – murder.

Eamonn stomped out the remaining sparks, then motioned for his friend to follow him back down the hill. The dampness of the night glistened off the rocks. The wet briny air making Will wish for his bed. A dog barked as they passed a white plastered house with a thatched roof. Moving quickly to the street below, Eamonn hurried to the bay side. Thirty feet below the road, murky water lapped noiselessly against the rocks. Headed towards the mall they followed the lonely road around the bay. Eamonn stopped and flashed his torch towards a clump of thorns near the water, then started down a jagged pile of rocks.

"Wait for me," Will said, clambering over the last giant boulder towards a darkened entrance into the hill.

"Are you okay?" Eamonn asked, bumping into his friend.

Will felt his coat catch on sharp thorns, "Damn," he mumbled, "let's take a break."

"Aye, that's a good idea."

Handing Eamonn a piece of chalk, Will whispered. "As we go in, we should mark the way out." Holding up his lantern, he went over to the cavernous wall and made an arrow pointing to the exit. Except for lapping waves there was no sound. *Like being in a vacuum, he* thought.

Darkness seemed to eat up the light from their lanterns. Eamonn tied one end of the large ball of twine to a branch just inside. If they were going into this unknown world, it was best to have all avenues of escape available. If Will's lantern or his torch failed, they could feel their way back using the string. No telling how many tunnels there were or where they led. The only sound they could hear was the ringing in their ears.

As ready as they could be they started into the tunnel, crouching to avoid the ceiling. Cut from solid rock, the cavern was no more than two meters wide by one and one-half tall. While Will led the way holding the lantern, Eamonn unwound the twine behind them, the black void absorbing the tiny lantern flame. Darkness surrounding them, Will strained to see as they inched forward. Descending slowly into the hill the tunnel widened, allowing them to walk side by side. Still the going was slow as Eamonn continued to trail the string behind.

The stifling air reminded Will of rotting things, long dead. Eamonn stared into the darkness, trying to see further than one meter ahead. Slowly they crept forward. The tunnel had opened into a large room with a wall dividing it into two different caverns. Eamonn stopped, trying to decide which path to take. To the left it rose steadily, the right continuing downward. Thinking of the tales his dad had told him, he was sure the entrance to the right was the way to go. Will watched as he marked the wall where they stood and just beyond the new tunnel entrance. Even though this one looked like it went further down, Eamonn was sure it was the correct one. Under ground, nothing was as it seemed. Their exit marked, Eamonn followed the dim shadow of his friend, as Will held the lantern high in the air. Their path had grown considerably larger with the cavern ceiling much higher now. A warm breeze brushed their faces as they continued. Their equilibrium off a little, neither noticed when the path had started a slight incline. Stopping to mark the tunnel, a soft whimpering echoed through the passageway. Eamonn straightened up quickly. Straining to see ahead by the scant light of the lantern, both held their breath as they listened intently. From behind the faint sound of footsteps stopped.

"My God, it's all around us," Will said, looking back. "Could be the wind blowing through the rocks."

"Aye, rocks with feet. You wouldn't hear that sound unless it was a banshee."

Will looked at his friend's serious face, then patted him on the shoulder. "If it is, we'll beat the hell out of it and send it on its way."

Eamonn smiled weakly, rolling his eyes. "You're turning into a bloody Irishman, Mate."

Neither had moved for fear of missing any sound, but precious minutes had ticked away and there still wasn't anything they could put their finger on. Taking a deep breath, Eamonn motioned Will to continue as he unwound the last of the twine. *With luck our lights won't burn out,* Will thought, *hopefully, we'll be able to find the boulder Eamonn's attached the string to.*

The going was easier with Eamonn at his side. The path had become decidedly steeper as they moved steadily upward. At what felt like a thirty-degree angle, Eamonn figured they should be directly below St. Anne's Church.

Still, the air was becoming more and more humid. A baby's scream startled Will. Stopping, he put his hand on Eamonn's shoulder restraining him from running wildly up the tunnel towards the sound. Trying to make as little noise as possible they hurried forward.

In the distance a pinpoint of light reflected off the tunnel walls. Unsure of what they were dealing with, it was decided to put out the lantern and leave it next to a giant rock. Will drew a crude picture of it with an arrow pointing downward. Eamonn turned off his torch as they crept forward towards the light.

The sound of footsteps other than their own interrupted Will's thoughts. Closer than before, both men froze in place. Nothing moved. The only sounds were small snatches of breath from each of them. Signing, Eamonn indicated they should continue. Will nodded. *Even at a snail's pace it's better to keep moving, We've got to get into the light.* It seemed to take forever as he followed the tall man.

The walls of the tunnel melted away as they neared a massive room. An old woman in a rainbow-colored dress, a shawl covering her head, sat in a wicker chair rocking back and forth. As Eamonn and Will came into view she stared at them with her one good eye. Smiling a toothless grin she sang a ditty,

"Fine's the folks that stay alive, but them that takes must always die.

For each that's gone, one must stay, for each that's here, two must pay."

The shrill cackle of her voice rang out, reverberating off the walls. Torches glowed dully about the dimly lit chamber.

Impatient for answers, Eamonn moved a few feet closer. "I've come looking for me daughter, old woman. Do you know where she might be?"

Putting a pointed finger to her ear, she seemed to be thinking.

"Do you know where me son is, pray tell? I've been lookin' for him," she replied.

"Your son?" Eamonn said, his voice full of anger. "What son would you be having?"

Small eddies of wind-blown dust appeared here and there on the rock floor while he awaited her answer.

"Me son would be someone you met perhaps. An Irishman like yerself, or maybe a tinker."

Puzzled by what she said, Eamonn tried to think of any tinkers he knew. Seeming to read his mind, Will suddenly realized a truth.

"Unless it was that man in the fairy circle."

"Yes," the rasping voice agreed, "perhaps it was he. A tall man with a mustache. Might he have been me son?"

Standing now, she walked slowly around the chair.

More and more, bits of foul dirt filled the air in swirling spirals, grains of sand biting into Eamonn's face.

"You come here askin' fer what's yers, and it's I who should be doin' the askin', Eamonn Gallagher. It's I who should be demanding answers."

Not waiting for him to speak she pulled the shawl closer around her face as she continued. "You and yers have caused ma family to disappear off the face of the earth."

Walking closer to the two men she eyed Eamonn intently.

"Flynn was me son incarnate. Revenge now, an eye for an eye, he always said. His instructions were explicit. If ever he didn't come home, someone dear was to disappear."

Will listened to the old hag and remembered the spindly granny he spoke with in Mullaghmore.

"It was you near the jetty yesterday."

"That it was, Will Bonner, and a good source of news you surely be. Not that I'm owin' you anythin'. Scums and slimes you both be."

Eamonn started across the chamber towards her.

"What have you done with my Mollie?"

With all his strength he lunged at the wicked creature. She smiled a devious grin then pulled a rope near her chair. A clanging sound from above caused him to look up just as a large metal cage fell, banging to the floor with a loud thud trapping him within. Unable to stop his forward momentum, he hit the inside bars closest to the object of his hatred. Scrambling to his feet he shook the bars with all his might.

Unnoticed on the other side, Will had fallen to the rock floor. Sure he was in hell, he tried frantically to think of ways to save his friend. It was obvious the old lady had been expecting them.

The croaking voice was louder now. Looking through the cage past Eamonn, Will stared in disbelief as the shawl fell away from a purplish face covered with warts. Large red eyes protruded out of a head grown twice its size, straggly gray hair barely covering oversized ears. A bony finger scratched its long hairy nose. Skinny and slow moving, she looked at her prey much like a dog eyes its bone. The voice of a thousand years spoke to Eamonn, the hoarse whisper of death lingering in every word. "You are given to me, Master Eamonn, you and yer hidden friend are mine to eat, to enjoy, fer all the pain you've caused."

"And I'm wishin' you choke on your own spit," Eamonn screamed in frustration. "I know who you are, shape-changer. You're a goblin!"

Its eyes glowing, it nodded an evil grin, stretching its chapped purple lips. "I'm goin' to do the tell so, you can enjoy the time you have left."

Eamonn backed away from the bars as the goblin appeared near his face in the blink of an eye.

"You can spout stories 'til your tongue falls out and I'll not listen to your words," he said.

"Oh, you'll listen all right," she said with a wave of her spindly hand.

Eamonn covered his ears and pain filled his head. He reached for the monster torturing him and just as suddenly the pain ceased.

"Now you see dearie, don't cover yer ears and there'll be no pain."

Eamonn cursed the hellish thing as he listened.

"Thousands of years ago we wondered what it would be like to live in human form. Feel your greed, your lust. We did, but not without sufferin' the same human foibles our appetites growin' bigger. You humans left us alone for years until you started hangin' those that crossed you."

"Tinkers! You took the bodies of travelers?" Eamonn asked disgustedly.

"Aye, when they died early or in bed."

"Then it's you who are behind the deaths on this hill. Turning man against man, it's you who are the scum, shape-changer. I wish you and yours an eternity in hell."

Reaching through the bars with a long hairy arm, the goblin touched Eamonn's fist. He moaned in pain, jerking back from the searing burn of green acid-like fluid spreading across his shaking hand. Terrified, he watched the goblin beaming with hatred.

"For the loss of me own you must pay the price, and pay dearly you will."

Turning its head slowly it pointed at an opening in the cavern.

"See there by the wall, 'tis a final resting place. Somethin' of yers perhaps?"

Waving its hand Eamonn heard a baby's cry. A shaft of yellow light revealed a waist-high opening. Lying on a blanket Mollie cried out in fear as the light touched her face.

"I curse you for eternity. If I have an afterlife I'll come looking for you till the end of time. I'll crush your evil soul and you'll die one death for every year you've been on this wicked earth."

Near tears Eamonn lunged at the bars futilely, banging against them again and again until his body was bruised and bloody.

Eyeing the wounded man the goblin breathed a hateful sigh.

"You'll not kill yerself before you've seen what I've prepared for yer wee one."

The foul smelling thing looked at the ceiling. Hanging above the entrance to Mollie's prison was a massive boulder on a chain pulley, held taut by a thick rope. Underneath the knot was a candle which the goblin lit with a small torch. Slowly the flame grew, then reached hungrily for the hemp, blackening it as he watched. Energized, it engulfed the thick knot.

"You shall stay in this cage of me own makin' and watch the rope burn through. The stone will fall and shut yer precious seed in her tomb for all time. You will listen as she starves to death, beggin' for food, some small morsel, until she weakens and dies. Her organs will fail, then she'll choke on her own tears . . . "

"Enough, you monster!" Eamonn screamed hysterically.

Filled with fear and frustration he tried to think of some way to outsmart the ugly beast. *If I had some salt to throw on it,* he thought forlornly. *Damn the legends anyway, burning thorns didn't work, the remedies are worthless.* Looking at the goblin only reminded him of all the torturous stories he had heard. Vicious and cruel, a sadistic creature, he hated this abomination as he had never hated anything before.

"Could you not understand how I feel, you childless demon?" Eamonn pleaded.

Confused, it stopped for a second. With an almost benevolent look, it watched the bleeding man in the cage. "Childless? What're you sayin'? Two thousand years ago I was . . . "

Eamonn interrupted quickly, "Then you being so wise, you must understand how I feel."

"Oh, I understand all right. I understand that you and yer bit of fluff are goin' to pay."

Its eyes filled with disdain as it watched the defiant man glaring helplessly from the cage.

Crouched, Will listened, his heart aching for Eamonn and Mollie. Even though the demon from hell knew he was there, he was sure it had forgotten. Thinking of all the predicaments characters in his stories had been in, he tried to make a plan. Somehow he had to get to Mollie without that fiend touching him.

Behind him a woman's voice echoed through the chamber. "Aye there, goblin, how would you like to fight me?"

"And who might be callin'?" the scraggly hair creature said hoarsely.

Before there was any reply, it hobbled around the cage to a spot midway to the other side. A woman stood in the shadows of the tunnel entrance.

"Come closer and you'll find out, you horrible toad," the voice said firmly.

Moving into the light, Kate waved a thick tree-limb at the advancing menace.

"I want me baby and husband back or I'll knock that ugly lump off your foul shoulders."

Taken aback by the feisty woman's courage, the wily demon stopped for a moment sizing up its opponent. Kate stood with her legs slightly spread. A cruel smile crossed the goblin's large purple lips, eyes flashing thoughts of torture as it moved closer to Kate ever so slowly.

"So yer makin' demands, are ya?"

"That I am, you creature of darkness. I'm warning you before it's too late and I have to kill you."

Behind Kate's angry facade fear raced through her brain. She had never seen a goblin before and hadn't really believed in them. But then she had never seen leprechauns or fairies either. And now, in the space of a week, had seen all three. This thing with the rotted face seemed by far the most dangerous.

In the yellow light of the cave, everything seemed slow and unreal. Raising her club she watched the creature take another step forward, looking for traps in the rock chamber, something it had missed. The glow of the torchlight was poorly served by the shadows creeping into every corner. Seeing only the woman, in her red flannel shirt and long pants covered partially by seamen's boots, the goblin felt braver. This was no threat; it was just a frail human, a female, no match for its powers. *I'll cook her for breakfast,* it thought hungrily. *Aye, I'll cook her now. Me appetite's growin'.*

Deadly eyes of a predator stared into the fearless gaze of Kate Gallagher. *If I have to die, I'll crush its feckken head first. I'll save me Mollie.* Before she could think further, the goblin moved quickly towards her.

Hearing the creature talking to someone in the shadows, Will crept around to the other side of the cage. Rubbing his bleeding hands together Eamonn listened to the goblin talking to the shadows, unaware of Will moving quickly to where Mollie lay crying.

Across the way the goblin's wrinkled, contorted face spewed hatred at Kate as she suddenly attacked, swinging with all her might. The goblin groaned loudly from the impact to its large head. Though Kate's aim was true, it grabbed the stiff pole from her hands. Shaken, the frightened woman stepped back then rushed at the creature, her head down like a battering ram. The force of her body threw it off balance for a moment, as momentum carried her towards the other side of the cave.

"Ah, me little spider, you thinks you can get away perhaps. Yer luck has run out this day," it said, spinning around to search for its prey.

Lifting Mollie from the small opening, Will felt something bump him in the back. Looking around he saw Kate pointing upward. The rope knot was burning strand after strand of hemp-fiber, disappearing in a pile of ash.

Racing across the room at an alarming rate the goblin snarled at its victims. "I've got you now. Eat me enemies, take their essence," it said slobbering. "me vengeance will be complete."

Eamonn watched in horror as the withered thing headed for his wife and baby. *If only I could distract it,* he thought frantically. He searched the stone floor for a small rock, a handful of sand. Scooping up some dirt and pebbles just as the smell of death hurried by the cage, he threw it with all his might through the bars, peppering the deadly creature.

The small projectiles hit the goblin in the face like bee-stings. Howling like the wind, it turned on the trapped man. "You have sealed yer fate now me lad, you'll die shortly." Drooling, it lashed out at Eamonn spitting acid-like fluid through the bars.

He gritted his teeth from the pain of the droplets hitting his bare skin.

"You'll all die now!" the creature screamed, turning towards Will.

Will handed Mollie to Kate, trying to signal her with his eyes, looking up at the boulder. Putting Kate behind him, just off-center of the hanging rock, he hoped desperately that his ploy would work. He held his breath as the goblin came nearer hoping it wouldn't notice its position under the rock.

"Come and get us, if you dare," Will shouted angrily at the swift moving demon. He wished there was some way to trigger the rock to fall, as the half-burnt rope looked hopeless.

"I've got you now, Will Bonner. I'll add you to the pot, along with the baby, for flavor," the goblin spat out. Grabbing viciously, it touched his hand as acid-like goo burned his skin. Will closed his eyes, anticipating the horrible end that awaited him.

Suddenly from behind something pulled hard on his coat collar as a great rumbling emanated through the large chamber. Thunder shook the walls, as the massive stone swung on its tether.

Off-balance, the goblin tried to steady itself. Bulbous eyes looked up just as the stone broke free and crashed down upon its cowering form. Bones cracked and crunched as the heavy weight landed squarely. Bony fingers twitched, then were still. An ungodly gurgle was followed by silence.

In the cavern wall an opening appeared. In single file a group of small men dressed in silver coats of mail, carrying round shields, silently filled the cave. Near the end of the procession came the fairy king, dressed in lace and wearing a crown. A brightly colored majestic being, he walked directly to Will. "You are a busy man, I see."

"It would certainly seem so," Will replied, bowing slightly.

"The comings and goings on this hill are of no concern to me. The revenge of goblins seems best left to them." He stopped as though deep in thought, "But a debt is a debt. We live in different realities, Will Bonner. The Gaelic Sidhe will continue to live here until the end of time."

The fairy king looked at Eamonn still captive in the cage. Motioning to his subjects, they formed a ring around the enclosure and lifted it so he could escape.

Rushing to Kate's side Eamonn whispered words of affection and relief, thanking her for following them. "I don't know how to say I was wrong," pausing he looked into her eyes. "I love you woman."

Will cleared his throat, interrupting Eamonn as he looked at the little people standing there eyeing them. Eamonn turned to the fairy king.

"All me life I've heard about the Gaelic Kingdom, the legends . . . it was you who healed me in Connemara."

Eamonn looked closer at the serene face. "You're Finvana!"

"Aye, tis true, today and forever after."

Bowing, Eamonn spoke with gratitude, "I thank you with all my heart for saving my family. If ever you need me . . . "

The fairy king raised his hand to stop Eamonn from continuing.

"You needn't thank me, though your thanks are well received. It's your friend here you should be thankin'. He did me a service and I've but returned the favor."

Walking over to Will he spoke in a soft voice, "Now I say we're even, Will Bonner."

Will smiled, nodding at the little man. "Thank you, Sir, for saving us. If ever you visit Maine, I live in Steep Falls."

"Aye, I might," the diminutive monarch answered as he turned to leave. Stopping at the brightly lit opening, he turned and looked at Eamonn. "It is ended now."

Eamonn nodded, then hugged his wife and daughter as he watched the procession disappear into the rock.

Will looked down at the boulder, surprised to find there was nothing remaining of the goblin. It was gone without a trace.

"I think we should leave this place," he said. "Go have a spot of tea. No sense pressing our luck."

"Aye mate, some tae, that's a grand idea," Eamonn said. Kissing Kate on the nose, he turned to lead them out.

Fifty-seven—In to the depths

Will held the torch high as he led the way into the tunnel. Kate carried Mollie close to her bosom. Eamonn was in pain but determined not to show it, at least until they got out of this abominable cave. The going was slow as they retraced their steps. After a time, Will spied the marking on the wall pointing to the lantern he had left on their way in. After several attempts, Eamonn lit the fickle lamp. Holding it in his right hand, he raised it high. With the darkness of the cave devouring the light, it still afforded more than they had been getting.

The constant sound of dripping water intermingled with laughing voices made Will feel as though he was going nuts. Stopping for a moment, he signaled for the others to be quiet and listen. *Hopefully I haven't lost it. The stress of seeing a goblin may be too much,* he thought. Holding his breath, he strained to hear. Hearing a definitive sound would be better than his imagination working overtime. Looking back at Eamonn, he whispered, "Did you hear that?"

The Irishman stood still, blood caked on his face.

"I can't make anything out, maybe it's the wind."

Both stood listening as Kate rocked Mollie in her arms. Nervously Will signed for them to continue, following the string they had laid out on the way in. As the tunnel narrowed it became more difficult to stand upright, finally walking in single file as it gradually became smaller. It seemed to take forever to reach the fork in the passageway. The yellow light of the lantern revealed the arrow pointing to the exit. Will breathed a sigh of relief as they continued out the shrinking tunnel.

Eamonn took turns with Kate carrying Mollie. His head pounding, he prayed that they'd get out in one piece. He hadn't heard a sound since they had stopped to listen for someone laughing.

Suddenly a voice penetrated the darkness, "Are you in there, Eamonn Gallagher?"

Kate looked at her husband nervously.

"That depends on whether you be friend or foe," he answered.

"It's Officer Shankley and I'll not be playin' games."

"Aye, then it's me and we'd appreciate your assistance."

The angry looking garda came into Will's light, blinding them with his powerful torch. "You can thank Mrs. Bonner for havin' the good sense to call when the three of you didn't come home." Seeing Eamonn's battered and bruised face, he gasped. "Oh, Jaysus, what happened to you? You look thrashed."

Licking his cut lip, Eamonn shook his head tiredly. "You wouldn't believe the trouble we've run into. But the good of it is, I've got my wife and wee daughter back."

"I can see that, but I didn't know your daughter was missin'. Maybe you ought to take a break and stay home from now on."

Offering Eamonn his arm, the officer turned to leave. Eamonn smiled weakly and nodded in agreement as he, Kate and Will followed Officer Shankley out of the small tunnel.

Fifty-eight—Saying goodbye

Wind blew in from the sea, whistling through the cracks. Will felt a chill even though Kate had set a blazing fire of peat logs. The touch of the goblin had left its mark. Both he and Eamonn were strangely silent. Thunder rumbled in the mountains behind Ballyshannon. Will looked out the study window at the rain sluicing down the windows.

"We were lucky."

"Aye, that we were," Eamonn agreed somberly.

The burns on his hands and face had done more than hurt him superficially. They had etched a new reality in his mind.

"No one would believe us, Will."

"God, I wouldn't either. A leprechaun causing people to kill themselves."

He looked at Eamonn seated close to Kate, Annie smiling kindly from the rocking chair.

His mind reluctant, he continued, "Eamonn being stabbed; Kate stopping the tinker; then me and Kate almost being hung." He shook his head.

"Yeah, I reckon that leprechaun got more than he bargained for when he tried to snuff the Fairy King and you hit him," Kate interjected.

"At least he didn't kill the king," Will said tiredly.

"Lucky he owed you a favor," Annie added softly.

"Aye, that was lucky indeed," Eamonn said in agreement. "That goblin would surely have done us in."

Rain poured down as the four friends sat in the safety of the large house. Even though Will thought of what a great story this would make, it seemed too close to home. *Home,* he thought, *Steep Falls.* He missed his garden, his writing. There'd always be another story. Annie brushed his arm, pointing to the clock. Reluctantly they got ready to go. For once he felt old, *well at least sixty,* he thought, smiling to himself.

"Eamonn . . . Kate . . . this has been one of the most unusual vacations I've ever had."

"Yes, and if anyone ever asks did you see a fairy, you can say with some authority you certainly did. As a matter of fact, you can say you met several." Annie whispered, giving his arm a squeeze.

Shy to say goodbye, Will started to shake Eamonn's hand as the Irishman gave in to his emotions and gave him a big hug.

"If ever you want to come stay with us again you're surely welcome, Sir William."

"Aye, and you as well, Annie," Kate piped in.

Rubbing the mist from his eyes Eamonn nodded sadly in agreement.

"You can stay now if you like. Things won't be the same . . ."

"We've got to go, my friend, but we'll be back," Will said with affection.

"We'll be back because Ireland's in our blood now and we love you guys."

They turned and hurried through the rain to the green Fiat at the curb. The pouring rain seemed a fitting end to an exciting trip. Tonight they'd stay in Mullaghmore one last time, then head for Dublin Airport in the morning.

Fifty-nine—Lost in memories

Seated in the den Eamonn watched the clouds roll across the sky. A day had passed. His friend should be on his way home by now, somewhere over the coast of Nova Scotia. He felt good, *nothing strange will ever happen to us again,* he thought. He and Kate had seen sights that mere mortals would never believe. Thankfully Mollie was asleep and safe in her own little bed, the trauma of the last few days soothed over by familiar surroundings and love. Finished in the kitchen, Kate came and sat by her husband.

"I'm glad you're home, Mister," She said, snuggling on Eamonn's shoulder.

"Aye, me too. I've missed being here with you."

"I've missed more than that, Mr. Gallagher," she replied warmly.

Hugging each other, neither noticed the steady drumming of the rain on the roof. Secure in their house, Eamonn held Kate tightly. "I love you," he breathed into her neck.

Kate rose and motioned him to follow. Wordlessly they went upstairs to their bed. So much had happened it was important to reaffirm their closeness, reclaim their love.

Eamonn watched as Kate took off her sweater, the fullness of her breasts seeming greater than before.

Filled with desire they disrobed, shedding the last remnants of their fears. Each in their own way admired the other's body.

Lying together, Eamonn caressed his woman, moving to her warm mound. He kissed her lips and neck, the scent of her sex like fresh rain. Caressing her breasts, he softly embraced one. Together they held each other tightly, finding their rhythm, they moved as one. Kate whispered her love for this man, her warrior, her lover, as he exploded inside her.

Fireworks flashed through Eamonn's mind. Trying not to vocalize, he buried his face in Kate's neck. Not quite there yet she guided him slowly at first, then faster as she gasped in pleasure.

Holding each other in breathless wonder the two lovers gazed into each other's eyes, windows to their souls. Together now and forever, they held each other close.

Sixty—Home again

The next day seemed more a dream than reality. Annie read road signs to pass the time as they drove to Dublin, some four hours away, *two-hundred-twenty kilometers* Eamonn had said. While Will drove, Annie jotted amusing road signs in her day-planner as they passed the misty lakes and streams along the way. Try as he might, he couldn't stop thinking about the fairies.

"Listen to this," Annie interjected, deep in the throes of her notes, "*Speed kills, kills*; *loose chippings*, that's gravel I guess; *surface dressing* for blacktop. *No overtaking*; *traffic calming ahead.* Have you ever heard of such signs? Have you?"

No, I haven't luv," Will said, trying to sound Irish. "How about a hug and a jug, Mrs. Bonner?"

"How about you watching the road until we get to the airport, then we'll talk about a hug and a jug," she said laughing.

Time slipped by as they finally arrived at Dublin Airport. Waiting for their flight took forever, as announcement after announcement reported yet another delay. Finally boarded, Will followed Annie down the aisle to their seats. *The sky is clear as a bell, he* thought dreamily, *no rain.* As the giant L10-11 gained altitude over southern Ireland and headed out over the Atlantic towards America, Will wondered if it had all been a dream, a figment of his over-active imagination as Annie always said.

A voice interrupted his musings, "Would you care for anythin' from the bar, Sir?"

"Yes, I would please, Old Bushmill and water."

Busying herself, the stewardess filled his order. "Here Sir, take an extra just in case."

"Thank you," he replied gratefully.

"Did you enjoy your stay in Ireland?"

"Yes, I did," he said, rubbing the bandage on his hand.

"Did you run into any fairies?" she said with a twinkle in her eye.

"Yes, we did," Will replied, giving Annie's arm a squeeze, "many."

Maybe it was just the drinks, but the flight home seemed shorter. The shuttle from Logan to Steep Falls breezed along, summer heat radiating through the half-open windows.

It was late by the time they finished putting their things away and got into bed; a relief to turn off the lights and settle in. The sound of crickets sifted through open windows, filling the room. Sleep came quickly to the tired travelers.

Footsteps gently creaking on the stairs slowly penetrated Will's dream-filled mind. "Did you hear anything?" he whispered to Annie.

"What? Hear what?" she replied, half asleep.

"It sounded like someone coming up the stairs."

Both lay frozen for a second listening, hearing only the chorus of crickets. Convinced it was nothing, they snuggled together as restful dreams of another time and place filled their heads.

From somewhere below a small voice whispered, "Sure and they're home safe, sire."

Mollie's Song

Child of life, Rise up! Rise up!
Fair damsel be, delight with simple vices.
For out of love has come your song.
Never mind the winds so fair,
for out of love has come your peace.
With cheer and song to the sky,
be free, my love, to always be.

Will Aebi
The UnGnome Author

Soon to be released UnGnome Stories

The Cat & the Rooster

An Irish girl in North Ireland learns life's lessons from her cat and the rooster her da kept for raisng chickens. What insights and truths she uncovers change her life forever.

The Son's of Stone

Laura Stone fights for her life and family in an ugly turn of events that threatens to eliminate mankind. Though a hard worker by nature, life in Aroostook County, Maine presented many difficulties. Like her father, Homer, and his father before him, she was a farmer in 1926 struggling to live.

Deranged Commuter

A bizarre twist down insanity lane. Fifteen years of driving, compressed into a one-week composite of warped humor, lunacy, despair and destruction.

About the author

A long time ago, he was born to average parents who loved him dearly. Taking pen in hand in his fifties, he's found a magical life in his alter ego the UnGnome Author. Living in Milwaukee until he was six, then in Arkansas until he was ten, then San Diego until he was twenty-three, he became suitable unstably to write fictional stories. He hopes you enjoyed this tome and will read others he's penned. As an author Will Aebi is deeply committed to writing interesting stories. As there are thousands upon thousands of writers trying to do the same thing, this puts his chance of success at little or nil. To that extent he has created an alter ego to write his stories. His dear friend, The UnGnome Author, creature of fantasy though he may be, affords some interest to the reading public. So, as this alter ego, let me do the author bio.

Born with a well-structured mind, being an UnGnome has been a treasure trove of fun, with the exceptional good luck of having big ears and a very long nose to sniff out things of interest. Keenly interested in human behavior, he writes about the mysteries of life. An avid traveler, he moved about the world, leaving his home in Ireland to relocate to the forests of Maine in 1998. He now calls the woods and hills of Salem, South Carolina his home.

A wee bit advanced in age, (well over 300 years) he enjoys entertaining and has devoted his life to writing novels for the ladies. He enjoys a good game of hide and seek, and prefers a tasty lunch of dried mushrooms and bark. To you he wishes love and happiness and, of course, great new stories for your entertainment.

UnGnome Facts

There was a time long ago when writing was a solitary art.

Husbands make better writers than a stone.

Peas & Carrots are as good as cucumbers.

When an Ungnome wife sez no, she means it.

None are as happy as a gardener planting flowers.

The written word is more precious than silence.

Excerpt from the 'Sons of Stone' coming out in 2008

Nicholas Stone had worked hard all his life. Aroostook County, Maine had its difficulties. His father, Homer, had been a farmer and his father before him. Now here it was, 1926, and he had inherited the farm, his father's dream.

A chemist by trade, Nicholas had reluctantly returned to work the land. Producing two hundred acres of potatoes had turned out to be difficult at best. The planting season in northern Maine was short, starting in late May, or after the last frost, ending sometime in October. He hadn't been able to earn enough to support his wife Margaret and sons; Matthew, the light of his life, Mark, named after the second book in the New Testament, serious minded Luke, and John, who made everyone laugh. Luckily they all loved potatoes, so there was no end of dishes his wife could prepare. Fried, baked or in casseroles, they always cleaned their plates.

A Christian, Nicolas found his faith faltering of late. It seemed his prayers had been ignored by God for five years now. _God's just too busy,_ he thought.

Seated at his desk in the corner of his dilapidated storage building he opened a book of poems by Edgar Allan Poe and read from the Raven.

Feeling depressed, he wondered if the devil would listen and answer his prayers if God was too busy. A chill made him look up. Startled, he watched as a dark cloud formed in the corner, the smell of rotten eggs permeating his nostrils. Nervously he started talking aloud, "My luck's been down, the price of potatoes is less than an empty can. Bugs ate eattin' the plants before they can bloom. I'd be eternally in your debt if you'd help." Feeling foolish, he closed his eyes and listened for some sign that he wasn't just talking to the wall. A cold wind blew across his desk, lifting a piece of paper onto his lap. He picked it up and read the words which appeared there as if by magic.